Trail Rides & Starry Eyes

Also by Katrina Emmel

Near Misses & Cowboy Kisses

Trail Rides & Starry Eyes

KATRINA EMMEL

Delacorte
Romance

Delacorte Romance
An imprint of Random House Children's Books
A division of Penguin Random House LLC
1745 Broadway, New York, NY 10019

penguinrandomhouse.com
GetUnderlined.com

Library of Congress Cataloging-in-Publication Data is available upon request.
ISBN 978-0-593-90406-0 (pbk.) — ISBN 978-0-593-90407-7 (ebook)

The text of this book is set in 11-point Sabon Next.

Manufactured in the United States of America
1st Printing

The authorized representative in the EU for product safety and compliance is
Penguin Random House Ireland, Morrison Chambers, 32 Nassau Street,
Dublin D02 YH68, Ireland, https://eu-contact.penguin.ie.

To Jody,
for your constant love and your unfailing belief in me.
My dreams are possible because of you.

CHAPTER 1

Cassidy

THE HEAP OF carrots in front of me shrinks as I peel them for Sunday dinner. I've already finished with the potatoes, which are cubed and in a pot on the stove, ready for boiling and mashing. I'm so used to peeling, dicing, and slicing up veggies for dinner that I barely think about it anymore.

When I was younger, the piles of vegetables seemed insurmountable, and I used to get blisters where the ancient metal peeler rubbed against the soft pad of my palm. Now that I'm seventeen, I have years of experience and hard-earned calluses to protect me.

Rough skin.

Ragged nails.

Rope burns.

A hand model, I'll never be.

I toss the carrots with salt, pepper, olive oil, and a few sprigs of fresh rosemary from the garden before spreading them in a baking dish. The cowboy steaks are seasoned and marinating, ready for Dad to throw on the grill as soon as he and Grandpa get back from riding out to the south pasture to check on the cattle.

Hardly anything goes to waste here on the ranch—not if we can help it—and the hogs are more than happy to snack on our kitchen scraps and week-old leftovers. I use the back of the knife to scrape the vegetable peels off the cutting board and into the antique enameled slop bucket. I can remember my grandmother having me hold the bucket for her while she scraped kitchen trimmings in. The kitchen is full of reminders of her.

A collection of tea tins.

Hand-tatted doilies.

The kitchen witch she made hangs over the sink, the doll's frizzy gray hair billowing out under a crooked black hat. She sits on a broomstick of sticks and dried wheatgrass. When I was little, Grandma and I would gather up twigs, herbs, and bits of leftover twine, and we'd sit on the back porch while she taught me to make little brooms that I'd leave as gifts for all the fairies I was sure lived out by the duck pond.

Grandma's been gone for two years, but sometimes the grief rushes at me from out of the blue.

I blink back tears and grab the slop bucket. The handle squeaks as I make my way from the kitchen to the mudroom. My sturdy red rubber boots are on a mat by the door, snuggled between Dad's old work boots and Mom's gardening Crocs. I slide my feet inside the boots and clunk over to the screen door, where a warm, soft breeze floats in.

June in Wyoming smells like warm grass and sunshine,

with just a hint of barnyard. It's my third favorite smell after Mom's fresh-from-the-oven wild huckleberry pie and the scent of sweet pea blossoms on a dry summer day.

The dirt path from the main house to the pigsty cuts through the kitchen garden where we grow most of our produce. Honeybees hover around the fragrant lavender blossoms. Cucumbers, peas, and beans grow up trellises, and watermelon and cantaloupe vines attempt to flee the raised-bed planters and stretch toward the goat pasture.

Like me, their roots are firmly planted at the ranch. Ever since I can remember, I've been fed stories, along with my peas and carrots, of the intrepid Sterlings who traveled from England to Wyoming in search of a better life. What started as a sheep farm in the 1860s eventually became a cattle and horse ranch. And, as an only child, I'll be expected to take over someday.

I love it here. I do. But lately I've also been wondering what lies beyond the soil at my feet. Beyond our kitchen garden. Beyond Silver Stallion Ranch's ten thousand acres.

It's not like I've never left the ranch—Jackson's only a little over an hour's drive away. We make monthly shopping excursions into Casper or Salt Lake City. And there's always our annual New Year's trip to Denver for the National Western Stock Show.

Sometimes it just feels like I live in a completely different world.

Maybe I do.

At least, compared with the other students in my online distance learning classes, who are always chatting about the things they do for fun.

They play on sports teams. I play mechanic on the old tractor.

They go to concerts. I go on cattle drives.

They act in the local theater's plays. I act like life on the ranch is . . . enough. And it should be, right? It was enough for Grandma, who left behind her life in New York City to marry Grandpa after a love-at-first-sight chance meeting while she was vacationing in Denver. It's been enough for Grandpa and Mom and Dad. But there's a voice in the back of my mind that reminds me it wasn't enough for Uncle Alex.

That it might not be enough for me.

Trouble, one of our farm cats, is sunning herself between the rows of bee balm and lemon balm. She peers at me with suspicious yellow eyes, her calico tail swishing.

"Cause any chaos today?" I ask.

She replies with a salty "Meow."

We originally named her Sweetie, before we knew just how much of a menace she can be. Shortly after we got her, she climbed Mom's brand-new lace curtains in the living room, completely shredding them in the process. We're still finding tiny white strands of thread that haunt us like old Christmas tinsel. A few days after the curtain catastrophe, she ran into the main house with a live squirrel and then let it go right in the middle of dinner. Imagine our shock when the squirrel ran across the table, knocked over the gravy bowl, and then flipped Grandpa's plate right onto his lap.

In his frustration, Grandpa wiped a clump of mashed potatoes from his cheek and exclaimed, "That cat is trouble with a capital *T*."

And the rest is history.

I take the path between the rustic greenhouse Uncle Alex built from old doors and reclaimed windows and the cozy guest cottage that sits next to the duck pond. I wonder if Uncle Alex dreamed of building his new life in California while he was hammering in the nails. Was he thinking of Hollywood when he cut the scavenged hardwood to size?

The goat pen is straight ahead, but I turn and head toward the pigsty. A few of our hens peck at the dirt and cluck to each other. Most of them ignore me, but Birdzilla, an ornery Rhode Island Red, fluffs up her feathers and stomps her foot. Usually, her bawking is worse than her bite, but she's definitely one to watch out for.

Hogwash squeals as soon as she sees me coming, and the sudden burst of noise sends Birdzilla scampering back toward the chicken coop. Hogwash jumps up against the wooden plank next to the gate, and immediately Pigsly and Lizzie Boarden join her, snuffling and grunting and making a ruckus. Duchess of Pork rises from her mud bath, gives a little regal shake, and struts across the pen to preside over the commotion with a bellowing oink.

"Afternoon, ladies," I say. "How about a little snack?" I upend the slop bucket into the trough to a deafening chorus of oinks and grunts. The minute the scraps land, the pigs line up in a row and their anxious squeals turn to happy slurps.

As I turn to head back to the main house, a commotion catches my eye. Trouble must have followed me over from the garden. Usually, the farm cats and the chickens get along, but Birdzilla is uppity today and Trouble is . . . well, trouble.

The hens are not happy to see a cat strutting through their terrain. Like mini-velociraptors, the chickens fan out in a circle to surround her. Trouble sits and glances around, her tail twitching. Birdzilla mock-charges and Trouble gives her a lazy blink before lifting a paw and licking it.

A few of the chickens lose interest and go back to pecking at the dirt. Birdzilla scratches an itch. Trouble yawns.

Then all hell breaks loose when Sergeant Peeper and Tyrannosaurus Pecks rush over.

Trouble jumps up, her back arched, and hisses.

The agitated hens flap their wings and charge.

The yard becomes a whirlwind of flying feathers and dust.

Mrrreeeeooooow!

Ba-gawk!

I wrap my arm around Trouble before she can pounce on Birdzilla. Trouble twists away from the attack chickens. When I set her down behind me, she bounds off toward the goat pen.

Crisis averted.

Or not.

Trouble is gone, but Birdzilla's still out for blood. Her beady black eyes fix me with a cold stare. I stare back. It's not the first time we've squared off, and I'm sure it won't be the last.

Birdzilla comes at me with all the fury a six-pound chicken can muster. When she's in arm's reach, I grab her as gently as I can, flip her upside down, and tuck her into my side like a football. Birdzilla wiggles for a bit and then calms enough that I can set her back down without worrying that either of us will get hurt. The minute her feet hit the ground, she rushes off toward the coop in a huff, leaving a trail of feathers behind her.

Mom's in the kitchen rolling out buttermilk biscuit dough when I get back to the main house.

"Hi, Ma," I say as I return the slop bucket to its home, on

a shelf hidden behind a red-and-white-checked gingham skirt beneath the large cast-iron sink.

Her long brown hair is coiled in a messy bun at the back of her head and held in place with one of Dad's tattered old blue bandanas. "What happened to you?" she asks, looking up from the counter.

"Birdzilla and Trouble happened," I say.

"That explains this," she says, plucking a fluffy auburn feather from my hair, which is a few shades lighter than hers. "You look like a mess."

"I feel like a mess." My flannel shirt is splattered with potato starch and carrot juice and covered in a fine coating of barnyard dust. "I'm gonna go get cleaned up for dinner."

Upstairs, I wash the smudges of dirt off my face and do my best to comb the remnants of the barnyard melee from my hair. All I need now is a fresh top.

Sunday dinner isn't a formal affair, but Grandpa insists that everyone's neat and presentable in a clean shirt and their best jeans when we sit down to eat. Even though Dad's taken over most of the ranch's operations since Grandpa retired three years ago at the age of seventy-four, Grandpa still presides over the dinner table.

No phone calls or texts are allowed during meals.

You don't get served dessert until your plate's clean.

And there can be absolutely, positively no mention of Uncle Alex before the table is cleared. (Unless Grandpa brings him up first.)

Just as I reach the bottom stair, Dad's phone rings. I walk into the kitchen to find him standing next to the sink, staring down at his cell phone with a torn look on his face.

"Don't answer it," Grandpa warns from his seat at the head of the dinner table. "We're about to eat and I don't want my steak to get cold."

Dad looks over at Grandpa with a furrowed brow. This is Dad's decision-making face, which means he's seriously considering taking the call. Must not be a telemarketer, then.

Grandpa pulls his cloth napkin into his lap. Clearly he doesn't expect Dad to defy him.

Dad's phone rings again. He presses a button before lifting it to his ear. "Hello? Is everything okay?"

There's an excruciating pause as we all look at Dad.

"Well, now, that's a mighty big favor," Dad says, dragging a hand through his short salt-and-pepper hair. He listens for a second and then his eyes lock with mine. "I understand, Alex. Right. Well, I'm not sure. I'll have to run it by Cass."

There's a warm breeze coming in through the open window, but a shiver of unease snakes its way down my back, all the same.

What on earth does Uncle Alex want from me?

CHAPTER 2

Wilder

LIGHTS.

Camera.

Action.

And a face full of fake snow.

Thankfully, wardrobe gave me a pair of dark aviator sunglasses to protect my eyes. A gust from the wind machine tousles my hair, and I step forward, my boots sinking into a thick layer of cellulose snow. When I hit my mark, I casually pull off my sunglasses.

Gaze at the camera.

Tilt my head.

"Flannel-lined to keep you comfortable in the cold," I say, making sure I enunciate each word.

"Good," the director calls. "Cut." He steps out from behind his live feed monitor. "Let's do it again. I want more snow this time."

I slide the sunglasses on and walk back toward the fake snow drift that separates me from a giant green screen.

This time, when the director calls "action," I'm greeted with a massive flurry so thick I can barely keep my eyes open, even with the sunglasses.

"Cut. A little less snow."

It might look like a wintery wonderland in here, but it's almost summer in SoCal and this set is hotter than hell. Not to mention, I'm severely overdressed. The fake snow isn't melting, but I sure am. Still, this commercial will be a perfect addition to my demo reel.

A makeup assistant rushes over and dabs at my face. A trickle of sweat slides down my back and soaks into my already-drenched T-shirt.

"Backpack," the director calls. "He needs a backpack. Teens these days are always walking around with a backpack."

While the props department scrambles to find a backpack, the pause in shooting offers me a prime opportunity for a quick cooldown. I stand in front of the giant fan meant for the fake snow and pull open the flannel-lined canvas jacket the wardrobe department dressed me in.

After a couple of minutes, I'm back on my spot with a backpack slung over one shoulder to give me an "authentic high schooler vibe."

The backpack's not the problem, dude. Reality is.

I haven't been to a traditional school in years—between having on-set tutors and doing remote learning—but I don't know anyone who'd be caught dead in a flannel-lined anything outside of a paid gig. But this is L.A., land of year-round warmth and sunshine, so what do I know? The coldest thing here is the ice rink where the Los Angeles Kings play.

We run a few more takes until the director's satisfied and then break for a set change. Usually I'd head straight for craft services but it's a short shooting day, so instead I make my way to the tiny cube of a room they've assigned me for wardrobe changes. As far as a dressing room goes, it's nothing spectacular. Four dingy white walls and scuffed linoleum floors. There's a rack of clothes in one corner, labeled by scene, and a creaky metal folding chair. A cheap mirror hangs on the back of the door.

It's not the dressing room of my dreams by a long shot. But at least I have one.

I simultaneously kick off the heavy work boots and toss the jacket over the chair. As I change into clothes for the next shot, I picture the dressing room Future Me will have.

A big window looking out onto the movie lot. A comfortable couch. A fully stocked mini fridge.

Or, better yet, maybe Future Me will have my own trailer.

I'll be the lead actor on a big budget film.

Get a star on the Hollywood Walk of Fame.

Someday.

Until then, I just need to keep grinding. Smiling for the camera. Memorizing lines. Adding clips to my demo reel to prove I have what it takes to break out from kiddy fame into the big leagues.

I'm proud of what I've accomplished so far, don't get me wrong. But now that I'm almost eighteen, I'm tired of toothpaste commercials, slapstick comedies with laugh tracks, and goofball tween made-for-TV movies. What I'm doing now's not riveting stuff, but I keep reminding myself: You gotta start somewhere, right?

Take Bryan Cranston, for instance. His first gig was for Preparation H and look at his career now.

DiCaprio hawked Bubble Yum.

Keanu Reeves . . . Corn Flakes.

This thirty-second outerwear commercial won't be my big break, but it could help me land a part in something that can really show off my acting chops and propel me to the top.

But at this point . . . I'll take whatever my agent can book me.

"Wilder. We're ready for you." A petite woman with bright orange hair calls me into the makeup room and points to a chair in front of a large mirror illuminated by LED lights. "I'm Dee."

"Hey," I say with a nod.

"Ready to get messy?" Dee asks.

"That's what I'm here for," I say, giving her a confident smile.

I settle into the seat and pull out my phone while Dee gets to work. Usually it doesn't take much to get me ready.

A bit of under-eye concealer.

Maybe a dab of color correction.

Some powder and I'm good to go.

But this next scene has me working on a dirt bike in a barn. It'll be a far cry from the squeaky-clean face I presented for the acne facewash commercial I shot last week, that's for sure.

Dee pulls out a tub of Vaseline, a canister of instant coffee grounds, and a small bowl from a cabinet. "Time to mix up some grease."

The mixture's cold and sticky, and I try not to squirm as she applies it to my face with a brush. It reminds me of that medicated stuff my mom used to rub on my chest when I was sick as a kid, but it smells a million times better.

I stare at my reflection in the mirror, pulling out my best tough guy face. There's a dark streak angled across my forehead. A smudge on my cheek. I look like I've just spent hours in a garage ripping apart an engine.

Badass.

My phone rings just as Dee starts messing with my hair. I glance down at the caller ID.

Alexander Sterling.

My agent.

My finger hovers over the screen.

Please be good news.

Please be good news.

Please be . . .

"Hey, Alexander," I say, fighting to keep my voice chill. I recently auditioned for a couple of different roles, and an unexpected call from him means there's news.

My pulse races. Is it good news? Bad news? It could go either way.

"Wilder, hello," Alexander says in that laid-back way of his. "How's the shoot going?"

"Good," I say. "Thanks for booking it for me."

"Sure thing," he says. "Wardrobe fit you okay? You liking the jeans and boots and all that stuff?"

Okay, this is kind of weird. Alexander's never asked me about my feelings on rugged outerwear—or any of the wardrobes I've worn for past projects.

"They're fine. A bit hot with the flannel-lined jacket," I say. "But not as bad as that sloth costume." I hope to hell that I never have to film a high school prom-com again.

Alexander laughs. "I'd have never survived a Wyoming winter without it. Well, the flannel not the fake fur." He clears his throat. "Summers there are downright pleasant, though. You'll see."

Like that'll ever happen. No one *actually* films in Wyoming anymore, do they? Unless it's for work, I can't think of any other reason to go.

"You remember that historical Western miniseries *Outrider?* We sent in an audition tape a few months back. The thing with all the cowboys?"

"Yeah," I say, my pulse kicking up a notch. There are a few supporting cast roles that would be great exposure for me. But if I could land a lead role? That would be epic.

"Well, the studio's been dragging their heels for weeks. You were short-listed to play Deacon Slade, the broody and misunderstood rancher's son. It was down to the wire, between you, Jackson Miller, and Cam Sheffield. They finally decided to cast *you* this morning. Congratulations."

Holy crap.

I got a part.

"It's one of the lead roles," Alexander continues.

Double holy crap.

It's one of the leads.

Blood races through my veins and I clench the chair's arm

to keep myself seated. If it wasn't for Dee and the pair of shears she's using to trim the hair around my ear, I'd be jumping sky-high. Instead, I swallow and sink into shock.

Because it's finally happening. I've been cast in a serious role. And I beat out two other legit actors for the part.

"Wow," I manage.

"Shooting's planned to start early August up in the Santa Clarita Valley. It's scheduled to take about three months, so get used to all those rugged clothes. You'll be wearing plenty of 'em. But I'm getting a little ahead of myself." He chuckles. "What do you think?"

"I think it's great. It's awesome. It's . . ."

It's a good thing someone else will be writing my lines for the show, because right now, I'm practically speechless.

"So it's a yes, then?"

"Yes," I say, because how could I say no to an opportunity like this?

Alexander clears his throat. Coughs. Then it sounds like he's shuffling papers around. "There's just one thing . . ."

My racing heart screeches to a halt and I'm pretty sure my rib cage collapses from whiplash. Based on the tone of his voice, whatever this "one thing" is, it isn't great.

Still, "one thing" could mean a lot of things.

I might have to shave off my shampoo-commercial hair.

I might have to share an on-set trailer.

There might be a nonnegotiable clause in the contract that says I can only shower once a week.

"Have you ever ridden a horse?" he asks.

I barely hear Alexander over the ringing in my ears.

A *what*?

It takes a second for my brain to catch up. A horse. "Umm ... no?"

One of the set runners peeks their head into the makeup room and holds up their hand, fingers splayed. I have five minutes to get to set. I nod in acknowledgment and they disappear down the hall.

"I figured as much," Alexander continues. "The production team wanted to cast someone familiar with horses for the role. Someone who knows how to ride. I told the casting director you were practically born in the saddle."

"I was born at Cedars-Sinai." Which is about as far from the saddle as it gets.

"Ordinarily, I wouldn't have fudged the truth," Alexander says, sounding truly remorseful. He's cool and he's tough, but he's always been a straight shooter as long as I've known him. This lie is way out of character for him. "But Jackson's allergic to horses and hay, and Cam doesn't know how to ride, either. Sure, you might not be able to ride now, but I'm confident that come August, you'll be riding with the best of 'em and no one will be the wiser."

"I'm sorry," I say, rising from the chair. I quickly check my reflection in the mirror. While I've been distracted on the phone, Dee's managed to make my hair look both mechanic garage greasy and fashionably messy. I don't hate it. "But how am I supposed to pull that off?" I ask.

I know how to look the part. Learn lines. Act with emotion. Whenever I have to do something unfamiliar for a role, I stick with the old saying *Fake it till you make it.* Or fake it until the director tells you what they want you to do and how.

But there are some skills you just can't fake.

Fire eating.

Sword fighting.

And horseback riding.

"Don't worry," Alexander says. "I've already got that part figured out. There's a ranch up in Wyoming, in the middle of nowhere. It's the perfect place for you to learn to ride. By the time they're done with you, you'll be the best horseman on set aside from the trainers. And the best part is, it's so off the map, no one will ever know you've been there."

CHAPTER 3

Cassidy

WHILE DAD'S IN the office, finishing up his call with Uncle Alex, I help Mom set the rest of the platters out. Most nights, we fill up our plates in the kitchen and carry them over to the table, but Sunday night dinner is a more traditional family affair.

Mom transfers food to the same serving dishes Grandma used to use, except for the carrots, which come straight from the oven in their blue and white CorningWare baking dish. The steaks—grilled medium-rare—sit on a white, rectangular porcelain platter with a handle on each side. Fluffy mashed potatoes are mounded into a soft peak in an old yellow stoneware bowl with hand-painted gold trim. And the French-cut green beans glisten with melted butter in an oval-shaped piece of china that looks like it belongs at an English high tea and not on a ranch in the middle of Wyoming. Which is probably accurate, since Grandma brought it back to the United States from a trip to England she took a few years before she met Grandpa.

Grandpa sits in his chair with his arms crossed over his chest and a deep scowl etched on his face. From his stance, I can tell that more than the mashed potatoes are steaming.

"Steak's getting cold," Grandpa says.

It's not the only thing, I think. The breeze floating through the screen door was warm earlier, but the winds of change have arrived.

I set a basket of Mom's buttermilk biscuits on the table—they're nestled beneath a linen tea towel I embroidered with Wyoming wildflowers and bees, back when Grandma was trying to teach me to sew.

When Dad finally takes his seat, the biscuits are cold, too, and the atmosphere in here is downright frigid. One thing's for sure, dinner tonight will be an experience. And that's being generous.

Aside from the one time I ask Mom to pass me the green beans, no one says a word during dinner. I had no idea that silence could be so loud.

Bite.

Sip.

Scrape.

Repeat.

I spend most of dinner chewing on my steak. And chewing over why Uncle Alex called and what Dad needs to run by me.

Dad's got a steely glint in his eye as he slices his knife through a roasted carrot.

I'm up in a flash the minute Grandpa sets down his fork, rushing to clear the table just so I can escape. Even though we usually have dessert after Sunday dinner, as soon as I'm done washing dishes, I'm out of here.

Except I'm not.

Because before I can get the last plate loaded in the dishwasher, Grandpa asks Dad, "What did he want from you this time?"

My ears perk up. Maybe I should stick around for a few more minutes. Just to satisfy my curiosity.

Dad sighs and pushes his chair back from the table. "Why do you assume Alex only ever calls if he wants something?"

"Tell me I'm wrong. Go ahead." Grandpa snorts. "I'll wait."

I thought dinner was uncomfortable, but the silence that hangs between Dad and Grandpa now is downright excruciating.

"That's what I thought." Grandpa smacks the table.

While they've been at it, Mom's dished out plates of home-made huckleberry pie. She hands two to me and takes the other two to the table. I set one in front of Grandpa and then slide into my seat.

Grandpa stabs at his slice with a fork and then says, "Well, don't keep us waiting. What's so damn important that Alex had to call you at dinnertime on a Sunday?"

"He was asking if we needed a ranch hand for a few weeks this summer," Dad says.

"Has he finally come to his senses? Or has that hoity-toity Hollywood town finally finished with him?" Grandpa asks.

"He's not coming back to Wyoming, Dad. He made his choice a long time ago. Mom made peace with it. I've made peace with it. You need to let it go."

"I'll do no such thing," Grandpa says, his eyes full of fire. "He turned his back on us. On the ranch. Damn near broke your mother's heart."

"She forgave him."

"She'd forgive the devil if he asked nicely enough."

Dad opens his mouth to say something back, but before he

can speak, I ask, "What's this about a ranch hand? And what's it have to do with me?"

I'm not sure if it's curiosity that's gotten the best of me or if it's a desperate attempt to get them to stop bickering. But as soon as I open my mouth, they both stop staring each other down across the table. Now Dad's dark brown eyes and Grandpa's hazel ones are fixed on me.

Fun fact: I don't like being the center of attention. Especially not like this.

What was I thinking?

"I . . ." I cough. "It's just . . ." I take a deep breath and stare down at the flakes of golden pie crust on my plate. "Summer's a really busy time for us and it would be nice to have an extra pair of hands around here." Extra hands usually mean extra free time for me. The stack of unread books next to my bed is threatening to topple over and there's got to be at least a dozen shows and movies I want to watch before school starts up again.

In the past, we've usually hired a few seasonal workers by now, but Dad's been complaining how hard it is to find good help this year. He managed to put together a decent crew of cowboys to help him with the cattle, but there's always plenty of work around the homestead, too.

"I don't know," Dad says. He takes a swig of water and sets the glass down on the table with a dull thud. "I'm not sure it's a good idea."

"Finally, you're talking some sense," Grandpa says. "We'll have all the help we need once Matt arrives."

"About that." Dad reaches up to scratch his forehead. "Matt's not coming back. He got a year-round job at a dude ranch in Texas. He let me know last week."

"When were you planning to let *me* know?" Grandpa says, his jaw going hard.

You and me both, Grandpa.

It's not like I'm opposed to hard work or long days, but I would like to have *some* free time this summer. Without Matt around to help, I might not have any free time at all.

"I suppose I can make a few calls—" Grandpa says.

"I'm handling it," Dad says, cutting him off. "It's my job to worry about this stuff, not yours."

"Since when?"

"Since you retired," Dad says.

"If Matt's not gonna be here, we could use the help," I say, once again inserting myself into the conversation. "*I* could use the help. Mom's been spending more time in the stables. So far, we've managed to handle the day-to-day okay, but once the summer training season starts, she'll be even busier."

Dad drums his fingers on the table. "The kid Alex wants to send here . . . has no experience. He might be more trouble than he's worth," he warns.

"It doesn't take an advanced degree to muck out the stables or feed the hogs. Plus, Grandma always said Michelangelo couldn't paint the Sistine Chapel his first day on the job," I say. "Everyone has to start somewhere."

What I don't say is that if Uncle Alex called to ask us for this favor, it must be pretty important to him. Even though he and Grandpa have a complicated history, Uncle Alex has always been good to me. And taking on a new ranch hand for the summer isn't exactly a huge favor, not when it would be benefiting me.

When I look over at Grandpa, he's regarding me with watery

eyes. "You remind me so much of her sometimes," he says. He blinks and turns to Dad. "How much will you have to pay 'im?"

It's not a truce, exactly, but it's something.

"Nothing," Dad says. "He'll work in exchange for room and board. And riding lessons."

Riding lessons?

"Someone will have to show him the ropes," Grandpa says. "And teach him to ride."

"Are you volunteering?" Dad asks, but instead of the defensive tone he's taken most of the night, this time there's a hint of humor in his voice.

"Not me. I'm retired, remember?"

"I'm not the one who keeps forgetting." Dad glances at Mom and shrugs. "But Alex and I were thinking Cassidy might be up for it."

My skin prickles under the scrutiny of three sets of eyes suddenly fixed on me. "Who, me?" I say.

Dad raises his eyebrows. "You did just say you could use the help."

I swallow down a bit of nerves and nod. "I'll do it."

Now that that's settled, most of the tension that's been hanging around the dinner table has seeped away. Our forks scrape against our plates as we finish up our slices of pie.

"Has Alex told you anything about our new farmhand?" Mom asks.

Dad scratches at his stubble. "He's one of his clients. Name's Wilder something or another."

It's not exactly a common first name, and since I have Uncle Alex's client list memorized, I'm pretty sure I know exactly who our new farmhand is going to be: Wilder Nash.

★★★

When Uncle Alex called asking if we could take on a ranch hand for the summer, I didn't anticipate that he'd be putting him on a plane the same week, let alone two days later. Yesterday passed in a blur of the usual chores, with additional loads of laundry to make sure the guest cottage is stocked with fresh linens. I spent the morning helping Mom tend to the beehives and kitchen garden, and now I'm scrambling to get everything ready before our ranch hand arrives.

It's been a few months since anyone spent the night in the guest cottage, so it needs to be aired out and freshened up. On my way over from the main house, I clip a few sprigs of lavender to set on the kitchen counter. Lavender always makes things smell fresh and clean.

Trouble wanders over and rubs against my leg. I bend down to give her head a quick pat and she flops down at my feet, purring.

"How's my favorite little imp?" I ask, scratching under her chin.

A butterfly flutters past and Trouble jumps up and darts after it, her tail swishing behind her.

"Stay away from the chickens," I warn as she races off.

I continue along the dusty path to the guest cottage, stopping by the greenhouse to grab an old mason jar to use as a vase. As expected, stale air greets me when I push open the cottage door, which leads directly into the main room that serves as a combination kitchen, living area, and dining room. After setting the jar of lavender on the counter, I make my way through the little house to open the windows and check for signs of a vermin infestation. Thankfully, Trouble can stick to chasing butterflies around the garden today.

I work my way from the back of the cottage to the front. The window frame in the bedroom creaks as I force up the sash. A fine layer of dust coats the dresser. There's an impressive spider-web in the corner. And the bed needs making. Plenty to do but nothing I can't handle.

I pop in an earbud and listen to an audiobook as I work. While my feet are very much planted in Wyoming, my imagination transports me to San Francisco.

It's easy enough to get lost in the story as I tug a fitted sheet onto the mattress. To get caught up in images of fog swallowing the Golden Gate Bridge while I wipe the fog from my breath off the bathroom mirror. I dream about another life riding trolly cars instead of horses as I stock the pantry with staples and snacks. I've never been to a bay, let alone an ocean, and the descriptions of the scent of salty air and the waves breaking against the shore sound incredible.

But as much as I'd like to experience it myself, would I—could I—choose a life away from here? I think about the life in New York City that Grandma gave up when she married Grandpa. And then I think of what Uncle Alex gave up when he moved to L.A.

Is life at Silver Stallion Ranch perfect? No. But I'm not sure the grass is any greener on the other side of the fence.

CHAPTER 4

Wilder

WYOMING.

I've never given it much thought before now. Never had a reason to.

What do I even know about Wyoming?

The capital city is Cheyenne. I think. It's been a while since the on-set tutor had me memorize state capitals. Talk about excruciating. Lines are easy to remember. They have a flow and a purpose. But random facts about random places, ready to spit out on command? I'll pass.

I've heard from some of my castmates that Jackson Hole has good skiing.

Yellowstone has Old Faithful. Wolves. And a TV series named after it (even though they filmed in Utah and Montana).

And, according to Alexander, there's a ranch in the remote town of Cottonwood Grove where I can learn to ride.

26

After years of working with him, I trust Alexander completely, and he's always done right by me. Besides being my agent, he sometimes serves as my on-set chaperone when Mom has to work. But Wyoming?

"The days are comfortable, but the nights can get cool," he says as we make our way to LAX.

It's a good thing the wardrobe department let me keep all those outfits from the commercial shoot.

"And even though there's not much traffic, you'd be surprised how many times bison, moose, sheep, pronghorn, cattle, and geese cause delays."

"They all just . . . roam free?" I ask.

Alexander looks over at me and grins. "The wild ones do."

"Cool," I say, like an actor who is really, really good at pretending that everything is, in fact, cool.

Alexander pulls into the departures lane and stops in front of the terminal entrance. I grab my bags from the trunk of his giant Cadillac SUV, and he hands me a manila folder through the passenger window.

"Here's a copy of the release forms your mom signed and your itinerary. I've arranged for a car service to pick you up at the airport."

"Thanks," I say.

"You're going to love it there, Wilder," he says, his tone wistful. "You'll make a great cowboy."

"Right."

But with everything I have riding on this, I'm not so sure.

The nonstop flight is short—not even two hours—and only a little bumpy as we make our way over the Sierra Nevada mountains in California and then again over the Rocky Mountains in Wyoming. It's amazing to think that we can cross multiple states in the same amount of time it can take to get from our condo to a local film set on days when traffic in L.A. is particularly bad. It seems like the flight attendants barely have time to pass out our refreshments before the pilot announces it's time to prepare for landing.

I shove an unopened bag of pretzels into my carry-on.

Return my seat back and tray table to their upright and locked positions.

Gaze out the window at the massive mountains growing larger as we make our final descent.

The wheels touch down and the next thing I know, I'm stepping onto the Jetway. It's about ten degrees cooler here than it was in L.A., but the air is clean and refreshing.

My driver meets me at baggage claim with a whiteboard that says Wilder Nash.

"That's me," I say.

I wonder if someday I'll be so recognizable, my driver won't need to hold up a sign. Maybe they'll be asking me to sign something for them instead.

That would be epic.

Someone once told me that you know you've made it in Hollywood when they book you for *The Tonight Show*. I think I'll know I've made it when I'm recognized by a stranger in an airport. Or by pretty much any non-film industry adult.

"I'm Charles," he says.

Charles stands by while I pull my luggage from the conveyor belt. When I'm done, he takes my bags and then guides me to his shiny black Lincoln Navigator. Above us, the sky is clear and such a brilliant blue I'd swear it was created by a CGI special-effects team.

Charles doesn't say much on the hour-and-a-half trip to Silver Stallion Ranch. While he focuses on driving, I stare out the window at the passing landscape. Highway 191 cuts through flat fields with groves of deciduous trees, so different from the palm trees and desertscapes that I'm used to. Guardrails line the road at seemingly random intervals. Soon they disappear and the trees thin out until all that surrounds us is wide-open grassland with imposing peaks in the distance.

We pass the Grand Teton National Park sign.

We pass a long, dirt road that carves across the earth to an evergreen-dotted hill.

We pass a yellow sign with an image of a bounding deer. Caution. Next three miles.

I keep an eye out for wildlife, but aside from a few birds, there's no indication that we'll be held up in an animal traffic jam like Alexander warned might happen.

Instead, we slow for a very familiar kind of traffic jam. Cars crawl through an intersection, and as we ease forward, a town appears.

"Welcome to Jackson," Charles says.

"Where's the hole?" I joke.

Charles glances at me in his rearview mirror, but there's no change to his perpetually stony expression. "You're in it. Jackson's the town. The hole's the whole valley." The edge of his mouth crooks up, only the slightest hint of a sense of humor.

Jackson would be considered sleepy by L.A. standards.

We head east at Hoback Junction and the hills become rockier, with smooth cream-colored outcroppings and spindly evergreen forests. A few miles more, and those give way to rolling fields surrounded by fences and the ranches they belong to. I'm used to seeing vast expanses of land between mountains, but in Southern California, it's usually a pale, dusty desert with tan boulders and spiky yucca. In this part of Wyoming, it's a thick field with rolling hills and clumps of bushes. Turns out, watching the grass ripple in the wind is almost as mesmerizing as watching the waves lap against the shore.

I figure we must be getting close to our destination, and sure enough, ten minutes later we exit the highway for a paved but unpainted single-lane road. It's so narrow that vehicles traveling in the opposite direction have to pass on the shoulder. Charles slows the car as we approach a long dirt driveway. At the entrance, a black metal sign is affixed to a weathered post—a rearing horse and below it: Silver Stallion Ranch.

From the road, I can't see a house. Or a barn. Or any building whatsoever. If it weren't for the sign, I'd think we were in the wrong place.

Charles turns in and we drive up a sloped hill. We come around a curve and suddenly the landscape opens up to the valley below: a lush prairie with a stream winding across it.

"Wow." It's beautiful.

And intimidating, if I'm being honest. There's so much open land, I feel the opposite of claustrophobic . . . whatever that is. I'm totally out of my element here.

There aren't any cattle in sight.

Or horses.

Or Stetson-hatted cowboys.

But there's plenty of space and endless blue sky, just like Alexander promised.

A large white house sits prominently at the end of the drive, with a few other buildings behind it. I step from the car and stretch while Charles piles my luggage at the rear of the SUV. I suppose I should go knock on the door and let them know I've arrived.

I should.

But I hesitate.

Once I knock, that'll be it. I'll be fully committed. The needle on the speedometer of my life will go from "Fake it till you make it" to "Do or die."

What if I can't hack it?

What if I can't learn to ride? Or become a convincing cowboy?

I could hop back in the car and return to L.A. Maybe Alexander could find me a stunt double or a stand-in or . . .

If it were that simple, the studio would've hired a double. But then they could've cast Jackson Miller or Cam Sheffield.

But they didn't.

They cast me.

And *I'm* supposed to know how to ride.

Dammit.

"Wilder Nash."

My head swivels toward the sound of my name. A girl about my age strides toward me with a sense of authority and purpose. Her dark brown hair is pulled into a loose braid that sits on her shoulder, and her long, thick bangs hide most of her eyebrows. She's pretty in a fresh-faced and natural way. "I'm Cassidy Sterling. Welcome to Silver Stallion Ranch." She gives me a polite smile and holds out a hand for me to shake.

"Nice to meet you," I say automatically, as if it's been programmed into me. Which I suppose it has, thanks to my mother and her early lessons in manners when I first started out.

Cassidy's shorter than me by a few inches and athletically built. Her hands are rough and her grip is firm. Dusty cowboy boots peek out from under the fraying hem of her faded blue jeans.

I glance down at my brand-new, straight-from-the-commercial-shoot jeans. My barely worn dust-free sneakers. Of the two of us, she definitely looks like she belongs.

Her dark brown eyes widen when she takes in the pile of luggage stacked behind me. "Looks like you came prepared. Why don't I show you the guest cottage and you can get settled in."

I nod and grab two of my bags. She grabs the other two and motions for me to follow her. I'm surprised she's carrying the bags, when they have perfectly good wheels. But I soon find out the hard way that the path to the guesthouse is full of ruts and pebbles. It's a fight to keep my roller bags upright and moving.

Cassidy turns to say something to me and then realizes I'm lagging behind. I give up trying to drag my bags after a few embarrassing seconds where she watches me lose the wheel-versus-dirt path battle. I haven't even been here for ten whole minutes. The little voice in the back of my head whispers, *Fake it till you make it.*

That, I can do. I'm an actor, after all.

"I'll just come back for that one later," I say, as if it's the most natural thing to just leave a suitcase in the middle of a . . . vegetable garden?

She lifts a questioning eyebrow, then turns away to continue toward a small log cabin.

I fumble with the suitcase and hurry after her. Wow, she's fast. I'm almost out of breath by the time my sneakers hit the stairs that lead up to the front door. Cassidy doesn't even look like her heart rate increased a single beat per minute.

Damn, she's fit.

I straighten my shoulders, force myself to take slow, steady breaths, and give her my best camera-ready smile.

"Let me give you a quick lay of the land. The main house is there." She points to the large white house and then turns toward a red-roofed structure. "That's the stable. There's the green house. Our chicken coop. The pigsty and the goat shed. There are a couple of other buildings scattered over the south end of the property, which I'll show you later."

I nod. What am I supposed to say? It would be nice to have someone writing lines for me in real time. Nothing comes to mind, so instead I run a hand through my hair and lean back against the porch railing. If there's one thing I know how to do, it's look good.

Cassidy doesn't seem impressed. In fact, she barely gives me a look before pushing open the front door. I follow her inside, where the soft scent of lavender welcomes us.

"The bedroom's down the hall there. Bathroom's right next door. There are extra towels in the closet and some snacks in the pantry. You're welcome to eat meals with us up at the main house or you can make yourself something here. Although tonight, Mom and Dad would like you to join us for dinner."

"Sure thing," I say.

Cassidy glances at her watch and frowns. "I've got some chores to finish up. Dinner's at six tonight. Holler if you need anything."

Then, in the blink of an eye, she's gone, and I'm left standing alone in a cabin on a ranch in the middle of Wyoming wondering what the hell I've gotten myself into.

CHAPTER 5

Cassidy

COAXING OUR TOGGENBURG goats back into their paddock from the surrounding pasture is always tricky because these two are master escape artists with a playful streak. And they absolutely love attention.

As soon as Rambrandt spots me, he gets the zoomies and races around the fenced-in field like his tail is on fire. He lets out a few loud bleats as if he's a proud toddler who's just mastered a new skill. "Look at me, Maa. Maa. Maa." He's a blur of russet and white as he darts past.

Van Goat looks down his long nose at Rambrandt and sighs, as if to say, "Can you believe him?" He leans into my side and nuzzles my arm with his head, begging for a chin scratch. I wrap my arm around his mouse-gray neck to reach the area behind his white beard, and his tail swishes, gently tapping against the back of my leg.

Rambrandt and Van Goat are the ranch's mobile weed-control units. They graze around the property in portable mesh pens set up in specially selected areas, helping to keep the red-cedar from encroaching on the fields we use for grazing cattle.

Rambrandt eventually tires himself out. He lopes over and rams me with a playful headbutt. He's always been fond of ramming into people, which is how he got his name. "Maa," he says.

I reach down and scratch along his cheeks. His dark eyes stare into mine for a second and then his eyes close. If goats could smile, I'm pretty sure he'd be grinning from ear to ear.

I start walking toward the goat paddock, but neither of them follows. "C'mon," I say. "Time to head home now."

"Maa," says Van Goat, shaking his head no. Sometimes I wish I'd never taught him that.

"Maa," says Rambrandt, making a point by sitting down on his butt like a dog.

People say mules are stubborn, but clearly they've never met these two wise guys . . . er, goats.

"Okay, who wants to play on the seesaw?" I ask.

Both goats' ears perk up and soon they trot after me through the gate that separates this pasture from their pen. I latch it shut, double-checking to make sure it's locked, while Van Goat bounds over to the seesaw with Rambrandt following close behind.

When they're both on the board, they take turns jumping and bouncing. Rambrandt goes to the end and the platform sinks under his weight. Van Goat makes his way to the opposite side so that they're balanced in the air. It's been years since I taught them this trick and it's always fun to watch them play and perform.

When I glance up at the guesthouse, I catch a glimpse of

Wilder watching us from the window. It must be a strange sight for him, two goats on a seesaw.

He gives me a "what's up" head bob and then disappears behind the curtain.

I'm not quite sure what to make of Wilder. I expected him to be just as good-looking in person as he is on TV. And he is. Wilder's mid-length waves curl around his ears, the dark brown strands highlighted by sun-kissed blond locks. His striking eyes are more gray than blue. And he has perfectly straight, white teeth that were practically made for the most recent toothpaste commercial Uncle Alex booked for him.

Uncle Alex has always been proud of Wilder. So while I wouldn't call myself a fan girl by any means, I have paid attention to his career.

I'm well aware that actors are not their roles, so I expected Wilder to be different from the characters he usually portrays. A few years ago, I watched *Homecoming Hero*, where Wilder played the school heartthrob with a plethora of smoldering looks and swoony lines. There was *Ghost Ed*, where he was a suave spirit haunting the halls of Valley Glen High. And *Junior Prom Marathon*, where he played the hunky rent-a-date in a rental tux. In fact, I can't think of a single thing he's been in where he wasn't portraying a self-assured flirt with a charming smile.

No, that's not entirely true. There was that toothpaste commercial—no flirting or smoldering eyes, but plenty of smiling in a twenty-second ad.

So is Wilder simply a character actor, or is the incorrigible flirt aesthetic his entire personality?

I walk over to the fence and pull up a clump of blooming hawksbeard on the other side. The leaves remind me of a dandelion's, but the plant has very different yellow, star-shaped flowers. Of course, the goats are curious to see what I'm doing by the fence. Rambrandt gracefully leaps off the seesaw while Van Goat scrambles to the ground. I hold the hawksbeard out for them to munch. Happy with a snack from the other side of the fence, they trail me all the way back to the goat shed.

On my way out, I latch the gate and double-check the lock. As long as they're contained in the goat shed or surrounded by a proper fence, they can't get up to any mischief. It's keeping them contained that's the problem. The last time the goats ran wild, they ate all of Mom's sunflowers. The time before that, they discovered the laundry line. We found Van Goat wearing a pillowcase and chewing on a fitted sheet, while Rambrandt was gnawing on what used to be Dad's favorite flannel shirt.

I spin around and triple-check to make sure the gate's secure. With everything else we have going on right now, the last thing we need is two destructive escape artists wandering around the ranch.

It's almost time for dinner, and I figure I should check on Wilder to make sure he's settling in okay. The front door to the guest cottage is ajar, and I hear what sounds like shoes clicking on the hardwood floors inside.

That's strange.

I could've sworn Wilder was wearing sneakers when he arrived. Still, a lot of Uncle Alex's clients are multi-talented, so maybe Wilder's practicing a tap dance routine? Judging from the sound, he's not very good.

I rap against the door a few times to get his attention. "Wilder?"

I lean in to listen for a response, my hands braced on the door frame, but all I hear is *tappity, tap, tap. Tappity tap.*

I knock a little louder. "Wilder, it's Cassidy."

Everything goes quiet, and then I hear a cautious, "Maa?"

But that can't be, because Rambrandt and Van Goat are locked inside their pen for the night. I know. I triple-checked.

Except . . . there's a sinking feeling in my gut that's more than just an empty stomach. Just to be sure, I walk to the corner of the guest cottage and glance around the side, expecting to find the door to the goat shed firmly closed and latched as it should be because that's how I left it.

But it's not how I left it.

The door is now wide open, swinging in the breeze.

I turn back toward the guest cottage's front door and push it open all the way with my foot. "Wilder, you in here?" I call.

There's still no response. I can't see Rambrandt or Van Goat from where I'm standing, but I can hear the *tappity-tap* of their hooves on the floor.

Not good, not good, not good.

I have to get them out of here before they cause any major damage. Curtains. Door frames. Table legs. The chaos they could create is endless.

"I'm coming in," I holler, and then step over the threshold.

Nothing seems to be amiss in the living area. The couch cushions are intact, at least.

Rambrandt and Van Goat aren't in the kitchen.

The bathroom door is closed, so they probably aren't in there. That just leaves the bedroom.

I tiptoe down the hall and peer in.

"Oh, lord," I say when I take in the scene of destruction in front of me.

Van Goat stands beside the closet door, a packet of airplane snacks split open at his feet. Bits and pieces of mini hard pretzels and cheese crackers are strewn over the floor along with what's left of a shredded magazine. In his mouth is a bright white shoelace, which has been almost completely severed into two pieces. The frayed bits wave like prairie grass at the corner of his mouth, where Wilder's sneaker dangles precariously as Van Goat gnaws on the shoelace.

As for Rambrandt, he's on the bed, with the corner of the top sheet in his mouth. He pulls back, trying to yank the fabric off the mattress. It won't move because he's standing on it. With a stubborn grunt, he tries again, scrambling backward until the sheet begins to tear.

"Oh, no, you don't," I say, rushing over to extract the bed linens from his mouth.

Of course, Rambrandt thinks it's a game. He jumps out of reach and tugs at the sheet again.

"Get down from there," I say in my sternest goat herder voice.

"Maa," says Rambrandt, the goat equivalent of "make me." And then, with a defiant look in his eye, he starts jumping.

The bed creaks beneath him as he launches himself into the air over and over again, the sheet flapping beside him like a billowing sail.

"Stop it right now," I insist.

But clearly, scolding is getting me nowhere. Maybe if I can get Van Goat to cooperate, Rambrandt will follow his lead. "C'mon, let's go," I say, attempting to coax Van Goat toward the door. He stares at me, chewing the shoelace, completely un-impressed.

I should know better. Trying to catch a goat is like trying to catch a rainbow. It always seems like you're getting close, but you can never quite get there.

I glance around the room, looking for something . . . any-thing . . . that will spark their interest and help me get them out of the guest cottage.

Aha! A brown paper bag is tucked between the trash can and the wall. I reach out to grab it when I'm startled by a mas-culine voice behind me.

"Holy crap! Why are there goats in my bedroom?"

I spin around to find Wilder standing in the doorway, his hair dripping wet and his flannel shirt unbuttoned over a white tank top. He's got a towel in his hand and a scowl on his face.

"The front door was open," I say, as if that explains everything.

Wilder blinks and looks over at me, his brow furrowed. "What are *you* doing in my bedroom?"

As if it's not obvious.

"Trying to get the goats out of here," I say.

I try not to take offense that he seems to be more concerned with me being in his room than the goats.

I glance over at Rambrandt, but he's not about to cooperate. He gives me a long stare and lies down on the bed. Then he has the audacity to rest his chin on Wilder's pillow.

"What the hell is happening?" Wilder asks.

I'm not even going to dignify his question with a response.

I grab the paper bag, shake it open, and hold it up for the goats to see. "Doesn't this look fun?"

Both goats ignore me.

"Oh, man, my shoes. What have you done to my shoes?" Wilder says, reaching out to grab his sneaker. With a swift yank, he tugs it away from Van Goat. The shoelace snaps with a loud ripping sound. "These are brand-new."

Not anymore.

"Look," I say, "we can worry about your shoes later. Right now, we have to get the goats out of here before they destroy anything else."

Rambrandt takes it as a personal challenge. He fixes his gaze on the neck pillow hanging on the corner of the chair next to the bed.

"Don't do it," I say.

Rambrandt licks his lips.

"Don't you dare."

I make a grab for the pillow but I'm too late. Rambrandt chomps it with his teeth and the fabric splits open. Tiny white beads scatter everywhere like a localized blizzard.

"Stop," I say, trying to get the pillow away from him, but that just makes Rambrandt shake his head, sending more beads flying.

"Do something," Wilder says, waving his shoe at me. There's a panicked look in his eye and his voice is unsteady.

"What exactly would you like me to do?" I ask in frustration.

These goats might be domesticated, but they're not exactly obedient creatures. And it's not like I'm not trying.

Wilder lets out a frustrated grunt. "Shoo," he says, flapping his towel at Van Goat. "Get out of here."

But Van Goat isn't keen on having a tasty-looking towel waved in front of his face, especially by a stranger. He lowers into charging stance and takes off toward Wilder.

CHAPTER 6

Wilder

MY FEET ARE already in motion when I hear Cassidy call, "Watch out!"

The goat's hooves slip over the hardwood floor as he comes after me, his strange, scary eyes focused on my backside. I race toward the front door in bare feet, my heart thundering in my ears. There's a loud thud and Cassidy yells, "Rambrandt, no!"

Now the sound of eight hooves scrambling over the planked floor echoes behind me. I once had to get out of the path of a runaway golf cart in a home insurance commercial by swiveling around a lamppost. So, just like I'd done last year, I pump my legs harder and grab on to the first sturdy thing I come to: the door frame. I whip myself around and the goats barrel through the door behind me, clattering down the two front steps as they charge ahead. Pressed up against the side of the house, panting, I watch them stop in the middle of the dirt path that leads to the main house and look around.

Thank goodness for the stunt training.

Thank goodness for Safe Home Insurance.

"We cover it all" is their slogan. I wonder if that includes attack goats.

"Maa."

"Maa."

"Well done getting the goats out of there," Cassidy says, giving me a light smack on the shoulder as she jogs past. "You'll be a proper goat wrangler in no time."

Say what? I wasn't wrangling goats. I was running for my life.

But I can't bring myself to admit it. I give her a confident smile and wait until she's out of sight before my butt hits the deck and I drape my arms over my knees. Hopefully I look cool and relaxed, and not like someone who just saw their life flash before their eyes.

A few minutes later, Cassidy returns. Her cheeks are flushed, her hair's a mess, and there's a smudge of dirt on her jeans. "You okay?" she asks.

"Of course," I say as nonchalantly as possible. As if these chaotic, unplanned things happen to me all the time. "Do . . . um . . . your goats just wander free?"

Cassidy gives me a *look.* "Definitely not. Those two," she says, jerking her thumb over her shoulder toward the goat pen, "are much better off in containment." Her lips purse and she sighs. "I just can't understand how they got out. I know I latched the gate."

Before I can stop the words from exiting my mouth, I find myself saying, "About that . . ."

Where's a director to yell "Cut!" when you need one?

Cassidy's warm, brown eyes suddenly go flinty. She lifts a brow and it disappears behind her bangs.

"I . . . um . . ." I cough. Push myself up to standing. Roll the towel and wrap it behind my neck like I've just hopped off the treadmill at the gym. With the way my heart's pounding, it almost feels like I have. "I wanted to stretch my legs and I must have left the gate open. . . ."

Cassidy's hands clench and unclench at her sides. She takes a deep breath, as if she's forcing herself to stay calm. "Well, no harm, no foul. Just don't let it happen again."

"I wouldn't exactly say 'no harm.' My bed's a mess. My neck pillow's destroyed." I run a hand through my damp curls and flash her the same extra-wide smile I used for an anti-cavity toothpaste commercial last year. "I'm gonna need new laces."

Cassidy shrugs. "When the goats run free, there's always a fee. You're lucky all it cost you was a travel pillow and a shoelace."

Cassidy leads me into the main house through a side door. The hinge squeaks as the screen door pulls shut behind us. She kicks off her dusty boots into a black plastic tray and waits for me to do the same.

A moment later, my shoes join hers. I take a deep breath and smooth down the front of my flannel shirt. I don't have much experience with family dinners, since it's just been me and Mom for as long as I can remember. While I've filmed a few family dinner scenes, those were completely staged, so I'm not quite sure what to expect.

Fake it till you make it.

"This way," Cassidy says.

I follow her down a short hallway and through an opening that leads into a large country kitchen. My feet pause on the gleaming wood floors as the scent of fresh herbs and roasting chicken make my mouth water. My gaze skips over a giant butcher-block island covered in an array of baking dishes and pans as I step farther into the room.

"You're late."

I turn in the direction of the older, raspy voice, and I know immediately that it must belong to Alexander's father—Cassidy's grandfather. The man is probably in his early seventies, and he's shorter and more weathered than Alexander—with the same thick, dark eyebrows and strong jawline. His resemblance is clear.

"Sorry, Grandpa," Cassidy says with a wince as she makes her way to an empty seat at the table. "The goats were being goats."

The man grunts. "Food's getting cold."

I take a hesitant step forward and a middle-aged man turns to face me. I can't tell for sure, but he's probably only a few years younger than Alexander. "You must be Wilder. I'm Mitchell Sterling. Call me Mitch." He, too, shares the same Sterling eyebrows and jawline, but his hair is darker than Alexander's and his expression is less severe than his father's. "This is my father, Frank—"

"You can call *me* Mr. Sterling," snaps the older man.

Mitch ignores him and continues. "And my wife, Julianne. Of course, you've already met Cassidy."

"Welcome to Silver Stallion Ranch." Julianne greets me with

a warm smile. She points me toward the remaining empty chair at the table, the one between Mitch and Mr. Sterling.

"Food's not getting any warmer," Mr. Sterling says, looking pointedly from me to the seat.

I hustle over and sink down onto the worn wooden chair. It squeaks loudly as I try to nudge it forward so that I'm a comfortable distance from the table. Heat creeps up from under my collar.

Mr. Sterling clears his throat and narrows his flinty hazel eyes at me. "So, you're Wilder Nash," he says, drawing out my name like it leaves a bitter taste on his tongue.

I freeze, trying not to shrink under his scrutiny. My spine presses against the chair back. "Yeah. Hey," I say with a forced smile, but before I can say anything else, he cuts me off.

"Hay is for horses."

For some inexplicable reason, I start to laugh but then swallow it down quickly because he's not joking. In fact, with the look he's giving me, I'm not sure this guy even knows how to joke.

My father's a bit prickly, Alexander had warned me. *Prickly* was a complete understatement. This guy's a giant saguaro cactus with extra spines.

Mitch pushes his chair back from the table and a tense moment passes between him and Mr. Sterling. Then the older man reaches for a ceramic platter holding a whole roasted chicken. "I'll carve tonight," he says, reaching for a giant, glinting knife. "Light or dark meat?" he asks me.

Is this a trick question? "Oh, um . . . both?" I manage.

Mr. Sterling grunts and tosses a chicken leg onto my plate.

Everyone else gets nice, manageable slices. I'm still trying to decide if I should attempt to cut the meat off the bone or just go full Medieval Times on the chicken leg when my phone buzzes in my pocket. "Oops," I say apologetically as I move to answer it.

Mr. Sterling thunks his water glass down on the table. "I don't know how things are done in Hollywood, kid," he says, his voice as sharp as the carving knife. "But here in Wyoming, we don't take calls during dinner."

I force down a swallow. "It's probably my mom checking in," I explain.

"Then you'll kindly inform her that dinner here is at six p.m. sharp. And if you choose to dine at my table, you'll arrange to check in with her at a different time. Or you'll be checking right out of the guesthouse and heading right back to where you belong."

What am I supposed to say to that? I think I mumble something like "Right, sure," but my mind is spinning.

The rest of dinner is awkward as hell. Julianne and Mitch attempt to make polite conversation, which I appreciate, but most of the topics are things I know nothing about. It doesn't help that Mr. Sterling watches me with hawk-like eyes.

"Carmichael called earlier," Mitch says to his father. "His compact disc isn't working."

Finally, a conversation topic I can contribute to.

"Did he try rubbing some toothpaste on it?" I ask.

Even though practically everything's digital these days, Mom still insists on using her old, beat-up CD player every December to play a stack of her favorite holiday albums. Last year, she discovered a scratch on *The Carpenters: A Christmas Portrait* and showed me the toothpaste trick to fix it.

"Toothpaste?" Cassidy asks with a furrowed brow.

Everyone else is staring at me with blank faces.

"Toothpaste." I pause to wipe my mouth with a napkin. "You put a little dab on the disc and rub it with a soft cloth. Clean it up and pop it back in and it should play just fine."

"Toothpaste? For a compact disc?" Mr. Sterling's look changes from stern appraisal to confusion.

I'd thought trying to join in on the conversation might reduce the tension, but clearly, opening my mouth was a mistake. This is why I hate going off-script. "It probably works for DVDs, too," I say.

"Oh," Cassidy says, understanding dawning on her face. I'm pretty sure she's stifling a smile, based on the way the corner of her mouth is twitching. "Here on the ranch, a compact disc is a piece of farm equipment that's pulled behind a tractor. It's kind of like a tiller."

Great.

As far as first impressions go, this is by far the worst I've ever made. And what's more, I still have at least six more weeks to go.

After a restless night of tossing and turning, I pull on a still-stiff pair of dark-wash jeans, a soft cotton T-shirt, and a flannel shirt. The work boots are heavy compared to my sneakers. Based on my reflection in the bathroom mirror, I look every bit a ranch hand. Or at least, how I think a ranch hand is supposed to look. I've never been cast as one before.

I could use a cup of coffee and something to eat. Julianne

told me the kitchen in the main house is open during "normal rancher's hours"—whatever that means—and I'm sure they have coffee there. And hopefully breakfast.

As I head along the path to the main house, Cassidy walks toward me, carrying a metal bucket. Her hair is tucked under a threadbare blue bandanna and she's wearing a bulky hoodie and faded jeans. "Morning," she says when she spots me. "Ready to get to work?"

"Oh. Um." My stomach growls. "I haven't eaten breakfast yet."

"Neither have the animals," she says matter-of-factly, walking past me on the path that leads to the barnyard.

I jog a few strides to catch up. "I do my best work when I'm fed," I explain with a sure smile that usually gets me whatever I want.

Cassidy seems immune to my charms. "So do the chickens. If you expect to eat breakfast, then you need to feed the animals that provide it. You can't make an omelet without eggs."

"Who said anything about an omelet? A bagel would suit me just fine. Even cereal will do."

Cassidy doesn't respond but she does give me some serious side-eye. Maybe she's just not a morning person?

I follow her to a squat wooden structure with a slanted roof.

"Hello, ladies," Cassidy says to a chorus of oinks and grunts. She dumps the contents of the bucket into a long trough as four very large pink pigs hurry over.

"Now what?" I ask.

"Now we feed the goats."

Oh, hell no.

"Yeah, about that," I say, reaching up to run a hand through

50

my hair. After last night's run-in with those two beasts, I want nothing to do with them. "I'd rather not be impaled first thing in the morning."

"Impaled?" Cassidy gives me a puzzled look. "With what?"

"Their horns." *Duh.*

"Rambrandt and Van Goat are polled," she says.

Last I checked, goats can't vote, so what the heck is that supposed to mean? "So?" I ask.

"*Polled* means they were born without horns. It's pretty common for their breed."

Does that change anything?

Not really.

Even without horns, they look like they could do some serious bodily damage. They're basically battering rams on four legs.

"I'll just stay here," I say. "Out of your way." I pull my cell from my pocket and glance at the screen. There's only one bar of service, but maybe if I wander around, I'll get better reception.

Cassidy shrugs. "Suit yourself."

Maybe I could feed something else? I glance around and my gaze lands on the chicken coop. "I could feed the chickens."

"I'm not sure that's a great idea, Wilder," Cassidy says.

"They're chickens, not cheetahs."

"Yes, but—"

I cut her off before she can say anything else. "How hard can it be?" I straighten my spine and lift an eyebrow. "Just point me to the chicken feed."

I've jumped from a burning building, thrown the game-winning touchdown, and crashed into a mailbox while riding a skateboard on film, so feeding a few football-sized birds is sure to be a breeze compared to all that. Granted, there were special effects, plenty of choreography, and a stunt team involved, but the action was all me. They didn't even have to use a double.

Cassidy shrugs again. "Fine. If you're determined to feed the chickens, you can feed the chickens." She leads me over to an ancient, yellowing deep freezer. Inside is a bag of feed pellets and a small bucket. She fills the bucket and hands it to me. "Pour this inside the feeders. You can leave the door to the coop open, because unlike the goats, our chickens *are* free range." The edge of her mouth curls up into a smirk.

My ears grow hot, so I double down and flash my biggest grin. I grab the bucket from her and reach for the door. The goat incident was a one-time deal. Feeding these chickens will be a piece of cake.

"Wait," she says, "Wilder . . ."

I ignore her. Squaring my shoulders, I step into the coop and look around for the feeder. There are a pair of white tubes, about two feet long, hanging on the wire fence to my left, each with a little feeding tray at the bottom.

"You pull off the lid at the top and pour the feed in," Cassidy calls.

"I'm good," I call back.

I'm an actor, not an idiot.

I reach over to remove the caps on the feeding tubes. *Pop, pop.* Suddenly, all the hairs on the back of my neck stand up. It's feels like I'm being watched. Of course I am, because Cassidy is standing right over . . .

I glance back at where I expect to find Cassidy admiring the view, only to see her heading to the goat shed.

Hmm. I must still be out of sorts from the goat incident. Totally thrown off my game. I spin around, only to find that I'm being stared at by at least eighteen tiny, beady eyes.

Just outside the hen house, three chickens stand at the front of the flock, with another six or so behind them lined up in an arc. One chicken steps forward and flaps its wings at me. "Bwak."

They're probably hungry and can't wait for their food. I grab the bucket and fill the two feeders. "There you go," I say, setting the caps back on. "All—"

"Ba-gawk."

The chickens fan out around me, bobbing rhythmically as they shuffle closer, their feathers ruffled and chests puffed out. They occasionally dip down to peck at the dirt or preen, but they all keep a watchful, wary eye on me. And the ones in the front, they have danger in their stares.

"Ba-gawk," the meanest-looking chicken says.

"Bwak. Bwak," her friends reply.

I hold my hands up to try to calm them, but they must take it as an aggressive move. The closest chicken rushes at me, her two buddies on her tail.

It's like *Angry Birds.*

But in real life.

I wasn't a voice actor in that movie, and I've barely played the game, so I'm not sure what to do.

The ringleader dives at me again. I manage to dart out of the way using a dip-and-slide dance move I learned for *Junior Prom Marathon.*

It gets me out of the immediate danger zone, but now the other hens are riled up. The coop fills with loud, angry bwaks.

Feathers.

Dust.

The first peck on my shin is more painful than I expect it to be. I'm not about to wait around for another. Sprinting to the door, I slam it closed after me. The hens line up on the other side, watching. Waiting. Daring me to come back for more.

I pull up my pants leg to find a beak-shaped dent in my skin. Are all the animals here out to get me?

CHAPTER 7

Cassidy

FROM THE SADDLE atop Land Sailor, my dapple-gray gelding, I can just make out the sparkle of a spring-fed stream hidden behind a thicket of sagebrush and shrubs. We've ridden to the top of a grassy ridge, a weathered wooden split-rail fence before us. At just over ten thousand acres, Silver Stallion Ranch is covered with babbling brooks, silvery streams, and a serpentine creek, all of which are fed by snowmelt and springs.

I've spent hours out here on the trails that weave their way through the ranch. Inspecting fences. Driving cattle. Stargazing.

Today's perfect for a trail ride under a pale blue Wyoming sky streaked with wispy white clouds. The air is warm but the breeze is refreshing, and the June flowers are a riot of yellow and blue blooms: balsamroot, with their golden daisy-like petals; buttery groundsel blossoms atop tall stems; lemony clumps of hawksbeard; with the occasional splash of purple from a showy larkspur or delicate mountain bluebell.

It's almost time for Wilder's first riding lesson. If he even shows up. After his run-in with Birdzilla and the rest of the flock this morning, he stormed off toward the guest cottage muttering curses under his breath.

A tinge of guilt eats at me. I probably could have done a better job of trying to warn him about the hens. And I could have stuck around to make sure he was okay before heading to the goat shed. But ever since he showed up, he's been acting like he's all good looks and no common sense.

If he pulls the same "How hard can it possibly be?" routine and doesn't listen to my riding instructions? That could be dangerous for both him and his mount.

My gaze goes to the smaller stable that we use for the Sterling family's horses: Grandpa's red roan gelding, Zeus; Dad's palomino, Will Post, Mom's brown mare, Nutmeg; my Land Sailor; and our two old trail horses, Jupiter and Ginger. There's an exercise paddock attached to the stable, which is where I plan to teach Wilder the basics until he's comfortable enough in the saddle to venture out onto the trail.

A few weeks isn't a lot of time to teach anyone to ride well, let alone ride like they've done it for years. Usually, it takes about six months to get beginners ready for the trail and a few years for a rider to be proficient. Given Wilder's apparent general unfamiliarity with animals and farm chores, I don't have high hopes that he'll be anything close to a prodigy at horsemanship. Still, I'm determined not to let Uncle Alex down. Even though he and Grandpa have a *thing*, Grandma was always adamant that "family comes first, no matter what." She would have wanted me to help Uncle Alex. No matter what.

Plus, Uncle Alex's always been good to me. Sending gifts

on my birthday and for Christmas. Proofreading my English papers. Emailing me regularly to make sure I'm doing okay or when he knows I could use a bit of cheerleading. I smile when I think of the last message he sent before finals:

Cassidy Jane—
Sterlings always do our best.
So sharpen those pencils and kick butt on your tests.

My smile falters. What if my best isn't enough? What if my best is no match for what Wilder brings to the table? Clearly the guy's in over his head.

I know I am.

I've only ever assisted Mom when she gives riding lessons. I've never been the primary instructor. So why did Uncle Alex send Wilder here and specifically ask for me to train him and not Mom? There must be a ton of places closer to L.A. where he could learn to ride from seasoned pros.

I suppose it doesn't matter, since he's here now. Looking like the cover of *Western Wear Weekly* and acting like he has less common sense than Trouble, and that's saying a lot.

What will happen when I get him near a horse? Grandma used to say, "Good or bad, things always come in threes."

First the goats.

And then the chickens.

Worrying about the what-ifs won't make any of this go away.

I sigh and close my eyes, letting the sun's rays warm my shoulders like a comforting blanket. Birds chirp around me. The scent of damp earth clings to the breeze. I can almost taste the freedom of the wind in my hair as Land Sailor and I gallop across the fields.

But not today.

I open my eyes and brush a hand over Land Sailor's mane. "You'll be gentle with him, won't you?" I ask, coaxing him around so we can head back to the stable.

He dips his head as if to say yes.

"There's a good boy." I give him a nudge and he takes off in a happy trot.

I've just finished grooming Land Sailor when Wilder arrives looking like he just walked off a movie lot. He's ditched the canvas jacket he was wearing earlier and has opted to tuck his shaggy curls under a baseball cap. The new boots he brought with him peek out from under dark jeans that still have creases.

He's too put together. Too polished for a place like this. But . . . I don't hate it.

I wish I did.

Wilder glances around, his dark eyes surveying the stable. "Hey . . . um . . . hi," he says, shoving his hands into the front pockets of his jeans. He's the picture of cool and confident, but the way his eyes keep darting around make me wonder how comfortable he really is to be here.

Interesting.

I set a bucket of grooming tools on a nearby shelf. "Ready for your first lesson?" I ask.

Wilder shrugs. "Ready as I'll ever be." He cocks an eyebrow and fixes me with a sparkling gaze. "Ready to make me a cowboy?"

Some people will tell you that cowboys are born, not made. I have no idea if it's true or not, but we're about to find out.

"Ready as I'll ever be."

The corner of his mouth twitches and he reaches up to adjust his ball cap. Now that he's pulled it down low, it's hard to see his eyes in the shadow, but he seems to be taking stock of Land Sailor. I'll bet Wilder's never been this close to a horse before.

For a moment, I picture what it would be like if the roles were reversed. How would I feel being shipped off to Hollywood to learn how to act on a movie set? I've seen enough television and heard enough of Uncle Alex's stories to know I'd be surrounded by sound stages, cameras, and boom mics. I bet I'd be wide-eyed and gawking. But ... I don't hate the thought of it. I ignore the little voice in my head whispering *What if?* I don't have time to daydream about ridiculous things when I have a job to do.

"Okay, then," I say as I run my hand down Land Sailor's withers and give him a gentle pat. "Today we'll go over some basics to get you familiar with horses and the concept of riding."

"Whoa," Wilder says, causing Land Sailor to still. "So I won't actually ride today?" Wilder swallows and shifts his weight. I can't tell for sure, but I get the sense he's nervous.

"We have to get you properly outfitted before you sit in a saddle. Plus, you should get to know the equipment and your horse first."

Wilder nods and some of the tension drains from his shoulders.

"This is my horse, Land Sailor," I say. "He's a sixteen-year-old Morgan gelding and a great trail horse. I ride him around the ranch to check fences, monitor pastures, and drive cattle." Land Sailor nuzzles his face against my shoulder. "Let's get you two acquainted."

Wilder takes a slight step back, tilts his head, and squares his shoulders. "I'm Wilder Nash," he says, like he's being interviewed on the red carpet.

"That was . . . okay," I say, trying to stay constructive. "But when you meet a horse, you need to let them see you and smell you. Why don't you walk over to me and I'll show you how to do the horseman's handshake."

Wilder's body stiffens even though he casts me an easy grin. "Just walk over to you?"

"Yep."

"Is he friendly?"

I catch only the faintest of cracks in Wilder's facade, but I think I get where his reluctance is coming from. After the incidents with the goats and the chickens, he probably thinks all the animals on the ranch have it out for him.

"Land Sailor is a sweetheart," I say with a nod. "He's very calm and gentle."

"Right." It sounds like Wilder's trying to convince himself more than he's agreeing with me.

"First, take a deep breath. Horses can sense tension and anxiety, and you want to have an easy introduction."

"I'm not anxious," Wilder's quick to respond. He rolls his eyes and lifts his chin. But he also crosses his arms over his chest and rocks back on his heels.

"Look, I don't care if you're anxious or not. But Land Sailor will pick up on your tension"—I snap my fingers—"like that. Horses are prey animals, and they've evolved to read signals from their herd for survival, which means they can be sensitive to human emotions. Land Sailor is pretty even-keeled, but he doesn't know you yet. Any anxiety on your part might be misconstrued as a threat. So take a deep breath and come stand next to me."

I'm not sure if he inhales because he's frustrated or if it's because he's actually listening to me, but either way Wilder closes his eyes. He pulls in a deep breath through his nose. Exhales through his mouth. Then he very calmly makes his way over to stand next to me.

"Good. Now reach out slowly and extend the back of your hand to Land Sailor so he can give it a sniff. Like this." I lift my hand like I'm in one of those historical movies, offering it to a gentleman for a kiss.

Immediately, my brain calls up a scene from *Ghost Ed*, where Wilder's character, Edward Kneeland—a young man who died of scarlet fever in colonial New England—becomes corporeal and brushes a kiss over the back of the main character's hand.

I ignore the swoony butterflies that flutter as the movie clip plays in my head and nod to indicate Wilder should try holding out his hand.

Wilder lifts his arm and brings his hand toward Land Sailor's muzzle. Land Sailor dips his head down and brushes the tip of his nose over Wilder's skin. He puffs out a warm breath of air and Wilder jumps back.

Land Sailor snorts like he's laughing at Wilder.

"I think he likes you," I say.

Wilder manages a small, relieved smile in return. I think it's the first genuine smile I've seen from him, and it's a million times better than that plastic poster boy one he's always flashing. Or maybe it's a million times worse, because it's the kind of smile that sets my pulse racing.

"Now that you've been introduced, why don't you try

petting him. Stay in his sightline and place your hand on his neck, here." I set my palm on Land Sailor. "Move in the same direction as his coat."

Wilder tentatively runs his hand over Land Sailor. After a few passes, the horse gives a contented sigh. Apparently even horses aren't immune to Wilder's Hollywood charm.

"Do you have any experience tying knots?" I ask.

Wilder lifts a shoulder. "I know how to tie knots for, like, shoelaces."

I ignore the bitter tone of his voice when he says "shoelaces."

"Have you done any sailing or scouting or . . . ?"

"No. But I did play an extra in this movie where I was a hostage tied to a chair. My rescuer used a paperclip and a nine-volt battery to get the knot untied."

I give him a blank look.

"Probably doesn't count."

"Not really," I say. "But learning how to make a quick-release knot is pretty simple. And it's an important knot to know when you're a rider. There's some extra rope in the tack room. You can practice while I feed Land Sailor and then I'll give you a quick tour of the stable."

I put Land Sailor in his stall. Then we walk across the grooming area and stop outside the door to the tack room. "This is where we store the saddles, blankets, halters, bridles, ropes, and other supplies we need for the horses." I lift the latch, push open the door, and slide a cinder block in front of it to hold it open before flipping on the lights. A bulb flickers overhead and then glows brightly.

"C'mon in."

CHAPTER 8

Wilder

THE FIRST THING that hits me about the tack room is the scent: leather and oil, with a hint of musk and dirt. The room is small and reminds me of a miniature version of the props room on set, with all the different objects lined up on shelving racks with little information tags on them. In here, one wall is covered with hooks for ropes, leather strips, and metal parts I can't identify. In the far corner is a floor-to-ceiling iron post with alternating branches coming off it to hold saddles. Beside it is a shelf full of colorful, folded woven blankets. Wooden crates and chests are stacked against the walls and there's an old plank-topped worktable with a few drawers and a rickety-looking stool.

I follow Cassidy inside and my heavy-soled boots thunk over the old, worn floorboards while her cowboy boots make a smoother rasping sound. A silver stallion on a rusty metal sign catches my eye and, as I step forward to get a better look, the toe of my boot bangs into something hard and heavy. I lurch forward as the object scrapes over the floor and manage to catch my balance on a crate before I completely wipe out. Thank goodness these boots have reinforced toes.

Cassidy spins around in surprise.

Grateful that I'm still upright and that she didn't see me almost fall, I give her a confident-yet-charming grin. This is the smile that usually gets me a call back after an audition.

But not today.

Instead of admiration or interest or approval, Cassidy's eyes go wide with shock as the sound of squeaky hinges echoes through the room. She looks past me, over my shoulder, and dives toward me. "Don't let the door . . ."

Swish.

Thud.

Click.

"Shut," Cassidy says. She glances at the cinder block I've accidentally kicked out of place, and sighs. "Well, that sucks."

"What?" I ask, looking down at my boot and the cinderblock. Neither of them appears to be damaged. The floor might be a bit more scratched up than it already was, but it's not like we're talking gleaming hardwood here. One could argue I just added a bit of character.

Cassidy walks over to the door and pulls.

It doesn't move.

She grips the handle and leans back with all her weight.

Nothing happens.

She rests her forehead against the wood and sighs again. "Welp, we're locked inside."

"What? How?" I say, pushing away from the crate that saved me from a face-plant.

"There's a latch on the other side. I think I heard it click into place when the door shut," she says, giving the door another unsuccessful yank.

"Oh." I glance around the tack room, but there's only the one door.

No windows.

No other way out.

The room seems to shrink around us. It feels warmer in here all of a sudden. I unbutton the cuffs of my flannel shirt and roll the sleeves up to the middle of my forearms. "So, um, what do we do now?"

"We wait for someone to come let us out," Cassidy says matter-of-factly.

Like it's no big deal to be trapped in a tiny room.

How is she so calm?

I pull at my collar and swallow. "How long will we have to wait?"

Cassidy glances over her shoulder at me, her dark brown eyes meeting mine. "Probably a few hours, at most."

"Hours?"

That seems . . . excessive.

I massage the back of my neck, hoping I look more relaxed than I feel.

Cassidy pulls two tan-colored ropes from a hook and turns to face me. "Dad rode out to Little Bend Creek to check on cattle. He won't be back until dinner, maybe later. Mom's in the arena working with the yearlings. And Grandpa?" She looks at her watch. "He's probably napping in front of the TV while some PBR rodeo rerun plays on the Cowboy Channel."

I rub my fist over the growing tightness in my chest. "Can we call someone?"

"Service is spotty out here, so I don't usually carry a phone with me." Cassidy tucks a loose strand of hair behind her ear. "Do you have one?"

I pat my pockets and groan. "I left it charging in the cabin." The battery has been draining more quickly than usual because cell service *is* spotty out here.

Even though my stomach is a pit of churning acid, I sink down onto one of the dusty chests like I don't have a care in the world. I drape my elbow on a nearby crate. Rest the ankle of my right leg on my left knee. Clear my throat. "This has happened before?"

Cassidy nods. "The first time, I was in here most of the day. I was seven or eight at the time, playing hide-and-seek with the foreman's twins. I went from believing I'd found the best hiding spot in the world to wondering if I was going to die before anyone found me. I worried I'd never make it out and get my ears pierced." She pauses to twist the small diamond stud in her right ear.

"So just the one time, then?" I ask. My knee bounces up and down with nervous energy and I press it down with the palm of my hand to get it to stay still.

"Uh, no. The last time I got locked in here was three years ago, maybe? It was only a few hours that time."

The silence that follows seems to swallow up all the air in the room. I force myself to take measured breaths, but I can't seem to get enough oxygen. "If you keep getting locked in here, why don't you use a different lock?" I ask.

"Grandpa's not big on change." Cassidy shrugs. "Plus, no one's been locked in here since we started using the cinder-block as a doorstop." She gives me a pointed look as if to say that *I'm* the reason we're stuck in here. "Until today."

"Don't go blaming me," I say, crossing my arms over my chest.

"Look, it's no big deal," she says. "Land Sailor can wait for his supper, and he has plenty of water."

Water.

My mouth goes bone dry at the thought.

I glance around, hoping I overlooked a pallet of water bottles, or a sink, or a spigot, or something.

Nothing.

Damn, it's like a sauna in here. I unbutton my flannel shirt and pull it off. The cotton T-shirt below is damp and clingy. The scent of leather, which was so welcoming earlier, has turned sour.

"Wilder," Cassidy says, coming over to sit on the crate next to me. Her eyes soften as they scan my face. Her lips are soft and full, and for a moment, I'm completely distracted. "Are you okay?" she asks.

"I'm fine," I say, sitting up straighter and giving her a confident, toothy smile. "Totally fine."

"Totally," she says, shaking her head like she doesn't believe me. Her shoulder bumps mine and some of the weight on my chest falls away as a comforting warmth cascades over my skin. "Why don't we start your first lesson?" she says, her tone brightening. "By the time we get out, you'll be a whiz at quick-release knots and one step closer to riding."

My plan to fake it till I make it isn't going well.

Turns out, you can't fake tying a knot.

No number of dazzling smiles, sparkling eyes, or smoldering looks is going to save me.

The rope's foreign in my hand and I can't quite seem to get it to twist and turn the way Cassidy can each time she walks me through the process. It feels like I've tried it a million times, and I still haven't been able to do it yet. A frustrated growl rumbles through my chest when I accidentally drop the looped part that is supposed to go . . . somewhere.

I toss the rest of the rope into my lap and gnash my teeth together. This is impossible.

On film, I've made the championship winning touchdown. Repaired a dirt bike. And even battled giant alien creatures with laser beam eyes.

But in real life, I can't tie a damn knot.

And if I can't even tie a damn knot, I'll never learn how to ride a horse. And if I can't ride a horse—no, not just ride—ride like I was born in the saddle . . .

Then how in the hell am I supposed to hold on to the role of Deacon Slade?

My hands clench into fists.

In the back of my mind, a clock ticks down like the timer on a bomb, reminding me that I only have so much time to get my shit together. This is the biggest role I've ever landed, and if

I can't pull it off, it could very well be my last. My mind swims with visions of "Forgotten Child Star" lists.

"Wilder," Cassidy says, yanking me out of my spiraling thoughts. "Don't worry. You'll get the hang of it, and pretty soon you'll do it through muscle memory." Her eyes sparkle as an idea seems takes hold. "Memory . . . You're good at memorizing lines, right?"

"Yeah." You kind of have to be, to be an actor.

"Maybe coming up with a mnemonic device will help?" She nibbles on her bottom lip as she considers the idea. "I still remember the bunny rhyme from when I was learning to tie my shoes."

"There's a shoe-tying rhyme?"

"Oh yeah." Cassidy grins. "Over, under, around, and through. Meet Mr. Bunny, pull and through," she singsongs.

"That's something," I say dryly.

"I didn't come up with it," she says. "But it helped me remember the steps. And I bet it would work for you, too."

"I already know how to tie my shoes."

"Ha, ha," she says, giving me a playful smack on the arm that makes my skin tingle. "We can come up with something similar for the quick-release knot. Let's see . . ." She gestures for me to pick up the rope. "Okay, first step is to make a circle. Then you need to make a bunny ear. Bring it through the circle like this." Her fingers brush over the back of my hand as she guides me through it. I catch a faint trace of citrus in her hair as she leans in. "Okay, then push this part up to tighten the knot."

It takes us a little while to come up with a rhyme, and finally, *finally,* I'm able to make the knot on my own.

Make a circle.

Doubled end through.
Snug up the knot.
Pull and set loose.

I repeat the steps to the little rhyme we created. Each time, my hands are a bit faster. My movements surer.

Cassidy holds up her hand for a high five, and as our palms press together, I get the unexpected urge to weave my fingers through hers.

My gaze goes to her mouth, which is curved up at the sides in a soft smile.

When her lips part, I'm tempted to lean in and kiss her.

She leans closer, as if she's thinking of kissing me, too.

But that's ridiculous. There's no room in this script for a romantic subplot. Cassidy's supposed to be teaching me to ride, that's all. I didn't come all the way out to Wyoming to be distracted from my lifelong goal of being an A-list actor. And I'm definitely not here to fall for some girl.

CHAPTER 9

Cassidy

I GLANCE OVER at Wilder. His head is dipped down over the rope as he practices making a quick-release knot, his lips moving as he mouths the rhyme we made up. Wilder's good-looking, with perfect cheekbones and striking eyes that belong on movie posters. But here in this dusty room, with bad lighting and stale air, he's a total hunk. The sleeves of his black T-shirt hug his slightly muscled arms. Dark curls spill out from under his backward baseball cap, and I wonder if he always wears his hair medium-long or if he's growing it out for a part.

I look away before he can catch me staring.

Wilder hasn't said a word to me for a while, not since I offered him a high five for successfully completing his knot. The minute we touched, the air around us seemed to fill with tiny sparks. His eyes locked with mine and his lips parted. My blood felt fizzy.

But then, when Wilder glanced away and drew back, it was

like a switch had been flipped. His eyes grew flinty. His lips pressed together in a thin line. The moment—if you could even call it a moment—was gone.

Not that it matters.

Wilder's only here for a few weeks and then he'll be back home, surrounded by beautiful, airbrushed people. Surrounded by girls who pair designer clothes with fancy shoes, not Sunday-best jeans with good, better, or best cowboy boots.

I reach up and tuck a chunk of loose hair back into my ponytail. Soon he'll be back in Hollywood with girls who actually spend time on hair and makeup, whereas I usually have the fresh-from-the-trail windblown look and my makeup is limited to Mom's homemade beeswax lip balm.

Wilder's life is in L.A.

My life's here on the ranch.

But there's a voice in the back of my head—one that has nothing to do with Wilder, not really—saying *It doesn't always have to be.*

Chores.

Breakfast.

More chores.

The morning flies by as I flit from one thing to the next in the never-ending quest to stay on top of things on the ranch.

Wilder and I didn't speak earlier this morning while we fed the animals. I'd just finished with the hogs when he wandered into the barnyard with a baseball cap pulled low over his brow so that it shaded his face completely. I caught a glimpse of a dark gray Henley under his canvas jacket, blue jeans, and work boots.

While I took care of Rambrandt and Van Goat, Wilder contended with Birdzilla and her flock. By the time I finished moving the goats into their mobile pasture, he was already done and gone.

There are still a few more hours until Wilder's lesson, and Dad's asked me to go check the fences over by Pebble Creek pasture. Following a well-worn path through the fields, Land Sailor and I make our way over a grassy ridge. We look down over a large pond stocked with rainbow and brook trout where Grandpa likes to fish, then cut east to get to the pasture.

When we arrive, we ride along the wildlife-friendly post-and-rail fence to make sure there aren't any breaks or gaps that need repair. Pebble Creek pasture was one of our fallow fields last year, but Grandpa and Dad are planning to use it later this summer for the cattle.

As we meander over the gentle slopes, I can't stop my thoughts from veering off course. I should be focused on the fencing, but instead I can't seem to get Wilder off my mind. Yesterday when we were trapped in the tack room, he did a pretty good job of pretending everything was fine when he knew I was watching, but I caught glimpses of worry, frustration, and something else I can't quite put my finger on. There's definitely something weighing on him deep below the surface.

Or maybe it's not that deep?

When Mom finally unlocked the door, he couldn't seem to get out of there fast enough. And earlier today when we were doing chores, it was almost as if he was avoiding me.

I occasionally dismount from Land Sailor to flag a fallen

rail and mark down the approximate location in my notebook. Aside from a few broken rails and a split post in need of repair, the fence seems to be in good condition. Soon, we're back on the trail that leads us home.

Of course, my thoughts continue on the trail that leads to Wilder.

I picture his dark hair with its unruly curls.

The depths of his piercing eyes.

The smiles that I know are calculated and practiced but still somehow manage to make me melt like a Popsicle on a hot summer day.

I give myself a mental shake.

It doesn't matter what Wilder thinks of me. Or how I feel about him. He'll be gone in a few weeks.

By the time we near the stable, my hair is a windblown mess, my face is flushed from riding, and Land Sailor's coat is slick with sweat. We canter as we come around the bend in the path and slow to a walk as we enter the yard that leads into the stable.

Wilder's already there, leaning back against the fence surrounding the exercise paddock, elbows over the top rail and feet crossed at the ankles. As always, he looks as if someone's posed him in the perfect position for maximum hotness. He glances up to watch us approach, his face neutral. Even expressionless, he's attractive in an aloof, man-of-mystery kind of way.

Land Sailor and I ride up next to him, and I marvel at how the sunlight glides over his face when he tips his head up to greet me, causing his skin to practically glow.

"Hey," he says before grimacing and saying, "Hi."

Grandpa sure did a number on him at dinner.

Wilder pushes away from the fence, letting his arms fall to his sides. He takes a step closer and then stops, as if he's not exactly sure how close he should get to us. The sleeves of his green flannel shirt are rolled up, revealing a tanned strip of skin from his wrists to the middle of his forearm. His arms aren't muscle bound, but they look strong enough, and I wonder what it might feel like to be wrapped up in them.

"Whoa," I say, partly to stop Land Sailor from continuing on but also to stop myself from getting carried away.

We've already established that Wilder's attractive. There's no sense in dwelling on it.

"You're a bit early for your lesson," I say after glancing at my watch. I'd planned to get back to the stables with plenty of time to groom and feed Land Sailor before Wilder arrived.

Wilder shrugs. "I was bored."

The snarky side of me thinks, *That must be nice.* I'm not sure I've ever had the luxury of being bored on the ranch. Sun. Snow. Sleet. Ice storms or thunderstorms. Birthdays and holidays. It doesn't matter what's happening, there are always animals that need feeding, equipment to maintain, or chores to do. Ranch work is nonstop. And on those rare occasions when there's a break, I always manage to find something to fill up the spare time. Sometimes that means exploring the outskirts of the ranch with Land Sailor. Getting lost in a good book set in a faraway place. Stargazing out at the old cowboy cabin on Hunter's Ridge.

I force a polite smile. "There's plenty to do around here."

Wilder looks around as if searching for something to entertain him. "Like?"

I try to see things from his point of view. In L.A., there are probably stores and restaurants on every corner. Movie theaters. Museums. Pop-up markets. It must be strange to have all that at your fingertips and then find yourself in Wyoming, where the closest grocery store is the kitchen garden and the milk is delivered in glass jars from Gallagher's Dairy. Maybe he's not so much bored as he is . . . unaware of all the activities Silver Stallion Ranch has to offer.

Hiking.

Fishing.

Kayaking.

Although, that's not really why he's here, is it? He's here to learn how to be a cowboy. So if he's bored, that's on him.

Wilder blinks up at me, waiting for a response.

"Well," I say, "right now, you can help me groom Land Sailor. That was going to be tomorrow's lesson, but we'll get a jump on it today."

"Great," he says without an ounce of enthusiasm.

I gather the reins in my left hand and pull my right boot out of the stirrup. With my left hand over Land Sailor's withers and my right hand on the saddle horn, I bend my right leg and kick it over Land Sailor's back to dismount. Just as my foot clears his croup, the heel of my boot unexpectedly connects with something fleshy and hard.

"Oof," Wilder says.

His hand grabs at my waist and tugs me off balance just as I manage to pull my left foot free of the stirrup. Instead of hopping gracefully down to the ground like I normally would, I'm yanked backward. Arms flailing, I release the reins. Land Sailor shies away with an angry snort, sidestepping a few paces from us. I'm twisted around and then Wilder and I are falling.

When we land in a jumbled heap of arms and legs, the wind's knocked out of me.

Beneath me, Wilder's flat on his back, with one arm wrapped around my waist. He sucks in a ragged breath and then coughs. "Ow," he groans.

My shoulder burns where it slammed into the hard-packed dirt as I push myself up to hover above him. Wilder glances up at me with wide eyes full of surprise. Our faces are only inches apart, and I can't help but stare back at him. Up close, I can see the golden flecks in his dark eyes. The small scar on his chin. It's hard to breathe, and I can't tell if it's because of the fall or because of who caused it.

Wilder's gaze goes to my lips, and the arm wrapped around my waist tightens as if he's about to pull me in for a kiss. He lifts a shaky hand, and for a moment, I think he might press his palm to my cheek or brush a strand of hair from my face. The shallow breath I've managed to take catches in my chest. The ache in my bones is masked by a tingle of excitement at being held by a gorgeous boy. The rest of the world falls away. It's not so much gravity that has me dipping my head but the irresistible, magnetic pull of Wilder Nash.

Cool air brushes over my heated cheek as his hand whispers past my face. My skin sparkles with anticipation, but Wilder doesn't make contact with me. Instead, he presses his palm over a red mark on his forehead that looks suspiciously like the shape of my cowboy boot's heel.

He blinks and the dazed look in his eye disappears. "What the hell?" he says with a snarl, loosening his grip on my waist.

I scramble off him and roll to my side, my chest heaving from post-fall adrenaline and ridiculous near-kiss disappointment.

Above us, the brilliant blue sky is brushed with wispy horsetail clouds.

"Exactly," I manage to say.

"You kicked me in the face," he says, like I did it on purpose.

As if I was supposed to magically know that he'd moved away from the fence while my back was turned.

"What were you doing standing behind me while I was dismounting?" I bite back.

"I was trying to help you down," he mumbles.

That's both incredibly sweet and stupid. What am I supposed to say to that?

I glance at Wilder out of the corner of my eye. His hand is still pressed over his forehead and his jaw is tight.

"Well, it's a good thing I wasn't wearing spurs," I say.

Wilder winces.

Land Sailor grunts and nudges my foot with his muzzle.

"I'm okay, buddy," I say, sitting up. I run my hand down the side of Land Sailor's face before pushing myself up to standing. "How about you?" I ask Wilder, reaching a hand down to help him up. "You okay?"

He peers at me with narrowed eyes. "I'll be fine," he says.

But when he pulls his hand away from his face to take mine, there's a lump forming beneath the boot mark.

Ouch.

"We should get you some ice for that," I say.

CHAPTER 10

Wilder

I'VE NEVER FELT so incompetent before. Up to now, I've always been able to scrape by with a bit of direction, good looks, and luck. Acting's always been easy for me. I learn my lines, show up, and deliver. But now that I'm out of L.A., the things that served me so well before are failing me now.

How is it that I'm almost eighteen and the only skills I have are toothpaste smile, intense gaze, and line memorization?

Why did I think I could just show up in Wyoming with my country western clothes, hop up in a saddle, and be done with it? Getting where I need to be to pull this off is going to take hard work and focus. A flicker of doubt races through me. So much is riding on my ability to ride a horse, and based on how things have gone since I arrived, I'm not sure I'm cut out for it.

My boot scrapes over a rut in the path and I stumble. Cassidy reaches out a hand to steady me, her fingers wrapping around my arm until I regain my footing.

"I'm good," I say, waving her off while trying to look completely chill.

But am I?

My head pounds. My tailbone smarts. And there's a tingling sensation where her fingers were pressed on my arm. The physical stuff is one thing, but it's these unfamiliar feelings that really have me out of sorts.

This sudden surge of self-doubt.

The pressure I'm under to learn to ride.

The way I can't seem to resist Cassidy Sterling. How I almost kissed her back there. How much I still want to.

I glance over at Cassidy. Her cheeks are rosy pink, her hair is a mess, and she has a smudge of dirt on her cheek. She's hasn't been airbrushed to perfection, and yet she's absolutely stunning.

Cassidy's not plagued with self-doubt and trying to hide it.

She's completely calm under pressure.

And it's pretty clear she sees through my calculated smiles, given the lack of flirtations in response.

She's the whole package—cute, cool, and capable—and I'm just the packaging. For the first time, I realize Cassidy's way out of my league. I can't imagine what she must think of me.

We trudge up the steps to the cabin and I push open the door. Cassidy follows me inside. She heads straight for the kitchenette while I flop down on the couch like a stunt dummy.

She returns with a ziplock bag of ice wrapped in a kitchen towel. "Here, this should help," she says.

Our fingers brush as she hands it over. A tingle races over my skin, and there's no sense in trying to fool myself that it's just the chill from the ice and nothing more.

When I reach up to push my bangs out of the way, Cassidy offers me a sympathetic grimace. "I'm sorry your head ran into my heel."

I press the ice pack to my forehead and wince. There's a dull throbbing above my eyebrow, and I'm sure I'll have a nice bruise by morning. Thank goodness I'm not due on set for a few weeks. The makeup team would have a real challenge cut out for them with this whopper. "I'm pretty sure *your* heel struck *my* head."

"*Your* head should have been nowhere near *my* heel," she says, but her tone is more playful than cutting.

Cassidy sinks down into the armchair and massages her shoulder. I don't remember asking if she was okay after our tumble, which was a real asshole move. It feels like it's too late to say something. What I wouldn't give for a script right about now.

"For future reference, you should never stand behind someone dismounting a horse. Or behind a horse, for that matter," she says.

"Noted." I adjust my grip on the ice pack.

"We'll skip today's riding lesson," she says.

I drop my head back against the couch and stare at the ceiling.

"Don't worry," Cassidy says, tapping my knee with her fingers. "There's still plenty of time left for you to learn."

Cassidy's many things, but a good actress isn't one of them. Although it's sweet that she's trying to pretend I'm not a hopeless cause. I must look like a complete wreck if this is what it takes to get her to soften toward me.

"We can always double up on lessons after morning chores," she says.

"I'm going to need a lot more than double-up lessons," I grumble.

"Definitely," Cassidy says with an impish smirk as she rises from the chair.

"What?" I ask, feeling the corners of my mouth tick up into a smile.

"For starters, you need a helmet," she says, giving the bump on my head a meaningful glance. "But right now, I bet you could use some Tylenol."

Cassidy disappears through the front door in a swirl of citrus and dust.

My phone buzzes and I pull it out, grateful to find that it's still in one piece. Thankfully, the cabin has a decent Wi-Fi signal.

Alexander: *How's Wyoming? Everything OK?*

Simple questions and yet they feel so loaded.

Should I tell Alexander that things aren't exactly going as planned? That I've unleashed devil goats, gone toe-to-toe with angry birds, locked myself and his niece in a tack room, and managed to get myself kicked in the head within forty-eight hours of arrival?

Ha, ha, ha. No.

Alexander isn't looking for drama; he's expecting results. And with his reputation on the line, too, I can't let him down.

But I'm not quite sure what to say.

Ready to ride.

Delete.

Yeehaw.

Delete.

So far, it's been a disaster.

Delete.

Words come so much easier to me when someone else is thinking of them.

My finger hovers over the screen and . . . I've got nothing.

Cassidy knocks on the door and pushes it open, a bottle of Gatorade in one hand and a container of Tylenol in the other. There's a thick document mailer tucked under her arm. "Here you go," she says, placing everything on the rustic coffee table in front of me. "Will you be okay by yourself for a while?" Her eyes narrow with concern as she scrutinizes me.

"Believe it or not, I'm not a complete mess," I say, setting the ice pack down on the couch next to me. I grab the Tylenol bottle, tap two rapid-relief gels into my palm, and swallow them down with a swig of Gatorade.

"Just a partial mess," she teases. The humor fades from her expression as worry lines crinkle on her brow. "I'm actually concerned you might have a concussion."

"I don't." Of this I'm sure.

I once had a guest role on a family drama show where I took a ball to the head in a soccer match. The scene called for an EMT to assess my character for signs of concussion, and I remember each and every one.

Nausea? Nope.

Double vision? Nope.

Ringing in the ears? Nope?

Sensitivity to light and noise? Nope and nope.

Headache? Yes, but not unexpected and not widespread.

I pause, realizing that I can add another life skill to my meager list: concussion assessment.

Yay, me.

After Cassidy leaves, I pull the document mailer from the table. I don't need to open it to know it contains a script. Even though a lot can (and will) change between this version, the table read, and filming, it'll at least give me some valuable insight into my character. Curiosity has me tugging the zip strip to open the package.

The cover page says *Outrider, Episode 1*, with a confidential watermark stamped in the background. In the upper right-hand corner, my name is written in blue ballpoint pen with my character's name, Deacon Slade, below it.

I'm not quite halfway through the script when Cassidy returns. This time, she has the handle of a large wicker basket draped over her arm.

"How're you feeling?" she asks.

The Tylenol and ice did a good job of managing the pain, but my stomach's been hollow for a while. "Hungry."

"Omelets okay?" Cassidy heads to the kitchenette and starts pulling an assortment of ingredients from the basket. "Birdzilla sends her regards," she says, holding up a light brown egg.

"You can't make an omelet without eggs," I say, remembering what Cassidy said yesterday. It seems like forever ago.

"You've fed the hens twice now. I figure it's time they return the favor."

I stand up and stretch. My tailbone is sore but I'm not woozy. "Can I help?"

"Can you cook?"

I'm no chef, but I do know my way around a kitchen. "A bit." Between Mom's hospital shifts and my filming schedule, I've learned to fend for myself.

There's an assortment of veggies on the counter: a yellow onion, a green bell pepper, a handful of crisp spinach, and a ruby-red tomato. "Fresh from the garden," she says. "And the greenhouse. And the root cellar."

"You grew all this?"

Cassidy nods. "We try to be as self-sufficient as we can, since it's not always possible to run out to the store for something."

"That's what Instacart is for."

She gives me a blank look.

"DoorDash?"

She shakes her head.

"Grubhub? Postmates?" In disbelief, I draw out the words "Uber Eats?"

She shrugs.

"I can't believe you've never heard of any of them."

Cassidy rolls her eyes. "Of course I've heard of them. I just can't believe you think they'd deliver *here.*" She bumps me playfully with her shoulder. "But who needs them when you can have farm-to-table food whenever?"

It feels good to laugh spontaneously. It's been a while.

I reach for one of the knives, but Cassidy swats my hand away. "Heck no," she says. "No more injuries for you tonight. Not on my watch."

"Hey," I protest.

"The nearest ER is thirty miles away. I'm Red Cross certified in first aid, but I'm also really terrible with a needle and thread. The last time I had to stitch someone up . . ." She scrunches up her nose. "Well, it wasn't pretty."

My mouth drops open. "What happened?"

I've had a few unfortunate incidents already, but exactly how dangerous is this ranch Alexander shipped me off to?

"A goat bit Jasper once."

Based on my experience with the goats, I am not at all surprised that they have a history.

Cassidy scrapes chopped peppers into a bowl and reaches for the tomato. "He almost lost his whole arm." She looks over at me with a wicked glimmer in her eye. "I should probably add that Jasper was my stuffed bunny and I was seven at the time." She smirks. "It's *possible* my sewing skills might have improved since."

"I'd rather not find out," I say, shaking my head.

"Same." Cassidy pulls open a drawer and rummages around. "Here you go." She hands me a wire whisk. "Can you handle the eggs?"

"Yes, Chef," I say, brandishing the whisk and giving her a salute.

Cassidy slices and dices while I crack eggs into a bowl. We work quietly, the sound of her knife whispering over the wooden cutting board punctuated by the sound of cracking eggshells.

"So . . . um." I open my mouth to continue, but words fail me. What am I supposed to say when it's not already planned out for me? I wish I had a script page in my back pocket. A teleprompter. A cue card. Anything to help me fill the awkward silence.

I grab another egg, and just as I'm about to tap it on the counter, I lose my grip. Before it can completely slip from my grasp, I tighten my fingers. Too tightly. The eggshell smashes into pieces in my palm. Egg white and yolk spray between my fingers, smacking me in the face.

You can practically hear the goo drip down my cheek in the silence that follows. I risk a glance at Cassidy. The edge of her mouth quirks up into a smile.

"What?" I ask, wiping a paper towel over my face.

"I was just thinking . . . how *egg*stremely difficult today has been for you." Under Cassidy's dark eyelashes, her eyes sparkle. "You have a goose egg *and* a chicken egg on your face."

"Ha, ha."

"Here, let me." Cassidy takes the paper towel. She leans in, her breath tickling over my cheek, and brushes it over my face before stepping back to survey her work. "Eggcellent."

For a moment, we just stand there staring at each other. There's a perceptible electricity in the air between us. I take a half step forward, closing the distance between us, and reach up to brush a lock of hair from her face.

Cassidy stills, her eyes going wide, as I tuck the hair behind her ear. When I draw my hand back, I realize my fingers have left a shiny trail of egg goo on her skin. She reaches up to touch her face and cringes.

Not exactly the smooth move I was going for. Panic surges through me. My mouth opens and I blurt out the first thing that comes to mind.

"Now the yolk's on you."

CHAPTER 11

Cassidy

AFTER OUR MORNING chores are complete, Wilder and I agree to meet back at the stables for his first riding lesson of the day. I'm hoping we can get him comfortable with Jupiter, a fifteen-year-old black quarter horse gelding who's solid, calm, and patient. Jupiter's an experienced trail horse who Grandpa has described as "bombproof." As long as he gets plenty of love and attention, Jupiter will be the perfect mount for Wilder. And since I have no clue what horses Wilder will be riding on set, I hope we'll also have time for him to try a few of our more . . . temperamental horses.

Land Sailor greets me with a friendly snort as I pause to give him a handful of fresh snow peas I picked from the garden on my way over. "I'll be back for you this afternoon," I promise as I run my hand down the side of his face, just the way he likes. He presses his head against my palm and sighs.

Ginger pokes her head out of her stall as I approach but

then disappears back inside when she sees it's only me. She's not too keen on Mom or me, but she loves Grandpa and Dad. She's got a thing for human males, and I can almost picture her batting her eyelashes at Wilder. Like Jupiter, she's an excellent trail horse and is good with beginners. But given the high possibility that she would follow Wilder around with moony eyes, I think a distraction like that would only complicate lessons.

I make my way to Jupiter's stall. When I open the door, he nickers a greeting.

"Hello to you, too," I say, reaching out to run my hand along his withers. Beneath my fingers, his coat is warm and smooth. "How are you?" I ask.

Jupiter blows out a puff of air and steps forward to rest his head on my shoulder. This big guy is such a love bug.

"I have someone I'd like you to meet. He's come all the way from California to learn to ride, and I was hoping you'll help me teach him. What do you say?"

Jupiter flicks his tail, which I interpret as a yes. He dips his head down for me as I slip on his leather halter and stands still as a statue while I secure a lead line. Unlike other horses who can get impatient to get out of their stall, Jupiter's content to take things as they come. He doesn't rush. He doesn't fuss. He's ice cold under pressure. I'm kind of hoping some of his laid-back demeanor will rub off on Wilder, who seems to have a constant undercurrent of tension flowing beneath his carefully controlled facade.

Jupiter clip-clops across the stable and then we make our way outside through the large rolling barn door that leads into the fenced-in paddock. The air is warm and fresh, and the blue sky is dotted with large, puffy clouds. The combination of fresh air and sunlight is magical, and I wonder if anywhere else in the world could ever be so beautiful. The thought gives me pause.

I'm aware that there are other places in the world that people find beautiful. I've seen pictures and watched movies and read books. But I can't possibly know for sure if I never explore the world beyond the northwestern mountain states.

Out of the shadow of the stable, the short grass is fresh and green.

The grass is always greener . . .

It feels weird to be having these thoughts—almost deceitful. My whole life, I've known that my future is on the ranch. Someday I'll be expected to take over for Dad. I haven't questioned it or even really considered *What else?* For me, it's just always been a given, like the fact that my eyes are brown or that cilantro tastes like soap.

From what I gather, Uncle Alex always had a healthy dose of wanderlust. Sometimes Grandma would tell me about his youthful adventures, like the time when he took off with some of his buddies to backpack along the Oregon coast. Or the summer he joined a Shakespeare troupe that traveled across the country doing outdoor performances in city parks. Based on what I've heard, Uncle Alex jumped at every opportunity he got to leave the ranch.

But I'm not like Uncle Alex. I'm perfectly happy right where I am.

Aren't I?

Of course I am. I'm only having these thoughts because . . .

Wilder.

Our eyes meet across the yard and I'm surprised to find he's already waiting for us in the paddock. Today he's wearing a charcoal-gray Henley that sets off his dark eyes and another pair of jeans that look brand-new. I'm pretty sure everything he's worn so far is fresh off the rack, based on the lack of wear and, in some cases, the deep folding creases. If this is Wilder's Wyoming style, I wonder what his typical California clothes look like.

Board shorts, tank tops, and flip-flops?

Sweatpants, hoodies, and sneakers?

A suit, tie, and patent leather shoes?

I can easily picture him wearing each style and owning it because he's had an array of wardrobes for his various movie roles. He's like a chameleon, able to change to adapt to his surroundings, but if he were the subject of a National Geographic documentary, I wonder what his natural environment and appearance would be.

Behold, the elusive Wilder Nash. . . .

Without a hat to hold his hair back, the breeze ruffles the long curls that fall just above his eyes and hide the tops of his ears. The edge of his mouth quirks up into a cocky smile. There's no doubt he's destined to be the next Hollywood heartthrob based on how wildly my heart is beating just from that look.

I take a deep breath. *Pull it together, Cassidy.* Wilder's here for riding, not romance.

Not that it matters. If I've done my job well, he will be literally riding off into the sunset in a few weeks. The last thing I need is to be left harboring a crush on Wilder Nash after he's gone.

I lead Jupiter across the enclosure and bring him over to where Wilder leans against the split-rail fence. Wilder straightens up as we near and the smile fades from his face. Instead, his lips pinch together into a tight line, a mix of determination and apprehension on his face.

"Wilder, I'd like you to meet Jupiter. He's a solid trail horse and is very good with beginners."

Jupiter is half a hand shorter than Land Sailor, but his stature is slightly more imposing in spite of his gentle disposition.

"Hey, buddy . . . er, Jupiter," Wilder says. He takes a deep breath and then lifts his hand slowly to present it to Jupiter for a sniff.

"Jupiter, meet Wilder Nash. He's an actor and has been cast to be a cowboy in an upcoming show. You'll be helping me teach him to ride."

Jupiter breathes in Wilder's scent, wriggles his nose, and nods.

Wilder breathes out what sounds like a sigh of relief and takes a half step back. He shoves his hands into the front pockets of his jeans and gives me a confident nod.

Okay, then.

With introductions out of the way, I go over basic horse safety, taking extra care to make sure I don't miss anything since it seems like Wilder's an incident magnet. "Jupiter weighs over a thousand pounds," I say. "That's about the same weight as a golf cart, but instead of a steering wheel, you'll have reins, voice commands, and physical cues to maneuver Jupiter when you ride. All horses have a mind, personality, and temperament of their own. Riding is teamwork. It involves trust and cooperation, so it's important to know how to read a horse's physical cues and establish a relationship with them."

Wilder nods. "Okay."

"Some horses, like Jupiter, are pretty laid-back. They're good with almost anyone and are patient with beginners. Other horses get frustrated and only want to pair with experienced riders. My mom's horse, Nutmeg, is like that."

"Oh." Wilder swallows. "I . . ."

There's a flash of fear in Wilder's eyes that he quickly masks with a confident stare.

"I'm sure they'll pick a horse like Jupiter for you," I say. Honestly, I have no idea how it works in Hollywood, but I expect that trainers would only want to use horses that are as predictable and cooperative as possible. "Once we're done training, you should have enough experience to handle more challenging horses, too."

Wilder pushes his hair back from his face, giving me a glimpse of his bruise, and flexes his jaw. "Do you really think there's enough time to teach me to ride?"

"That depends," I say.

"On?"

"How quickly you pick things up. How serious and focused you are. How much time I can dedicate to teaching you around my other responsibilities."

"Time is something . . . I . . . I don't have a lot of." Wilder trips over his words a bit, and a hint of color darkens his cheeks.

Sympathy surges through me. Yes, he's cocky and full of himself, but he's also way out of his element here. It's not easy to learn a new skill, especially one as challenging as horseback riding. And, on top of that, there's the added pressure of knowing that the trajectory of your career depends on how you perform when you're seventeen.

"Uncle Alex's plan for you to be a seasoned rider in a few weeks *is* ambitious," I say. "But . . ."

Wilder glances up at me, his lips parted. He looks a bit lost.

I want to wrap his hand in mine and give it a reassuring squeeze. My fingers twitch but I don't move.

"It's not impossible," I say. I look away so I don't get caught up in his dark eyes and parted lips and impossibly tempting curls. "But I have plenty of chores around here to keep me busy. If you lend a hand, the work'll get done faster and I'll have more time to train you."

Wilder's quiet while he considers my offer. Which, now that I have time to think about it myself, was maybe not the best idea. I've been warning myself about the dangers of crushing on Wilder Nash, and yet here I am, offering to spend the better part of my days with him. Because that's not tempting fate or anything.

"I'm also supposed to study the script and develop my vision for the character while I'm here," he says.

I risk a glance at Wilder. Total mistake. He's got this broody thing going on, with his brow furrowed and his flinty eyes focused on the horizon. My traitorous heart beats double time.

"You can run lines while we work," I find myself saying. "Multitasking for the win."

When he turns to look at me, his dark eyes are full of hope. "That could work." A hesitant smile plays across his lips. "Are you sure?"

My heart does another pitter-patter. "Yes," I say.

No, I mean.

"Cool," he says.

"Cool," I echo.

Jupiter snorts.

Wilder's faint smile morphs into a full-fledged grin. This

one doesn't belong to a character. It's not called up on cue. It's not played up for an audience of one.

This is Wilder's actual smile. Warm. Dazzling. A bit lopsided.

And absolutely devastating ... because there is zero chance I'll make it through the summer with my heart intact since it turns out I'm already crushing pretty hard.

CHAPTER 12

Wilder

FOR THE FIRST time since I arrived, I think things might actually be going my way. I've made it a whole morning without any accidents. Plus, there's a plan in place for me to learn how to ride and spend time preparing for the other aspects of my role. Before, the summer seemed to be shrinking by the second, but now it feels spread out in front of me and full of opportunity.

Cassidy explains the basics of using a lead line and gives me a quick demonstration. The midday sun gives her dark-brown hair a honey-gold sheen. She looks over at me to check if I'm paying attention and I blink, forcing myself to concentrate on what she's saying and not on the soft curve of her cheek.

"It's customary to stand on the left side of a horse," she says. "Horses' eyes work differently than ours. They can't see anything below their face or right behind them, so you should always try to stay where they can see you so you don't scare them." Cassidy points to a spot on the ground. "You go there."

I take a few steps toward Jupiter and stop when I'm even with his shoulder.

Cassidy shakes her head. "You have to get closer than that." She steps in front of me until we're toe-to-toe and places her hands on my upper arms. I'm getting major school dance vibes, which are only compounded when she looks up at me from under a dark fringe of eyelashes and says, "Step toward me." I step forward while she takes a step back, so that I'm standing even with Jupiter's neck. "Now step to your right."

We move together like we're slow dancing. There's no music, no lights, no formal clothes, but it kind of feels like a prom moment. I never had the opportunity to go to a real school dance, but I have filmed a few prom scenes. Those involved intense choreography and specific camera angles, but with the way we're moving in pseudo–dance steps with Cassidy's face tipped up to mine and my hands at her waist and—

Hold up.

How did my hands end up on her waist?

I immediately pull my hands away and brush my palms on my jeans. There's a buzz in my nerves like there is when I'm doing improv, which I hate because there's no script and I usually have absolutely no idea what I'm doing.

Should I say something?

Laugh it off?

Pretend my hands on her waist never happened?

Cassidy looks up as if she expects something from me. An explanation? A kiss? A . . . What the hell am I doing?

I arch my eyebrows and give her my most dazzling toothpaste-commercial grin. Nine out of ten directors agree.

Cassidy steps back. She presses her lips together. Blinks. If I'm not mistaken, there's more color in her cheeks than there was a minute ago. Or maybe that's a trick of the light.

"Okay, now you want your right hand just about here," she says. She grabs my shirtsleeve and lifts my hand to the rope, about twelve inches away from where it connects to Jupiter's halter. "You'll use your left hand to grip the extra length of lead line."

Warm fingers brush over mine as she hands me the loosely looped end of the rope. An electric feeling dances across my rib cage and Jupiter must sense it, too, because he does a little trot in place.

Cassidy puts a gentle hand on his neck. "Easy, there," she says in a low, reassuring voice.

Nothing about any of this is easy.

She eases away from Jupiter and stands to my left. Her elbow brushes against my arm and I find myself leaning into her touch. "Now we'll practice having you lead Jupiter along the fence. To get him to move, push your right hand forward slightly and say 'walk.'"

Now, taking directions is something I can do.

I gently push the lead line forward and say, "Walk."

Jupiter moves forward.

The three of us stroll along the inside of the fence. Birds chirp and chitter. The wind rustles the trees.

Jupiter breathes deeply with his head lifted up, occasionally curling his upper lip back, baring all of his giant front teeth.

I'm not going to lie, it's scary to see such big teeth on an animal that's not a carnivore.

Back in middle school, before I'd transitioned from community theater to more professional opportunities, I was cast as the woodsman in *Little Red Riding Hood*. I still remember lines from the show. Even though they were talking about the big, bad wolf dressed as Red's grandmother . . . a lot of the observations apply to Jupiter.

What big ears you have. Totally.

What big eyes you have. Yup.

What big teeth you have. Ditto.

Cassidy catches me flinching the next time he does it. "Jupiter's just caught a whiff of something interesting. When he lifts his lip like that, he's studying the scent."

"Oh."

Well, at least it's not a sign he's about to bite me.

"Let's practice stopping. To get a horse to stop, pull back slightly on the lead while you stop walking and say 'whoa.'"

I follow her instructions and Jupiter halts beside me.

"I just drove a horse." I don't realize I've said it out loud until Cassidy laughs.

"Your very own ten-horsepower, grain-powered vehicle," she says with a playful smile.

"Ten horsepower? Not one?"

She motions for me to start Jupiter walking again before she explains. "Horsepower is a unit of power. One horse can provide more than one unit. Actually, the maximum human output is about one horsepower."

"That's . . ."

"Confusing? Yeah. Tell me about it," she says with a shake of her head. "When I was little, I used to see those commercials on TV for fancy cars advertising, like, three hundred or four hundred horsepower. I'd picture giant herds of horses speeding along the highway. And then, you know, I took physics. Epic image shattered."

I clear my throat, unsure of what to say in response. I've always taken the easiest and fewest classes possible. Physics seemed like too much work. So instead of opening my mouth, I nod.

We make a few more laps around the paddock as I practice "walk" and "whoa" commands, and then Cassidy takes the lead rope from me. She unclips it from Jupiter's halter and then removes that as well. "Go on," she tells him, brushing her hand down his long nose. "We'll be back for another lesson in a bit."

Jupiter wanders off toward a patch of dark green grass and starts nibbling on it.

"Are we done?" I ask.

"For now," Cassidy says. "It's almost lunch and then there are some chores to do before our next lesson."

When I agreed to help Cassidy with her chores in exchange for more lesson time, I didn't realize her to-do list included mucking stalls.

I am literally up to my elbows in horse shit.

I have regrets.

The smell is one thing. The flies are another. And I'm pretty sure these jeans are ruined.

I flex my fingers inside the heavy work gloves Cassidy gave me and fill the shovel with more crap and dirty wood shavings from the floor of Jupiter's stall. Even though I can't see them, I'm sure blisters are starting to form on my fingers and the pads of my hands from all this scooping. Also, there are muscles in my back I didn't know I had until today, so that's fun.

I've barely finished with Jupiter's stall in the time Cassidy's done three.

"How often do the stalls have to be . . . mucked?" I ask, setting my sore arms on the shovel's handle to give them a rest.

"Every day."

Great.

"But we only have to do it once or twice a week. We have other ranch hands to help out, and this is one of their jobs."

My aching shoulders sink with relief.

Cassidy grabs a pitchfork and helps me finish up Jupiter's stall. She works quickly, expertly sifting and tossing. I'm a sweaty, stinky mess by the time we finish dumping the wheelbarrows full of manure and shavings on a giant compost pile. I'm an even sweatier, stinkier mess when we finish laying down a new bed of wood shavings for Jupiter.

"Thanks for helping," Cassidy says. "Ready for your next lesson?"

What I really want is a hot shower. A cold drink. And a nap.

"Yeah," I say instead.

We walk into the paddock and she lets out a high-pitched whistle. Jupiter, who's wandered to the other side of the enclosure, looks up from his grass snack and trots over. Cassidy slips on his halter and attaches a lead line.

"More driving?" I ask.

She nods. "We're getting to the good stuff now. I'm about to show you how to turn, reverse, and park."

We spend most of the afternoon working with Jupiter, who's content to put up with my attempts to turn him in clockwise circles, back him across the field, and get him parked back in his clean stall.

"You did really well out there today," Cassidy says, closing the door to Jupiter's stall.

"Thanks," I say.

"I was talking to Jupiter." She smirks as she turns to face me. "But you did well, too." The light in the stable is pale but her eyes gleam beneath the shadows. Cassidy tips her face up and a lock of hair falls free. My fingers twitch as I reach up to brush it behind her ear, but she beats me to it.

Now what?

I have to make a spit-second decision about what to do with my hovering arm before things get awkward, so I keep my arm moving and run my hand through my hair like I did that one time in a shampoo commercial. The brand was Suave. I'm not entirely sure that move was.

Cassidy steps closer.

My heart thuds in my chest.

Her eyes meet mine.

Her lips part.

I lean forward, wondering once again what kissing Cassidy would be like, because I can't seem to stop thinking about it. Are her lips as soft as they look? Is her skin as silky as it seems?

Even though I hadn't realized it at the time, I liked the way it felt to have my hands on her waist.

Cassidy glances at my mouth before looking up at me. Then her eyebrows lift as she reaches around me to latch Jupiter's stall door.

"I . . . uh . . ." Huh?

She takes a step back, reaches into her pocket, and pulls out a green and white swirled peppermint hard candy. She holds it out like she's offering it to me.

Oh, damn.

Do I have bad breath?

I brushed my teeth this morning and I haven't eaten anything with onions or garlic. Maybe I should have thought to toss a pack of gum in my pocket, just in case.

I swallow, trying to force down some of my embarrassment. "For me?" I ask.

"For Jupiter," she says. "Horses love mints. He worked hard today, so you should reward him for it."

"Oh, right."

I feel like I'm on a one-person roller-coaster ride and the whiplash is real.

My fingers brush over her outstretched hand as I take the candy from her. The cellophane crinkles as I unwrap the peppermint.

"Hold it in the palm of your hand and keep it flat when you offer it to Jupiter."

I lay the candy in the center of my palm and Jupiter takes the mint, his chin hair tickling my skin. He closes his eyes as he chomps on his treat. Pure bliss.

"Now it's time for your reward," Cassidy says. "Follow me."

CHAPTER 13

Cassidy

"REWARD?" WILDER ASKS with a small eyebrow waggle.

The way he says the word makes my skin flush and I quickly look away. Maybe I should have chosen a different word? Too late now.

"You did a good job today," I say, hoping to redirect the conversation into safer territory.

And it's true. Wilder managed to avoid any and all incidents, which is practically a miracle in and of itself. He did a decent job working with Jupiter. And much to my surprise, he didn't complain once about helping muck out the stalls. It's nice to know that his time on the California celebrity track hasn't made him too good for Wyoming hard work.

This bonkers plan of Uncle Alex's might actually work.

Maybe.

If I can keep my head in the game and my heart on the sidelines.

Unfortunately, there have been more than a few moments when I almost let myself get carried away with my growing crush on Wilder. No matter how hard I try to stay focused on the tasks at hand, it's easy to get distracted by his good looks and endless charm. And those instances where it's felt like something *more* might happen . . .

Maybe it would have in a different universe. Or an alternate timeline.

I might be a naive country girl, but I know better than to fall for good looks and endless charm. To let a carefully constructed smile make my insides gooey. To let a pair of smoldering eyes make my knees weak.

But, dammit, my insides are gooey and my knees are weak.

It's even worse in those moments when the real Wilder Nash breaks through. When his smiles aren't calculated. When his gaze isn't flirtatious. That's when my heart's in the most jeopardy.

As we make our way from the stable to the training arena, I try to keep my thoughts focused on what needs to happen next.

My heart says *Kiss.*

My brain says *Helmet. Boots. Spurs.*

Clearly, I'm torn.

Thankfully, we arrive at the arena before I can sink much deeper into my wayward thoughts.

I push open the door to a storage room filled with racks of boots, helmets, and competition outfits collected from years of rodeo rides, roping contests, barrel racing, and other horse-related events. While most of the clothes in here are flashy competition gear, there's also more traditional Western wear mixed in. Most of this stuff is in good condition, and Mom keeps it around just in case we need it. It's also great when one of her riders needs a last-minute costume for an event. I'm hoping we can find Wilder a pair of cowboy boots, a sturdy helmet, and maybe a pair of leather chaps for him to wear so he can have the full cowboy attire experience. We can worry about spurs later.

"Let's get you outfitted," I say. I wander over to the shelves of boots in a rainbow of colors and styles. "What's your shoe size?"

Wilder looks over at me from where he stands next to a full-body white riding suit bedecked with rhinestones and sequins, with long fringe along the arms and legs. It reminds me of something Dolly Parton would wear.

"I . . ." He glances back at the bodysuit.

For a guy who should be used to wearing costumes, he looks particularly afraid that I'm going to gussy him up like 1970s Elvis.

Like a rhinestone cowboy.

I ignore Glen Campbell's voice in my head singing one of Grandpa's favorite songs and point to the rack of cowboy boots behind me. "Shoe size?" I ask.

"Oh." A look of momentary relief passes over his face. "Eleven."

That's the same size Uncle Alex wears, and I'm sure we have a pair of his old boots kicking around here somewhere. I spot them on the lowest level, dusty and worn, with scuffed sides and tooled leather uppers. I pull them out and hand them over. "Here."

Wilder has a lot of hair, so he'll need a larger helmet than I wear. I walk over to a wall filled with pegs that display riding helmets in one section and a variety of felt, fur, and wool cattleman, Dakota, Gus, diamond, and even a few Mountie-style hats in another. Wilder pulls a chocolate-brown wool hat with a cattleman crown from the wall and sets it on his head. As he adjusts it over his curls, he tips his head down, casting shadows over the planes of his face. When he looks up under the brim, my heart threatens to stampede from my rib cage. He looks every bit the rough and rugged cowboy he's been cast to play.

I turn away quickly so he won't see the rush of color rising to my cheeks and busy myself with selecting a helmet for him. Pulling down two options, I hold out a plain black one and a navy-blue one for him to try. Both have a slight visor that looks a bit like a shrunken baseball cap brim and adjustable hook and loop straps. "You want it to fit snuggly," I say. "Kind of like a bicycle helmet."

Wilder tips the cowboy hat back and frowns at the helmets I'm offering. "Can't I wear this hat instead?"

"Safety first," I say. But I'm not entirely sure if I'm referring to the helmet protecting his head or my attempts to protect my heart. Because Wilder, in a cowboy hat, is dangerous.

"Fine. But if I have to wear one, so do you." He reaches around me to pull down a raspberry-pink helmet covered in bright yellow floral decals. Wilder sets it on my head and grins. "Fits you perfectly," he says. He reaches out and snaps the straps in place and all the breath whooshes from my lungs when the back of his fingers graze my chin.

For a moment, I'm lost in the dark pools of his eyes. I want to lean in closer, to press my lips on his, to . . .

I look away before he can see the raw vulnerability there and, of course, my gaze goes to a rack of leather chaps. The idea had seemed fun before I saw Wilder in a cowboy hat, but now it seems just plain perilous.

In fact, spending any more time with him right now feels as risky as playing with fire. I've helped with enough controlled burns on the ranch to know that no matter how well you plan and prepare, there's always a chance that the flames will rage out of control. There's definitely a spark between us, at least as far as I'm concerned, and I worry that if I get caught up in it, I'll only end up getting burned.

After morning chores, I head over to the stable to get Jupiter saddled up for Wilder's first lesson on horseback. For new riders, Mom typically has me spend a session or two going over proper saddling technique, saddle maintenance, and grooming before having a beginner climb onto a horse, but given the tight timeline, the sooner we get Wilder in a saddle and out riding, the better. Plus, on set, I'm sure there will be a team of trainers and horse wranglers who will be responsible for preparing the horses for filming. It'll be easy enough to teach Wilder the key safety checks to perform before hopping into a saddle, and I can teach him the other things he should know as the summer progresses.

My thoughts immediately wander to Wilder as I run a brush over Jupiter's back. I know it's a waste of time and energy, crushing on someone who'll be gone in a little more than a month. Someone very much a part of a world that my grandfather doesn't approve of. Someone I'll probably only ever see on a TV or movie theater screen after this. But try telling that to my heart, which has me daydreaming about kisses and hand-holding and cowboy hats dipped low over Wilder's strong jawline.

I'm a fool for crushing on Wilder, because it's so cliché.

But it was bound to happen, *because* it's so cliché.

Thanks a lot, Hollywood. Not only have you been the root cause of years of family drama, but you've also served up plenty of romance clichés. In fact, this exact situation is pretty much the plot of half the cheesy teen romance movies ever made, including *Summer Camp Chronicles*. In that one, Wilder played the outgoing jock who managed to win the heart of the shy bookworm who ended the summer with a major glow-up and a first kiss.

Ugh.

I pat down the saddle pad to make sure there isn't anything sharp or hard that might make Jupiter uncomfortable and then toss it onto his back so it rests just behind his withers. The saddle I've selected for Wilder is deeper than the one I use and meant for long-distance rides. It's a good saddle for beginners because it often makes a new rider feel more stable and secure.

Stable and secure. Two words that I would not use to describe a possible—make that entirely fictional—romantic relationship with Wilder. Because just like in *Summer Camp Chronicles,* our forced proximity and numbered days are a barrier to anything more than a summer fling.

No thank you.

Even though I might dream about the world beyond our Wyoming ranch, I don't have any intentions of leaving. When Uncle Alex went off to Hollywood, he broke Grandpa's heart and caused a huge rift in our family. There's no way I could just up and leave all this behind. I might be a fool for my crush on Wilder, but I know better than to make huge life choices revolving around a boy I barely know.

Still . . . there's a big old world out there to explore.

I set the saddle over the pad and reposition it so that it sits right where it ought to.

Is Wyoming right where *I* ought to be? I've always thought it was, or at least I never questioned it. But now I'm starting to wonder if it's really so terrible to want to see and experience life beyond our ranch. Is it so wrong to want the possibility of something more?

Not wrong, I think. But why dream of things that would only end up shattering our family even more? If I followed in Uncle Alex's footsteps, Grandpa would cut me out of his life, for sure. My parents would be left to suffer the brunt of his wrath, which wouldn't be fair to them. And the ranch would no longer stay in the Sterling family once Dad retires. Our family legacy would probably be sold in a land auction to the highest bidder.

I've just finished adjusting the cinch straps when Wilder arrives. As requested, he's wearing the cowboy boots I gave him instead of the work boots he's been clomping around in for the past few days. He carries the dark-black helmet by the straps, and it bounces against his jean-clad thigh as he strides closer in a leisurely, laid-back walk. A cool June breeze ruffles his hair, and the way the sun shines down on him makes it look like he's in the process of filming a character montage scene in the countryside. I can picture the image as the clip featured in the opening credits, with Wilder Nash written in golden lettering at the bottom of the screen.

Damn, it's just not fair. My heart doesn't stand a chance.

I look away and fiddle with a stirrup.

Jupiter swishes his tail.

"Hey," Wilder says as he steps into the stable.

"Hi," I respond, hoping I look more focused than frazzled.

Wilder makes sure to give Jupiter's backside a wide berth as he makes his way over. He offers a hand to Jupiter to sniff, his movements less robotic and more comfortable today than yesterday.

Progress.

My heart skips.

Or not.

"This is a Western trail saddle," I say, deciding the best course of action is to just dive right in. If I'm busy teaching, I won't have time to get carried away with daydreams and desires. I hope. "It's a traditional cowboy-type saddle, so they'll probably use a similar one for you on set. There are a couple of different kinds of Western saddles, but they all have similar features." I keep my attention focused on the saddle. "A horn for roping cattle. A seat. Stirrups. This one is good for beginners because it's got a suede seat, which will help prevent you from sliding around when you're riding."

I pull the lead line free from the metal ring on the wall and hand the rope to Wilder, careful not to let our fingers brush for longer than necessary. I ignore the tingle from even that slight touch and say, "Why don't you take Jupiter out to the paddock? You can practice some of the things we worked on yesterday."

I don't wait for Wilder to respond. I spin away and grab the raspberry-colored helmet Wilder picked out for me yesterday, Jupiter's bridle, and a wooden mounting block.

"Head in the game," I remind myself before I follow them out of the stable.

As if in response, my heart does a rebellious pitter-patter.

CHAPTER 14

Wilder

CASSIDY SWAPS OUT Jupiter's halter and lead line for a bridle with reins and then steps up onto the mounting block with the reins folded in her left hand. "You want to put your left foot in the stirrup first," she says, demonstrating. "Then push up with your left leg while you kick your right leg over the horse's back. Like this." Her movements are quick and fluid. "Make sure to slide your right foot into the stirrup before you sit. You want to ease into the saddle so you don't hurt the horse's back." She lowers herself down and rests her left hand on her thigh.

Cassidy makes it look so easy. She's so confident and sure, and I am the complete opposite at the moment. I'm always down for a pickup game of basketball or tossing around a football, but I'm no gymnast. And getting up into the saddle will take an awful lot of coordination that I'm not sure I have.

The familiar voice in the back of my mind reminds me to

"fake it till you make it." But that doesn't stop me from worrying that I might pull a groin muscle. Or fall on my ass. My streak of accidents seems to be over. . . .

But what if it's not?

I roll my shoulders, trying to release the tension pooling in my upper back. Better for my first attempt to be here with only one witness and not in front of a whole film crew.

Cassidy stands in the stirrups. Beneath her dark pink riding helmet, she fixes me with a look that's half serious, half teasing. "I'm going to dismount now," she says. "And I don't need any help."

"Understood," I say, stepping back to give her plenty of space. My hand automatically reaches up to touch what's left of the lump on my forehead. Even with my riding helmet on, I don't want to be anywhere near her boot.

As before, she kicks her right leg over Jupiter's back and then, instead of kicking me in the head, she hops down onto the mounting block.

Damn, she's good.

Once she's dismounted, I step closer. When she turns to face me, our eyes meet. Standing there on the block, she's only slightly taller than me. The breeze flutters the hair at the nape of her neck and there's a slight flush on her cheeks. Her lips are right there in front of me, soft and parted. I'd only have to take one step forward to kiss her.

"Are you ready to try?" Cassidy asks.

It takes me a moment to realize she's talking about me climbing into the saddle, not kissing her. I reach up and adjust my helmet. "Sure am," I say, shooting her a grin paired with

113

smoldering eyes that hopefully compensates for the lack of confidence I feel. I lean forward with false bravado, letting my arm brush against her side, and reach for Jupiter's reins.

Cassidy's eyes narrow, as if she can see right through the act I'm putting on. "Just take your time, Wilder."

The way she says my name sends a bolt of electricity through my heart.

She doesn't treat me like I'm the kid from that shoe commercial. Or that guy from that Disney Channel movie. Or an actor who might be worth cozying up to in case I ever manage to claw my way to the top. Somehow, Cassidy sees through my bullshit until it's just me standing there before her.

I'm not sure how I feel about it.

The smile falls from my face as the swagger seeps out of me.

Looking into her eyes, I can almost see her waging an internal debate. She blinks and her gaze goes to something in the distance behind me. Eventually, she takes a deep breath, and when she looks back at me, her expression is cool. "Okay, Wilder Nash," she says. "Let's get you up in the saddle." She steps down off the mounting block, gestures for me to climb up, and hands me the reins. "Left foot stirrup. Right leg over Jupiter's back and into the stirrup. Then gently lower yourself down into the seat."

I'm sore and tired by the time I make my way into the guest cabin for the night. Every muscle in my body screams from all the hoisting, hefting, lifting, and lowering I did throughout the day. My legs hurt the worst. All I want is to crash in bed, but my dirty clothes are starting to stink up the closet and I still have a bunch of the script left to read.

After a hot shower, my muscles aren't as tight as they were, although it still hurts to bend down to pick up a pair of socks from the floor. I toss them into a clothes hamper with everything I've worn since I arrived and carry it to the hall closet that contains a tall and skinny space-maker washer-dryer combo. Thanks to a laundry detergent commercial I shot when I was in middle school, I know I need to separate dirty clothes by color, and new clothes—especially blue jeans—should be washed separately. I toss the jeans in first, add some detergent, and plunk the lid down. I'm hoping I can stay awake long enough to throw in at least one more load tonight.

There's a can of cold brew coffee in the fridge, so I crack it open and take a long swig. Even though the caffeine hasn't had a chance to hit me yet, I'm already feeling more energized.

Grabbing the script, I settle onto the couch with a pen tucked behind my ear. Before I dig in, I pull out my phone to check my messages. Back in L.A., my cell was constantly in my hand—practically glued to my palm when I wasn't filming a scene or with the on-set tutor—but since the service here is spotty away from the main buildings, I hardly check it anymore.

I don't have much of a reason to. Right after I landed the role of Deacon Slade, Alexander recommended I hire a public relations firm to curate my social media and help with press and promo. Before I left, I shared a cloud folder with some random pictures the team could use for posts. It's been nice to have a break from constant self-promotion and trying to figure out how to game the algorithm, especially since I'm never quite sure what my followers or future followers might want to see.

I pull up my profile and scroll through what the PR team has posted so far. An old clip of me from when I was first starting out, with a spot in a grape juice commercial. A handful of still photos from the outerwear commercial I just shot to play up my rugged side. And a few Western-inspired teasers and photos to build excitement for *Outrider*.

There's been more interaction with the posts than before, so it looks like I'm getting my money's worth.

I swipe over to my email, but nothing important has come in. Most things are funneled through Alexander now anyhow, since he serves as both my agent and on-set advocate. I send my mom a quick text to let her know I'm doing okay and to check in. She's been working night shifts at the hospital for the past year, so we've gotten used to communicating via text, except for those rare occasions when she has a day off and I'm not on set. Besides that, there are only a few texts and group chats that I bother to respond to. Even then, I keep it short and vague, since I'm supposed to be on "vacation."

Ha!

This trip has been the complete opposite. I'm not sure I've ever worked so hard before in my life.

The ache in my bones makes me wonder if it's worth it. Will all this horse riding and shit shoveling get me one step closer to the big time? Or should I ask Alexander to find me a role that I'm better suited for? My finger hovers over the phone app, but I can't call him. There's no way I can back out of this now. If I quit, it might brand me as difficult. Unable to commit. Uncastable.

Then I think about Alexander. It's not just my reputation— my career—that's at stake.

The smart move is to double down. To work as hard as I can to become the best damn cowboy actor since John Wayne.

I toss the phone onto the couch beside me and flip open the script. I start over at the beginning and after a few pages, I'm reminded that learning to ride a horse like I was born to do it is just one of the many cowboy skills Deacon Slade possesses.

"You have got to be kidding me," I groan five pages later. Are there *any* skills my character doesn't have? It might be easier to list them than the ones I'll need to convincingly portray.

I'm distracted from my pity party when the washer chugs to a stop and a short beep lets me know the cycle's done. My legs protest when I push off the couch, and I hobble over to the closet to shift the wet clothes into the dryer above. After I get another load in the wash, it's back to the couch for a serious script study session.

Skills to learn
- Horseback riding
- Fire building
- Open flame cooking
- Navigating the Western frontier
- Old West first aid
- Herding
- Fence building
- Camping out under the stars

I thought I was tired before, but now I'm exhausted from reading over the list—all things I've never done—and I'm only halfway through the first draft of the script. I don't have to be an expert at most of these things. And I know there will be a team of people coordinating everything I do so they can get the best shot.

But I also don't want to disappoint the viewers. One of my biggest pet peeves is watching a film where the character is supposed to play the piano, but the actor doesn't know how. They use these cutaway shots to show the action, while someone else's disembodied hands are used in place of the actor's. Instead of a smooth slow pan or a zoom shot, the quick transition from the actor to a close-up of moving hands always pulls me out of the story. I find myself wondering *Whose hands are those?*

Even though my character doesn't play a guitar or a harmonica or whatever other instrument a cowboy might have in the Old West, there are plenty of scenes where I can picture the director using a disembodied-hand shot instead of a zoom shot of me. Striking a flint to set a campfire ablaze. Securing a torn-cloth bandage over a gaping wound. The thought makes me cringe.

Besides learning to ride, I'll need to at least become familiar with some of these other skills, too. Even if it's just to maintain some self-respect.

I yawn. My limbs are so heavy, it feels like lead flows through my veins. I force my eyes open and swing my stiff legs off the couch.

I definitely need to tackle those other items, but I'm not about to start on them tonight.

CHAPTER 15

Cassidy

I'VE DONE A pretty good job of staying focused on training Wilder to ride these past few days. I haven't let my developing crush distract me. I've steered clear of situations where our personal space bubbles might bump and pop and lead to accidental brushes. I've even stopped using lip balm ... when he's around. (Because it's one thing to have soft, kissable lips and another thing entirely to have cracked and chapped lips.)

Thankfully, Wilder hasn't needed as much direction to complete the chores, and we've fallen into a comfortable daily routine.

In the morning, he tends to the chickens and I take care of the pigs and goats.

When it's our day to clean the stables, he mucks out Ginger's and Jupiter's stalls while I take care of the others.

He weeds the vegetable garden while I take care of the herbs and plants in the greenhouse.

Once all the chores are done, we break for lunch and then meet at the stable paddock for his riding lessons. I'd prefer to use the indoor arena, but Mom's got it practically booked out for lessons and parties until August.

Wilder's lessons have largely consisted of me guiding Jupiter around the paddock while he gets comfortable sitting in the saddle. Sometimes I let him hold the reins while I call out instructions from a safe distance. It's been pretty easy to keep things completely compartmentalized and professional while I'm out of range of his dazzling smile and piercing eyes.

But Wilder's starting to get the hang of riding. I can't keep him in the paddock forever. It's time to take him out of the arena and onto the range.

Just the two of us and our horses.

Side by side.

On the open trail.

All.

Day.

Long.

Okay, to be fair, it's just past noon and the ride will be only a few hours, at most. But it's very much a change from our normal pattern, and I'm not sure how I feel about it.

From a riding instructor standpoint, it's great news. Wilder's learning everything he needs to portray a well-seasoned equestrian. I think Uncle Alex would be proud of his progress. Soon we'll be able head out on a full-day ride—or maybe an overnight—so he can get even more comfortable in the saddle.

But from a Wyoming country girl with a crush on a California actor-boy standpoint, I have serious concerns. There's the proximity issue. Excessive alone time. And my complete inability to not have romantic feelings for Wilder Nash to contend with. I'm basically Becca in *Summer Camp Chronicles,* except I'm guaranteed not to get a happy ending because this is real life and not a cheesy teen movie.

Damn Wilder's irresistible smile. His mesmerizing eyes. And his unruly mop of curls.

The day is warmer than it's been lately and the sun is a bright glowing orb in the cloudless sky. I've swapped out the raspberry-pink helmet for my favorite Western hat—a satin-lined, sand-colored, buffalo fur felt cowgirl hat with a chocolate leather band and a pinch-front crown. The brim is nice and wide, big enough to shade my eyes from the sun and to hide me from Wilder in case my face threatens to betray my feelings for him while we're out on the trail.

I've already saddled and bridled Jupiter, who stands beside Land Sailor with a level of patience that only an old, seasoned trail horse can have. His tail swishes lazily as he watches a yellow-breasted Western meadowlark hop along the top of the split-rail fence.

When Wilder finally arrives, I'm glad I opted for the big-brimmed cowgirl hat that will hide the color rising to my cheeks instead of the pink helmet that would only accentuate the heated blush I feel spreading across my face. I expected to see him carrying the dark black riding helmet he's been wearing, but instead, he has a coffee-brown cowboy hat pulled down low over his brow. There's a swagger to his stride, and the way he looks in a red flannel shirt tucked into dark wash jeans over worn old cowboy boots sends my pulse skyrocketing.

Like a slow-motion shot, Wilder lifts his head and tips his hat back to look me dead in the eye before dipping his chin.

Thank goodness I'm already in the saddle, or I might seriously be in danger of swooning.

"Howdy," he says in a low, deep voice that sends shivers down my spine. He glances up as he comes to stand beside me.

I realize now that he's wearing a hybrid felt cowboy hat helmet. At first glance, it looks like a typical felt hat, but instead of a leather band where the brim meets the crown, there's a polystyrene band and a helmet hidden underneath. I've seen them before at rodeos and livestock auctions, but never here, at the ranch.

"Nice hat," I manage, because it seems to be the safest thing to say at the moment.

"Thanks." He reaches up and adjusts it. "Alexander sent it along with a note telling me to 'lean into the cowboy aesthetic.' I guess he figured I'd be wearing plenty of cowboy hats on set, so I might as well get used to it."

I can get used to it, I think.

But I shouldn't get used to it.

I shouldn't even think it.

"Here," I say, holding out Jupiter's reins for Wilder to take. "Let's ride."

I've survived our last few trail rides, but just barely.

Now that Wilder's more comfortable in the saddle, we're able to head out on longer excursions, which is great for him. For me? Not so much.

It's been a hopeless battle, trying not to get caught up in my growing attraction to Wilder Nash. Maybe if he would just keep his face hidden under his cowboy hat and his mouth glued shut, I'd stand a fighting chance.

But no.

He has to keep his cowboy hat tipped up just enough that I can see the cut of his jaw whenever I glance over at him. Which is a ridiculous amount.

Now that he's grown more accustomed to riding, we're working to correct his cowboy slouch, where he sits slightly forward with his forearms resting on the pommel, Jupiter's reins in his left hand. But correcting his posture means constantly looking at him when all I want to do is avert my eyes.

This is a blatant lie I keep telling myself because the truth is so much harder to admit. I have it bad for Wilder Nash.

What's worse is that now he's running lines. I vaguely remember telling him that was something he could do while we were spending time together. Epic mistake.

At first, he was saying innocuous things like, "It's time for me to mosey on down the road," or "They're fixin' to cause trouble down at the old McCoy place," or "You're about as welcome as a rattlesnake at a square dance."

But now? Now he's saying things that are a whole lot less cowboy and a whole lot more romance-y.

"You deserve the world, and I will go to the ends of the earth to get it for you."

"I ain't never seen the stars sparkle as brightly as they do in your eyes."

"No matter how far I ride, you'll always be my final destination."

I know these are not his words. He's an actor. Memorizing and reciting lines believably is literally his job. I'm fully aware that the swoon-worthy quips and sweet nothings are vomit-inducing. Ridiculous. And intended for whichever character plays Deacon Slade's star-crossed love interest, not me. But each and every syllable Wilder utters is like one of Cupid's little arrows piercing my heart.

Thwack. Thwack. Thwack.

"No matter where I ride or how far I get from you—north, south, east, or west—you best believe all roads will lead me to you. I promise, I'll always come back."

My heart pinches in my chest and I blow out a steady breath in an effort to keep my composure. It's totally ridiculous for someone to make a promise like that. Deacon Slade is stupid for saying it. And whoever his love interest is, she's a fool to believe it. So many things could happen to keep them apart. Knowing that *Outrider* is a dramatic miniseries and this is only episode one, so many things will. I don't even need to read the script to imagine the possibilities.

Storms.

Injuries.

His overbearing father.

Her wrong-side-of-town background.

Filming schedules.

Press junkets.

Movie deals.

"Easy," I say in an effort to keep both Land Sailor and myself on track. I hadn't realized how far we'd wandered from the main trail or how off course my mind had gone.

Wilder and Jupiter stop beside us and together we look out over the sloping fields dotted with scrub brush and a smattering of trees. It's late in the day, and the sun has started to sink low in the sky, casting everything in a golden glow. I can't resist glancing at Wilder, who seems to be mesmerized by the view. His eyes are fixed on the horizon and his mouth curls up into a half-smile. He looks relaxed and at peace. My chest burns and I look away.

"It's breathtaking," he says.

You have no idea.

"Can we maybe stop here for a few minutes?" he asks.

I hesitate. Stopping here in the golden glow with the warm wind and my insatiable crush is not a good idea.

"I wanna run through mounting and dismounting without a block. I don't quite have the hang of it yet." He gives me a pleading look, but it's not the calculated one I'm used to. Wilder is serious about wanting the extra practice.

How can I say no to more practice?

"Okay," I say.

As soon as my boots are on the ground, Wilder dismounts. His movements aren't smooth, like they will be eventually, but he's definitely come a long way from the first day when he arrived, after being chased out of the guest cottage by Rambrandt and Van Goat.

Wilder wipes his forehead with the back of his hand.

I force myself to look away.

I keep my eyes pasted on the valley below when he comes to stand beside me. "When Alexander told me I was heading to Wyoming, I didn't really know what to expect. It sure wasn't this."

Wilder gently tugs at my hand, pulling me around to face him.

I'm frozen in the moment, not sure if this is real or if I've fallen off Land Sailor and gotten a horrific head injury. Have I been concussed? Or worse? Maybe I should have worn that raspberry helmet, after all.

"Thank you for helping me learn to ride," he says, giving my hand a sincere squeeze. "I know this probably isn't how you planned to spend your summer...."

Wilder's warm breath floats over my cheek and the world melts away. His hand brushes a strand of hair from my face as his gaze darts down to my mouth and then back up to my eyes as if he's asking permission to kiss me.

The setting sun highlights the planes of his face. The curve of his mouth. The heat in his eyes.

Drawn to him like a bee to pollen, I lean in.

Warm. Soft. Hesitant. Our lips meet and electricity shoots through my toes. Wilder tugs off his hat and wraps his arm around my waist to pull me in closer, deepening our kiss. One of his curls tickles my forehead. When I reach up to brush it back, I discover it's just as soft as I imagined it would be. My lips curl into a smile under his and I sink deeper into his embrace.

I let myself be swept up in the moment. The magic. The magnificence of this kiss.

It might be minutes or a millennium when we finally pull apart. I suck in a deep breath and stare up at him.

"I've been wanting to do that for a while now," he says, his voice low and gravelly.

CHAPTER 16

Wilder

I'VE KISSED OTHER girls in the past, but this kiss with Cassidy has blown all the others out of the water. It wasn't stiff and rehearsed like any onstage or on-screen kiss I've ever shared. It wasn't rushed and hidden, like the time Amanda Marbourgh and I kissed on a dare backstage at curtain call before we stepped out as Dorothy and the Scarecrow in a local theater production of *The Wizard of Oz*. And it definitely wasn't anything like the time I was blindsided by a kiss from Chloe Pikowski, who mistook one of the other actor's dads for a paparazzo and was hoping to stir up some interest for her career by getting "caught" kissing me on a Disney set. I just happened to be the closest teen actor. Lucky me.

Cassidy gazes up at me with starry eyes. I could get lost in those dark pools full of sparkle and spirit.

Her cowboy hat must have fallen off during our kiss. My

fingers twine in her hair and I lean in, brushing my forehead against hers.

This is the part in shows and movies when the guy says something smooth and charming, and the girl gets swept off her feet. I know I should do something or say something, but what?

It needs to be more charming than "Hell, yeah."

"Thanks" would be weird.

And I don't want to look too exuberant, either. I don't want Cassidy to think I'm a pathetic sap. I carefully school my features into a calm, cool expression with my eyebrows raised in a way that was once called "alluring" by a director for an acne treatment commercial.

But now what? The longer the silence draws out between us, the more pressure I feel to say the perfect thing. I try to remember some of the lines my previous characters had in moments like this for inspiration, but I'm drawing a complete blank.

I want to be the guy who says something smooth and charming.

I want to be the guy who sweeps Cassidy off her feet.

In the glow of the setting sun, with the wind whispering around us, Cassidy gazes up at me with those shimmering eyes and my heart almost bursts in my chest.

"You're the prettiest girl I've ever seen," I say in what I like to think of as my hunky leading man voice.

I lean in for another kiss, but just before my lips press against hers, Cassidy stiffens. I draw back and the dazed look in Cassidy's eyes fades.

She steps away with a sharp, stony expression on her face.

My arm drops from her waist. Cool air fills the space between us, making it feel like she's a world away instead of right in front of me.

The wind kicks up, sending a small dust storm swirling around our feet. A small acid storm swirls in my stomach.

Something's wrong.

But what? I thought our kiss was incredible.

Still, I don't need a script to see Cassidy's not eager for a repeat.

It can't possibly be my breath, because I popped in a mint earlier. Unless Cassidy hates spearmint.

Maybe it's my technique? No one's ever accused me of being a bad kisser before. But then again, it's not usually polite to badmouth a costar.

I never thought I'd miss having someone direct me through a kissing scene, but I'm not exactly killing it out here on my own. A little help would be nice.

Or what if it's worse? Way worse than bad breath or terrible technique? Did I completely misread the situation? Maybe all those quick glances and shy smiles weren't signs she was into me. Maybe Cassidy was just checking to make sure I wasn't about to fall out of the saddle. Maybe she was just being nice. Maybe she was just putting up with me as a favor to her uncle.

Shoot, I probably should have asked first before I went all in with the kiss. My shoulders sag under the realization that I might have just been *that guy.*

"Oh my god," Cassidy says, shaking her head as if to clear it. "Was that . . . a line?"

"No," I say quickly. That's not what I expected her to say, and now I'm thrown off again. I plaster what I hope is a reassuring smile on my face and swivel my cowboy hat helmet around with nervous hands.

Cassidy doesn't return the smile. Instead, she studies me like she's trying to assess the depths of a lie, even though I'm being completely honest with her.

The echo of my voice rings in my ears. *You're the prettiest girl I've ever seen.*

I've never been good at improv. Or spontaneity. Or going off-script.

That kiss. Those words. That was all me.

I swipe a hand through my damp hair and then set the helmet-hat back in place.

Cassidy pinches her lips together and looks up at the sky, her arms wrapped tightly around her torso. "You're a really, really good actor." The tone of her voice tells me it's not a compliment.

"Thanks?"

I feel so lost right now. Without a script. Without a mark. Without a freakin' clue.

"I shouldn't be surprised. You're repped by Uncle Alex. But that acting just now? That was next level, Wilder."

The way she says my name makes it feel like the wind's been knocked out of me. "You thought I was acting?"

She brushes her fingers over her lips as if trying to wipe the memory of our kiss away and nods. "Obviously. No one actually says stuff like that in real life."

I do.

I just did.

Talk about a crushing blow.

Here I was, trying to sweep her off her feet, and instead, she's pulled the rug right out from under mine.

Panic surges through me. My heartbeat thumps like *Mayday, Mayday, Mayday* in my ears. I have to save face. To minimize the fallout and buy myself time to figure out how to fix this.

"It's just an early script," I say with a careless shrug. I adjust my cowboy hat and smirk. "I'm sure there will be some revisions after the table read."

Now there's a glassy look to Cassidy's eyes, almost as if she'd hoped I'd deny it.

Would it be better if I had? Would I have been able to convince her of my sincerity? Too late now.

Cassidy blinks and looks away. "You deliver your lines well," she says in a monotone.

Too well.

If this was a scene, and it was falling apart so badly, someone would have yelled "cut" by now. We'd all reset and try again.

But this is real life. There are no do-overs. No second or third or however many takes until we get it right. None of the mistakes I make will end up on the cutting room floor.

"Ready to head back?" she says in an overly bright tone when she turns to face me.

She's not a very good actor because I can see the disappointment written all over her face. Her words run together like she needs to get them out before she bursts. "This doesn't have to affect our professional relationship, of course. We can just pretend it never happened. You were running lines and I just got caught up in the moment. We'll hop back on our horses, ride back to the stable, and focus on making sure you're as prepared as we can get you before you head back to California."

"I . . ." I don't know what to say.

I know that's why I'm here.

And I know that I still have a long way to go before I can convince anyone that I was "practically born in the saddle."

But now there's more at stake here than my Hollywood hopes and dreams.

Now my feelings for Cassidy are in the mix.

The ride back to the stables is beyond awkward. Cassidy keeps Land Sailor slightly behind Jupiter, so it's impossible for me to see her face. I try to sit up straight in the saddle and stay calm, but my heart thuds with regret in time with every hoofbeat.

When we reach the stable yard, I want to jump down from the saddle, march over to Cassidy, wrap her up in my arms, and kiss her again until I can't breathe. In my mind, it'll be like one of those epic cinematic moments, with soft lighting, swelling music, and a 360-degree shot. But that's the problem, isn't it?

This is real life. My actions have to be less cinematic and more sincere if I want her to take me seriously.

I thud down to the ground like a clumsy cowboy. The added embarrassment makes my stomach sink even further. Usually by this time of day, I'm famished. But my appetite disappeared back on the trail.

By the time I'm finished untacking and grooming Jupiter, Cassidy's already finished with Land Sailor and has taken care of the rest of the horses. She watches me with cautious eyes as I make my way over. "Are you coming to the house for dinner?" she asks.

I don't miss her momentary glance at my mouth before she averts her eyes.

I clear my throat and shove my hands into the front pockets of my jeans like I'm totally chill. Like I didn't just have my heart ripped from my chest and stomped on by Cassidy Sterling. "I . . . uh," I say, "I'm pretty tired, actually. I think I'll just fix myself something small."

Cassidy nods and her shoulders sag like she's relieved. "Okay. See you tomorrow."

"Yeah."

I sulk around the guest cabin for a while, discouraged by my lack of game and unsure what to do about it. I don't want to fall back on one of my old characters, because I want Cassidy to like me for me. Now that I've had some time to think about it, I'm pretty confident that Cassidy's into me, too.

Our kiss was way too intense for it to have been anything other than mutual attraction. I know when someone's feigning passion, because staged kisses are not at all romantic. Lips here, count to three, tilt your head, pull away, open your eyes. And there's all the people watching while it happens. It's weird.

But the kiss Cassidy and I shared, that was as real as it gets. Even if she doesn't believe it was.

I crack open a can of soda and take a long swig.

Now I just need to figure out why Cassidy was so quick to believe I was acting.

CHAPTER 17

Cassidy

I KNEW THAT Wilder Nash would crush my heart. I'm sure that's why it's called a crush in the first place. I just didn't think it would happen so soon.

I figured I would quietly pine after him, my feelings carefully hidden behind my rib cage. The flirtations we shared would fuel the longing, but I would keep everything carefully contained and compartmentalized. And then, like I always knew he would, Wilder would ride off into the sunset like the hero at the end of a love story. Ours was never meant to be a whirlwind romance with a happy ending. Wilder would leave for California. I'd stay in Wyoming. That would be that.

And the minute he left . . . that's when my heart would crumble.

But to have it smushed only halfway into his time here?

Unexpected.

Unfortunate.

Unfair.

If it'd happened the way I'd planned, I could have convinced myself it just wasn't meant to be. That he'd been so focused on learning to ride that he hadn't had time to develop feelings for me. It would have been romantic in an unrequited, Shakespearean kind of way.

Instead, I got played.

Oh, but he's good. So good.

And I'm stupid. So stupid.

How could I have not seen it coming?

No.

I did see it coming. I saw through every saucy smile. Every flirty look. Every overconfident remark. And I fell for it all the same.

And that kiss. Wowzers. It's practically burned into my brain. I had no idea that a kiss could go from sweet to swoony so quickly. I thought that movies put a cinematic spin on smooching to keep the audience watching, that a kiss like we shared was totally far-fetched in actuality. One of those impossible things created with movie magic and audience buy-in, like the hero who takes thirty punches to the face after being shot and stabbed and still saves the day. Or the heroine who wakes up with perfect hair and skin instead of a rat's nest and pillow wrinkles.

Movie magic, that's exactly what it was. Wilder brought some of that Hollywood razzle-dazzle here, and like a clichéd country bumpkin, I almost let it blind me to the truth. I always thought Grandpa's opinion of Hollywood and the people in the movie industry was extreme, but now I think he might have a valid point. Life at Silver Stallion Ranch isn't fancy or glitzy, but at least it's real.

This is exactly why I shouldn't be harboring thoughts of the great big world beyond the ranch. I'm too doe-eyed. Too gullible. Too ready and willing to fall for the first hot guy with a sly smile that I meet.

I bury my head in my pillow and let out a silent scream.

How am I going to survive the next few weeks? Wilder's going to expect me to act normal around him. Professional. And not like some naive girl who actually hoped—*no, believed*—that he was into her.

I take a deep breath. Count to four. Hold. Count to four. Exhale. Count to four. Repeat.

Mom teaches box breathing to some of her students who are prone to panic attacks prior to a competition. Right now, I'm hoping the technique will help reduce some of the anxiety that's coursing through my veins.

After a few minutes, I feel marginally better. Not good enough to banish my feelings completely, but at least I no longer have the urge to eat an entire pint of ice cream.

I'm headed downstairs to get started on morning chores when Dad calls me into the kitchen. "Morning, Cassidy," he says, handing me a mug of coffee made the way I like it.

The scent of French vanilla creamer perks me right up. "Morning," I reply, taking the steaming cup and giving him a questioning look. Usually we save the coffee break for after the chores are complete. Not that I'm complaining. The longer I'm in here with Dad, the longer I can avoid Wilder. Plus, an unexpected jolt of coffee is always a bonus. "What's up?" I ask.

"I know you've got a lot on your plate already, but I'm hoping you could lead a last-minute trail ride out to Boulder Creek today," he says. Dad takes a sip from his mug and glances at me over the rim. "Some tourists in Jackson were looking for a place to ride, and the other ranches in the area can't accommodate them. Winnie called down from the hotel and asked if we could help out."

Ordinarily, I'd be begging off something like this. I don't feel like an experienced enough guide to take a group of people of uncertain horsemanship out for a ride. But the trail to Boulder Creek has some of the best views on the ranch and it's a fairly easy path, so it's perfect for all skill levels. Plus, having other people to act as a buffer between me and Wilder wouldn't hurt. The less time I have to spend alone with him, the better.

"Are they experienced riders?" I ask.

Dad nods. "Winnie says they keep horses of their own back home."

That's promising. "How many people are we talking?"

"Three." He waits a beat for me to consider. "What do you say?"

Tipping my head, I ask, "What time are they set to arrive?"

Dad looks at his watch. "In about two hours."

"Told you she'd say yes," Grandpa says with a smug grin from his seat at the head of the table. He bites into a slice of buttered toast. "She's got the Sterling spirit."

Two hours is barely enough time to get the morning chores done, grab breakfast, and prep the horses, but I'll manage it somehow.

Dad sets his empty coffee mug down on the counter. "You can saddle up Ginger, Misty Morning, and—"

"Al," Grandpa says, cutting Dad off.

So that means one of the riders is a kid. I make a mental note to grab one of the pins Mom had made up that's shaped like an old-fashioned sheriff badge and says *Silver Stallion Deputy* in a circle around the word *Sheriff* in the center of the star.

I finish my coffee, give Dad and Grandpa a kiss on the cheek, and then head out to the barnyard with the slop bucket bouncing against my thigh.

Trouble bounds over from behind the greenhouse and meows until I stop to scratch beneath her chin. "I hope you're all the trouble I'm in for today," I mutter. She looks at me with impish golden-green eyes and purrs before darting off under a bush.

Thankfully, I'm too distracted by chores and adding to my mental to-do list for the trail ride to stew over Wilder or the crush I harbor. My heart squeezes when I catch a glimpse of him gathering eggs in the chicken coop, but I refuse to be distracted by him anymore. Not if I can help it. Uncle Alex is counting on me to get Wilder prepared for filming, and once he can pass as a convincing cowboy, he'll be back in California where he belongs. He'll move on and so will I.

Instead of heading for the family stables after breakfast as usual, Wilder and I go to the arena stables to get the additional trail horses for the tourists. Misty Morning and Al Caponey are middle-aged horses who are great on the trail. Mom uses Misty, a golden dappled palomino mustang, for the weekly equine therapy sessions she hosts for a group of ladies from Sunny Acres Assisted Living, and Al is our buckskin Shetland pony gelding that we often use when someone books the arena for a kid's birthday party and pony rides.

Dad's already pulled saddles and bridles from the arena tack room so we can get straight to it. After saddling them up, I hang the bridles and reins on the saddle horns for later. Then we slide halters onto the horses and lead them to the family stable. The walk over is quiet and the silence hangs between us. I hadn't realized how we'd slipped into a pattern of near-constant conversation until it stopped. I try not to miss the friendly banter or the sound of his laugh. I definitely don't remember the grins or the way he squints when deep in thought.

When we arrive at the stable, I run the ends of Misty Morning's lead rope around a hitching post. I allow myself a moment to watch Wilder tie up Al Caponey with a quick-release knot under the guise of supervision. I refuse to acknowledge how hot he looks when his jaw is set in concentration.

Ugh, crushes are the worst. Why can't they just automatically die when you discover the person you've set your heart on doesn't feel the same? Or worse, that they were just acting like they did. It would be so much simpler if there was an off switch instead of a hope-hinge that just won't allow the door to your heart to close completely.

In the time it takes Wilder to saddle up Jupiter, I've finished getting both Ginger and Land Sailor ready for the trail. The tourists should be here in about fifteen minutes or so, and I'm pleased that we'll be ready for them.

Wilder saunters out of the stable with Jupiter, with his cowboy hat helmet pulled down low over his face. He leads Jupiter over and gives me a nod. "Howdy, partner," he says.

It's such an utterly ridiculous and unexpected thing for him to say that I can't hold back the bark of laughter that escapes me. I force myself to look away so he can't see the heat rising to my face. I don't want to have these kinds of reactions when I'm around him. Why must my body betray me like this?

Wilder clears his throat. "I was hoping we could talk," he says in a much more serious tone.

The heat that was in my face a moment before drains away like I've just had a bucket of ice water poured over me.

"Oh, um, sure," I say.

This is me being cool. Calm. Totally in control of my emotions, which are roiling like a dust storm in my gut. I dig the toe of my cowboy boot into the dirt to try to get rid of some of the nervous energy that has my skin prickling.

"I wanted to . . ." he continues.

Of course, my stupid heart skips a beat.

Of course, a fuzzy, foamy feeling skitters through me.

Of course, Dad would arrive with the tourists before Wilder can tell me whatever it was he wanted to talk about. I'm not sure if I should be relieved or frustrated that he was interrupted.

"This is my daughter, Cassidy. She'll be leading you on the trail ride today. One of our new ranch hands, who's still in training, will be helping her out," Dad says, nodding to Wilder.

It's not lost on me that he doesn't use Wilder's name, which makes sense because Uncle Alex was clear that his time here was going to be under the radar. I glance over at Wilder to see him give Dad a grateful nod.

"These are the Stegemanns. Bernard, Francesca, and Max," Dad says.

"Pleased to meet you," I say, reaching out to shake hands.

Mr. Stegemann looks to be in his early forties, with a silver patch of hair at both his temples. He's about the same height as Dad, but not as slender. Mrs. Stegemann is a few years younger than her husband, with short brown hair and bright red lipstick. Max is probably eight or nine years old, with a gap-tooth smile and sandy-blond hair. All three of them are wearing appropriate trail riding outfits and riding boots that have some mileage on them.

Wilder steps forward and pulls off his cowboy hat. "Welcome to Silver Stallion Ranch," he says, like he's actually a ranch hand. "You can call me Wily."

Wily? As in deceptive, scheming, and artful. I can't think of a more appropriate nickname.

Max's eyes light up. "Like the coyote?"

"Sure." Wilder nods. "You like those cartoons?"

"Dad and I watch them sometimes."

"Me too," Wilder says. "What's your favorite episode?"

I feel slightly better knowing I'm not the only one to be snared by Wilder's easy charm.

CHAPTER 18

Wilder

MAX'S MOM WASN'T kidding when she said the kid's a talker. I'm not sure he's stopped to take a breath since we hit the trail.

"Hey, Wily," Max says.

"Yeah?"

"Would you rather shoot snowballs from your eyes or breathe fire from your mouth?" Max doesn't even give me a moment to come up with an answer. "I think I'd rather breathe fire because then I could roast marshmallows and cook hot dogs and stuff like that. My food would never get cold. I mean, snowballs are cool but they melt. What if you could do both? Just think, you could shoot snowballs and then melt them in mid-air. Pew, pew, aaaah."

Cassidy's at the front of our group, leading the trail ride at an easy, leisurely pace. She's too far ahead to hear all the chatter back here. Mr. and Mrs. Stegemann ride side by side in the middle, probably happy to have a break from Max and his mile-a-minute mouth. Max and I bring up the rear.

"Hey, Wily," he says again. "Who do you think has cooler superpowers? Spider-Man or Superman?"

"Hey, Wily. Where's the largest hole in Arizona? Where's the second largest hole?"

"Hey, Wily . . ."

"Hey, Wily . . ."

And the whole time I'm talking to Max, all I can think is that I'd rather be talking to Cassidy. I have to figure out some way to fix this, because there's no way I'll survive the rest of my time here with this heavy weight between us.

Cassidy leads us to a ridge overlooking rocky outcrops covered with yellow and purple flowers. The Stegemanns group together to take a few photos and I attempt to seize the opportunity for a bit of private conversation with Cassidy. I ride Jupiter up next to Land Sailor.

"Whoa," I say, bringing Jupiter to a stop. It's not second nature yet, but I am starting to get the hang of it.

Cassidy glances up at me. The sparkle in her eyes is gone and her lips are pressed into a tight line. My heart feels like it might shatter.

"So," I say, trying to find the right words. Words that don't sound like a line. "I wanted to—"

"Hey, Wily," Max says.

My head swivels around to find Max and Al Caponey on my other side. How the heck did they sneak up on me?

"What's up, little dude?" I ask.

I give Cassidy a brief look of apology, but she just gives a neutral nod and maneuvers Land Sailor away.

"Do you think that's a large rock or a small boulder?" Max asks.

"How many Cheerios do you think it would take to fill an Olympic-sized swimming pool?"

"Do sharks have nightmares?"

Where does this kid get all these questions? And how is it that he's not exhausted from all the talking he's been doing? My jawbone hurts just from listening to him.

Cassidy guides us down into a valley where there's a large, clear pond. "Let's break here for a bit," she says.

Finally. Maybe now I can get a moment or two alone with her.

There's a weathered-wood hitching post in a grassy area a little way from the pond. The group follows Cassidy over to it and we dismount. Thankfully, everyone's so focused on helping Max from his saddle that no one notices how awkward and off balance I am when my boots hit the ground. My body is still getting used to riding and I flex my leg muscles to help ease some of the stiffness.

Cassidy opens her saddlebag and pulls out a handful of halters and rope leads. "Wily," she says to the Stegemanns with a pointed look at me, "and I can take care of the horses if you want to stretch your legs."

They wander off to take some family selfies while we swap the bridles for halters.

Even though I've been trying to get some alone time with Cassidy all morning, now that it's just the two of us, I completely blank on what I want to say. I keep opening and closing my mouth like a gaping fish, but nothing will come out.

"Wily, huh?" she asks once they're out of earshot.

I shrug. "That's what my mom called me when I was younger."

"Hmm," she says before ducking behind Land Sailor so I can't see her face.

I'm getting faster at tying quick-release knots, and pretty soon we have the horses settled along the hitching post.

"I was—" I say at the same time Cassidy says, "Let's take Al and Misty for a drink."

"—just going to suggest that," I say. Total cop-out.

I take Al's lead rope and he dips his head down and starts forward. Cassidy follows behind with Misty Morning. When we get to the edge of the pond, we release some slack in the lead ropes so the horses can lean down to drink.

Max rushes over with a concerned look on his face, Mr. Stegemann ambling behind. "Hey, Wily. Mom says I can't drink from the pond. So, is it safe for the horses to drink the water?" he asks.

I shrug and defer to Cassidy, who avoids meeting my gaze.

"It is here," Cassidy says, directing her answer to Max. Then, to Mr. Stegemann, she says, "This is a spring-fed pond, and we don't use any pesticides or chemicals on the ranch. We also conduct biannual testing for watershed management purposes." Cassidy glances down at Max like she's about to share a well-kept secret. She leans closer to him and whispers, "There are plenty of frogs that live around this pond, which is usually a good sign that the water's safe for animals to drink."

Max's eyes go wide. "Frogs?"

Cassidy nods. "Loads of 'em."

"Can I catch one?"

"You can try," says Mr. Stegemann.

Max and his father move away in search of frogs. Again, I'm left alone with Cassidy. And again, words fail me.

After a few awkward minutes, Cassidy and I return Al Caponey and Misty Morning to the hitching post. "Can you take the other horses for water, one by one?" she asks. "I want to check the girths to make sure none of the saddles have loosened on our ride."

Now's the time to say something.

I should open my mouth.

I should say *something*.

"Yeah. Sure."

I'm a complete idiot.

Max hovers around the edge of the pond when I arrive with Land Sailor. He stands just where the grassy field meets the muddy bank. "Trying to spot a frog?" I ask.

"Or a turtle. Did you know that all tortoises are turtles, but not all turtles are tortoises? My friend Benny has a pet tortoise. I saw a painted turtle at the science center once. Have you ever been bitten by a turtle?"

"No. Have you?"

Max shakes his head. "Nah. Do you think there are any turtles here?"

"Maybe?" Cassidy would know. I glance back at her to see if I can wave her over, but she's busy fiddling with something on Misty Morning's saddle.

"What kinds of turtles are in this pond, do you think?" Max asks. "Box turtles? Snapping turtles? Painted turtles?"

Again, I have no clue. My knowledge of turtles is pretty limited to Michelangelo, Donatello, Leonardo, and Raphael. "I dunno. Maybe the Teenage Mutant Ninja kind," I say.

Max grins. "I love TMNT!"

"Heroes in a half shell!" I half sing, half say. I once auditioned for a voice-over part for the cartoon. I didn't get a callback but there're no hard feelings.

"If those guys were here, it would be amazing." Max takes a step closer to the edge of the pond.

"Hey, little dude," I say, watching the tips of his boots disappear in the loose mud. "Be careful. You don't want to go for a swim, do you?"

He glances over at me. "Do you know how to swim?"

"Yeah."

"I don't know how to swim," he says with a frown.

"That's a shame." I love swimming, surfing, and sunning myself at the beach, but that's easy to do because I live so close to the ocean. "Where are you from?"

"Kentucky," he says.

I don't know much about Kentucky, but I don't remember it having any large bodies of water.

"How long have you been riding horses?" I ask.

"As long as I can remember."

Sounds like Max was practically born in the saddle. I narrow my eyes and stare out at the horizon, trying not to be jealous of a nine-year-old kid who has the skills I lack.

"Do you think there are tadpoles? Or maybe fish? What else do you think might be in this pond? Snails? Snakes? Alligators?"

"Um . . ."

At this point, Max is basically talking to himself as he continues on with his search. I head back to the hitching post with Land Sailor. Cassidy takes the lead rope from me and brushes her hand down his neck.

Ginger is the next horse in line, so I grab her lead. When I lift my hand to adjust my grip on the rope, she swings her face toward me, pulls back her lips, and takes a deep breath. I startle a bit, not expecting to have her chompers on full display so close to me.

"Ginger's a flirt," Cassidy says. "Don't fall for her antics." The tone of her voice is cold and sardonic, as if her words are layered with meaning.

It doesn't take a rocket scientist to know what she's alluding to. I glance up at the sky, hoping for some inspiration on what to say to Cassidy. A hawk circles overhead in a lazy spiral. I've just decided that the best course of action is to confess my feelings, but before I can open my mouth, there's a giant splash. Across the pond, a huge plume of water rises, sending ripples outward.

Immediately, I look over to where I last saw Max standing, but he's not there. My eyes track all around the pond, and he's not anywhere along the shore.

I glance over to his parents. No Max.

I look at Cassidy. No Max.

"Shit," I say, realizing that Max must have gotten too close and fallen in. Suddenly, I see arms and legs flailing. Alarm bells ring in my head. Max doesn't know how to swim. "Shit, shit, shit."

It doesn't take a lot of water for someone to drown. While the pond doesn't look particularly deep, if Max is panicked, he might not realize he can just stand. His head pops up and then drops back down under the water as he keeps thrashing about.

I'm not a great runner, but I am a decent swimmer. I can

make it to him faster if I swim across the water than try to go around on land.

I drop Ginger's lead and race toward the pond. I vaguely hear Cassidy calling my name, but I have to get to Max. When I reach the edge, I kick off my boots. Cold water splashes up at me as I rush in. My breath is torn from my lungs when the frigid water hits me like a hammer. My feet sink into the silt, so I kick forward, my arms and legs slicing as I propel myself toward Max.

It's not a large pond, but it feels like I'm trying to swim from Long Beach to Catalina Island. The extra weight of my heavy clothes drags me down, but I press on. My arms and shoulders are stronger than they used to be. Thank god for all the manual labor Cassidy's had me doing since I arrived.

Max's arms and legs aren't moving as fast as they were, and I watch him slip completely under the surface. My heart thuds in my chest as anxiety spikes through me. A surge of adrenaline has my legs kicking harder. I finally make it to Max with a desperate burst of speed. Diving down, I slide my arms under his armpits, locking my hands in front of his torso. My feet scramble for purchase on the bottom of the pond as I fight to hoist him up. It's not particularly deep where we are, but my feet sink into the silt and rocks below. My wobbly legs threaten to buckle. I lurch forward, barely able to keep his face above the water. Grunting, I lock my knees and lunge backward toward the shore, trying to keep Max's head up and tilted back. Out of nowhere, he starts to thrash and kick.

I grunt when his heel connects with my shin. "Stop fighting me, Max."

When he hears my voice, he goes still. "Wily?" he gurgles.

"I've got you, little dude," I say.

One more giant step and we're out of the water. I fall back on my butt and Max collapses on top of me. He sucks in a giant breath and immediately starts crying.

"Oh my god!" his mom shrieks as she races toward us. She tears him off me and immediately starts checking him over to make sure he's okay. His father sinks down beside him, and they huddle together.

I close my eyes, fighting to catch my breath, and suddenly something soft, warm, and wet slides over my cheek. My eyes flash open and there, standing above me, is Ginger, looking much too pleased with herself.

CHAPTER 19

Cassidy

EVERYTHING HAPPENS SO fast. One second, I'm filled with anxiety and anticipation for what Wilder's about to say, and the next, he's tearing off across the field toward the pond.

When he splashes into the water, Ginger lets out a spine-tingling high-pitched whinny. She is not a fan of water but she is a fan of Wilder, and she's not about to let him out of her sight. She runs along the edge of the pond as he swims across it.

I chase after them both, my chest heaving as I pump my legs as fast as I can. Everything after becomes a blur, and I'm not sure how exactly I end up standing over Wilder with Ginger's lead rope grasped in my hand. She gives him another lick across the face and he cringes. When our eyes meet, my heart soars like a helium balloon.

I don't know what to do with the mixture of feelings floating and bobbing inside me, so I turn my attention to what's happening around us.

The Stegemanns sit together as a trio next to Wilder, with a waterlogged Max propped upright in his father's lap. Tears stream down the boy's ruddy face as he takes stuttering, shallow breaths. His mom brushes hair back from his forehead while she soothes him.

"Is Max okay?" I ask with a slight tremor in my voice.

"Aside from being soaking wet and scared, he seems to be," Mr. Stegemann says.

Thank goodness.

I turn my attention back to Wilder, who's splayed out like a starfish at my feet. He's sopping wet and more disheveled than I've ever seen him. There's a smudge of mud over his left cheek and some pond vegetation caught in his limp curls. Both of his hands rest on his chest, which quickly heaves up and down as he catches his breath.

"Thank you for jumping in after him, Wily." Mr. Stegemann gazes over at Wilder, his eyes full of gratitude and relief. "Max doesn't know how to swim," he says.

"He mentioned that," Wilder says.

So that's why he dove into the water so quickly.

Since Max has his parents fussing over him, I drop to my knees beside Wilder. "Are you okay?" I ask.

He opens his gorgeous eyes and looks up at me with an intensity that sets off a fluttering feeling in my belly. "I'm cold and wet," he says. "But I'll live."

Ranching is full of incidents and accidents. I've seen men get thrown from their horses. Angry cattle charge ranch hands with their horns lowered. I've bandaged cuts and bruises. Used superglue to close up gashes. And I've even helped stabilize a broken arm with some branches and a torn bandana. But a near drowning is a first for me.

I hope it's a last.

I take in the pond. The water's surface is deceptively smooth and calm, as if it couldn't possibly have the ability to kill. The distance across isn't far, but if I'd been the one jumping in, I doubt I would have made it to Max in time. I can swim—barely—and my doggy-paddling skills are a far cry from the powerful freestyle form Wilder used.

"I'm so glad you were here," I whisper. If it had been just me, would have gone a whole lot differently.

Wilder pushes himself up into a seated position. He trembles a bit, but I can't tell if it's from cold or exertion. Probably both. Either way, we need to do something about it. I stand and reach down to help Wilder to his feet. His fingers are cold and slick from the water, but his grip is strong. I'm tempted to lace my fingers through his, but instead, I slide my hand away.

I've spent time with Wilder, the actor.

I've caught glimpses of Wilder, the person.

But having seen Wilder, the hero?

Keeping things strictly professional no longer seems as achievable as it did before. Because, seriously, how could I not practically melt into a puddle of smitten goo for Wilder Nash after all this?

Despite these feelings bubbling inside, I still have a job to do. And now that the immediate danger has passed, I force my brain to focus on what's important right this very minute. I'll have plenty of time to consider the implications of free-falling for Wilder later.

I glance up at the clear, blue sky. The weather is fair, but it's not a hot summer day by any means. Max and Wilder are dripping wet and their clothes won't dry out anytime soon, especially not while they're wearing them. Getting back on the trail right away is probably not a great idea. Not only can wet clothes chafe, but I can't be sure that Max and Wilder are physically up for the ride back, considering what they both went through.

Still, we can't just sit here and do nothing.

"What's the plan?" Wilder asks. He runs the back of his arm over his forehead just like he's done time and again since he arrived, but this is the first time it looks natural. And when it's not contrived, it's oh so sexy.

But there's no time for those thoughts now.

Focus.

Mr. and Mrs. Stegemann look up at me, so I keep my attention trained on them. "I'll radio for assistance." My eyes betray me by looking back to Wilder. "Then we need to get you out of those wet clothes." A blast of heat flares in my cheeks once I realize what I've just said. Definitely not the time to go there. My eyes dart back to the Stegemanns. "We'll build a fire. There should be stone ring around here somewhere." I close my eyes and try to remember where we had that Fourth of July picnic a few years back. I didn't pay much attention at the time, but I do remember it being close enough that I'd come to the pond to skip rocks. I turn toward a slight rocky rise. "There," I say, pointing over to it.

"Hey, Wily, will there be s'mores?" Max asks in a snuffly voice.

Mrs. Stegemann laughs and plants a kiss on top of his head.

"No promises," Wilder says.

"I'll see what I can do." The emergency radio is in my saddlebag on the other side of the pond. The fastest way to get there is to take Ginger, who's currently resting her chin on Wilder's shoulder.

"Sit tight," I say, sliding my left foot into the stirrup. "I'll be right back."

Ginger and I return to the group with Jupiter and Al Caponey in tow. Jupiter carries my saddlebag. Al is loaded up with the saddle pads I took from Land Sailor and Misty Morning and an old picnic blanket I pulled from my saddlebag. I've got Wilder's cowboy boots in my lap.

"Easy," I say.

Mr. Stegemann walks over as I uncoil Jupiter's and Al's lead ropes from the saddle horn.

"Dry clothes and more blankets are on their way, but until they get here, you can wrap Max in this," I say, pointing to the picnic blanket. "Do you think he can ride if you lead the pony?"

Mr. Stegemann nods. "We can lift him onto the saddle and walk beside him." I hold out Al's rope and he takes it from me with a "Thanks."

"Do you think you can ride Jupiter?" I ask, handing Wilder his boots. "Or would you rather walk?"

"Is there a third option?" he asks as he looks at his wet socks and then back at the boots with a grimace.

"'Fraid not."

155

"Ride, I guess." Wilder plops down on the grass. He pulls off his wet socks and rolls up his pants legs as best he can, but the jeans are still soaked and heavy. It takes a while for him to work his damp feet into his boots.

When he glances up at me, my heart pinches with sympathy. He looks so uncomfortable and waterlogged. But also kind of swoony, in an adorably disheveled kind of way.

I ride ahead of the group to lead them to the fire ring and immediately start gathering as much dry brush and kindling as possible. Thankfully, there's a small copse of trees nearby with some dead branches. Mrs. Stegemann helps me collect a few armfuls while the guys peel off Max's wet clothes and wrap him in the picnic blanket.

We set about laying out the fire and soon there are small, crackling flames for us to gather around. Once Max and Wilder are settled comfortably, I wring out Max's wet clothes and drape them over nearby bushes. I wish we had something for Wilder, but the saddle pads don't offer much coverage.

By the time Dad arrives, Max and Wilder have both stopped shivering and their skin is no longer ashen. I meet him at the ATV and take the bags he holds out to me. "How's everyone doing?" he asks. I already filled him in on the details over the radio, so we don't have to rehash it all.

"Okay, considering."

"Good," he says. "I'll talk to the Stegemanns. You take care of Wilder."

"Wily," I remind him.

"Right." Dad grabs a smaller bag and a bundle of firewood, and heads over to the fire ring.

I catch Wilder's eye and motion for him to meet me by the horses. Barefoot, he limps over. "Here are some dry clothes," I say. "You can change behind that bush over there, if you want some privacy."

Ginger presses her nose to his ear and Wilder squirms. I can't help but laugh.

"Marshmallows?" I hear Max squeal. "All right!"

Wilder and I turn to see Max hugging a bag to his chest. Dad gives me a thumbs-up and goes back to chatting with the Stegemanns. Based on their posture and Dad's relaxed jaw, it doesn't seem like there will be any fallout from the accident. While we always have people sign release forms before a trail ride, that doesn't mean we won't get pushback if something bad happens.

After a moment, Wilder and I twist around so that we're toe-to-toe again.

"Thank you," I whisper.

A small smile plays over Wilder's pale lips and there's a mischievous glint in his eyes. He lifts his hand as if he's pretending to tip his hat and says, "Just doing my job, ma'am."

It sounds like a line.

It probably is.

But this time, it's different.

I don't get the sense that he's toying with my feelings. It's more like we're sharing a secret. Something fundamental between us has changed.

Wilder's gaze goes to my lips and my skin starts to tingle at the memory of our kiss. I find myself leaning forward. A dizzy feeling overtakes me, and I reach out to grab his arm, shocked by how cold and damp his sleeve is. His arm goes to my waist to steady me. I really, really want him to pull me close and press his mouth to mine.

The glimmer in his gaze tells me he's probably thinking the same thing.

Mr. Stegemann laughs and I jump back, surprised at how close I've gotten to Wilder. His hand falls away, leaving a burning trail where his fingertips glide down my side.

Across from me, Wilder looks down at my mouth and sighs. "I should probably . . ." He tips his head toward the bushes I pointed out earlier.

"Yeah," I manage over a cottony lump in my throat.

CHAPTER 20

Wilder

I'M NOT SURE where Mitch found the clothes he brought for me, but they're warm and dry, so I'm not complaining . . . exactly.

But considering that this is the weirdest ensemble I've ever worn—and I've had multiple appearances on both Nickelodeon and Disney Channel—that's saying a lot. I'm almost embarrassed to return to the campfire looking like this, but I don't want to get lost out here wearing this hodgepodge of clothes. Not only am I too young to die, but it would be an absolute tragedy if a photo of me in this outfit ever leaked to the press. Being famous is one thing. Being infamous is another thing entirely.

The cargo pants are slightly too long in the leg and too wide in the waist, but if I focus on how soft they are, then I can ignore the fact that they are fire engine red with images of sparkly, golden lassos all over. The collared, button-down shirt is the same fluorescent orange as a traffic cone, with lime green and eggplant purple patches sewn all over it. And the socks? Both of them are nearly knee-high. One is horizontally striped with rainbow colors. The other is salmon pink with teal polka dots. I briefly consider wearing the black and white checkerboard suspenders because the pants are so loose, I'm worried they won't stay up, but I just can't bring myself to do it. I toss them back into the bag next to a frizzy blue wig that I don't even want to ask about.

Gathering my wet clothes, I hike up my fancy pants and trudge back toward the fire.

Cassidy sees me first and her eyes go wide with shock. "Dad," she says. "You brought him the rodeo clown costume?"

Suddenly, everything makes sense.

Mitch gives me a sheepish look. "It was the easiest thing to grab and I was in a rush."

I get it, but still. I would have gladly waited for five or ten minutes for him to find something a bit less vivid. I'd thought some of the costumes in the arena wardrobe room were flamboyant, but this getup really takes the cake.

Max looks over at me and a giant smile lights up his face. "Oh, wow, Wily. You look *so* cool," he says. Sticky strands of marshmallow coat his hands and face.

Stage, screen, or random spot on the ranch, I live for an audience. And this kid is the perfect audience.

I give a little bow and start a short clown routine I remember from back in the day. I'd been hired to play a clown in a school talent show bit for a movie. I practiced for hours, but my scene ended up getting cut. At the time, it didn't bother me because I got to pocket a cool ten bucks after my mom put the rest of the thirty-dollar paycheck into my savings account.

160

I do a short mime bit.

I juggle a few marshmallows.

And then I end the performance with a joke.

"What do you call a drawing of a clown?" I ask. I wait a moment to draw out the silence before delivering the punchline. "A comedy sketch."

Mitch and Mr. Stegemann laugh, while Cassidy and Mrs. Stegemann roll their eyes.

"Tell another joke, Wily," Max says, shoving another marshmallow into his mouth.

His mom frowns and takes the bag away. "I think you've had enough."

Me too. I'm out of material.

I give a flourishing bow and the Stegemanns clap.

"Best. Day. Ever," says Max.

"I'm not sure about that, kiddo," Mr. Stegemann says as he ruffles Max's hair.

"At least he doesn't appear to be traumatized," says Mrs. Stegemann.

Cassidy comes over, the edges of her mouth quirked up in amusement. "That was quite the performance."

"You think?" I ask.

"I think you might get an Oscar nod. Or maybe a Razzie? It could go either way." She laughs and reaches up to tuck a lock of hair behind her ear. "Dad's going to take the Stegemanns back in the ATV. But that leaves us to get the horses back to the stables. Are you up for riding?"

Now that I'm warm and dry? "Sure."

"Great. Then would you like to learn how to pony a horse?"

"Wait what?" I scratch at my temple, confused. I wonder if

I got some water in my ear, but when I tip my head to the side, nothing comes out. "Aren't ponies horses?" I ask.

Cassidy pats me sympathetically on the arm, and I don't miss how her hand lingers before she pulls it away. "Ponies are small horses, but ponying a horse is what it's called when you lead a horse while on horseback."

"Oh." Who'd have thought? "Okay."

Honestly, I'm not completely sure I'm up for ponying horses given the day I've already had, but I am here to learn as much as I can about being a cowboy, and learning to lead horses from a saddle seems like a very cowboy thing to do.

I've never been so exhausted in my life after our ride back to the stables. Ponying horses (and a Shetland pony) isn't as difficult as I expected, but it definitely takes some planning and preparation. While I was in charge of leading Ginger back, Cassidy was responsible for Misty Morning and Al Caponey.

My joints crack and pop and my stomach grumbles. The trail ride was only supposed to be a few hours long, and even though I don't know exactly what time it is, I'm sure we missed lunch.

Julianne and Mr. Sterling are waiting for us when we arrive at the stables.

"Whoa," Cassidy says, slowing the horses to a stop.

"Whoa," I say.

"Whoa," Julianne says, her eyes going wide just like Cassidy's did when she takes in my outfit.

Mr. Sterling doesn't even bat an eye. He's still as rigid and humorless as he was when I first arrived at Silver Stallion Ranch. The epitome of a grumpy old man. Not mean or rude, exactly, but not very welcoming to me, either.

Julianne goes over to Al Caponey and begins unlooping the pony's lead rope from Misty Morning's saddle horn.

"You two look exhausted," she says. "I've got a casserole in the oven for an early dinner."

Cassidy and I dismount. My legs and arms are sore, and I stretch to work out some of the knots that are forming in my lower back and shoulders.

"I was wondering where my favorite shirt went," Mr. Sterling says gruffly as he takes Ginger's lead rope from me. He peers at me with steely eyes and such a straight face, I have no idea if he's serious or joking.

Mitch joins us. "Be nice, Dad," he says. "Wilder's had a rough day."

"I'm always nice," Mr. Sterling says, but when I catch Cassidy's eye, she gives me a look that says I have every right to be skeptical. Mr. Sterling turns to his son. "I know the kid's had a hard day. Just look at him. He looks like a clown." Once again, he turns his attention to me. "I'm not saying you should quit your day job—not now that Cassidy's got you becoming a proper horseman—but if things don't work out for you in Hollywood . . . if you ever come to your senses . . . I know a couple of rodeos or ranches that are always looking for help." I almost miss the slight curve of his lips that looks suspiciously like the beginnings of a smile.

Then Mr. Sterling turns on his heel and leads Ginger into the stable.

Julianne folds up the end of Al Caponey's lead rope. "I

know it doesn't seem like it, but Frank Sterling just paid you a compliment, Wilder," she says.

"He did?"

"Believe it or not." Cassidy shrugs. "Grandpa said you're becoming a proper horseman. That's high praise. He usually says things like 'There goes stupid in a saddle,' or 'Nothing more than a bunch of flea-addled nitwits' or, my personal favorite, 'That fella is all hat, no cowboy.'"

He *did* say I'm becoming a proper horseman, didn't he? A man of his experience would know. A flash of pride has me standing a little taller.

If a true cowboy thinks I'm becoming a proper horseman, I might really have what it takes.

Even though I'm famished, I can't get out of this rodeo clown costume fast enough. I hop in the shower to wash off the mud and pond weed caked in my hair. My stomach is pretty vocal that I need to eat. It hasn't stopped grumbling since I walked in the door, even after I inhaled a Gatorade.

I've just finished pulling on a soft cotton T-shirt and a pair of flannel pajama bottoms when there's a knock at the door.

Cassidy stands on the front stoop, my clothes carefully folded in one hand and a covered casserole dish in the other. "Can I come in?" she asks.

I step back and hold the door open for her.

"I brought food." She walks over to the little dining nook and sets the dish on the table. "Mom's famous chicken bacon ranch casserole." Cassidy lifts the lid to give me a peek, and the sight of creamy sauce over rotini pasta topped with bacon crumbles and thin slices of green onion sets my mouth watering. And the scent? Heavenly.

"I haven't eaten yet. Mind if I join you?"

How could I say no to the person who brought me such superb-looking sustenance?

Cassidy sets my folded clothes on the kitchen counter and starts rummaging around for plates and silverware. Soon she has the table set and is spooning a generous serving onto my plate. I grab two bottles of water from the fridge.

We dig in.

"This is fantastic," I say between bites.

Honestly, almost anything would taste fantastic at this point, but this really is good. After a few more bites, I'm full enough that I don't feel the need to continuously shovel food into my mouth like a ravenous beast.

Cassidy takes a long swig of water and then sets a warped and crumpled piece of paper on the table. "I was helping Mom with the laundry," she says. "I was pulling your clothes from the dryer and this fell out."

I reach over and pull the paper closer. Most of the ink has run, leaving a ghostly shadow beneath the few words that are legible. Some of my choppy scrawl imprinted on the opposite side of the page, making it impossible to read. The only bit that really stands out is *Skills to learn*.

"Was it important?" Cassidy asks.

"Not really." I toss the paper on the table and lean back in my chair. "It's just a list of things my character does in the first episode. I started making it on my first read-through so I'd have an idea of what I need to learn—well, besides riding."

Cassidy glances down at the crumpled paper and then back up at me. "You're pretty committed to this role, aren't you?"

I lift a shoulder. "It depends on who you ask. I'm not into method acting, which some people believe is the only real way to commit to a role. But really, I just want to do it justice. It's hard to explain." I spin the water bottle cap between my fingers. "I want viewers to watch the miniseries and be so drawn in that they only see Deacon Slade on the screen and not see that it's me portraying Deacon Slade."

Cassidy nods. "I think I get it. You want to be effortless and authentic so your acting doesn't draw people out of the story."

"Exactly. But there's a lot to learn besides horseback riding. And I'm not sure when or where I'll be able to do it."

"Can I?" Cassidy asks, her hand hovering over the list.

"Good luck reading it," I say.

Cassidy gingerly picks up the rumpled paper and squints down at it. Her brow furrows as she considers the list. When her warm brown eyes meet mine, my heart stutters. There's a look of fierce determination in her eyes. And something deeper, but I'm not quite sure what.

"Wilder Nash," she says with a raised eyebrow. "I think Uncle Alex sent you to exactly the right place to learn."

CHAPTER 21

Cassidy

THERE'S A REASON people say no good deed goes unpunished, right? I already know I'm going to pay dearly for this arrangement before it even begins.

It was hard enough to convince myself to keep Wilder at arm's length before, but now that I've gotten so caught up in gratitude and admiration after he rescued Max, I've completely lost all sense of reason.

While he was soaking wet yesterday, I almost kissed him like a pathetic fangirl.

Then I offered to help him tackle his *Skills to Learn* list.

What on earth was I thinking?

Actually, I'm pretty sure I wasn't thinking.

My head's been saying "Whoa, whoa, *whoa*," but my heart's been saying "Go, go, *go*!" And now we've zoomed past Crushville, taken the exit for Headover Hills, and are barreling toward a collision course with Lonesome Heart Central. It's not an ideal route at all, but my personal navigation system refuses to recalculate and my final destination is dialed in.

He's here to learn to ride.

My job is to teach him.

And that should be that.

Except it's not.

Today, Wilder and I are heading up to one of Silver Stallion Ranch's northern pastures to spend the day checking the fences. If we find any in need of mending, we'll attempt to fix them so that Wilder can cross the activity off his list. Either way, we'll get in a nice, long trail ride.

Just Jupiter and Wilder.

Land Sailor and me.

A dusty trail. Open skies. And a whole lot of romantic tension between us. *Yeehaw.*

"Ready to go?" Wilder asks as he leads Jupiter over.

"Almost," I say, my stomach a bundle of nerves.

How can I ever be truly ready when anything could happen out on the trail?

There might be flirting.

And more swoon-inducing lines.

And it's possible I might spontaneously combust from yearning for another kiss.

But what if Wilder *is* only acting? Maybe I want my heart to be right so badly that I've seen things that aren't really there. The extra softness in his gaze. The lingering looks. The change that's happened between us.

My pulse flickers in my veins. Whether he's that good an actor or not, my poor crushing heart is doomed.

I double-check my saddlebag to make sure there's an emergency radio and first-aid kit tucked inside. A container of water-proof matches. A Swiss Army knife.

The only thing that's missing is my dignity, because the minute I glance over at Wilder, I know that I don't have a shred of it remaining. Because today, in medium wash jeans, a light brown flannel, and his cowboy hat helmet, Wilder is the definition of hot.

We mount our horses and head out from the stable yard toward the trail that will take us north. Even though it's only been a few weeks, he's much more relaxed in the saddle. His shoulders used to be so tight. His mouth pinched in concentration. Now he lets his arms sit loosely in front of him while the edges of his mouth curve up. It's not a smile, exactly, but you can tell he's more at ease. Even his body, which used to jolt around in the saddle, is much steadier under Jupiter's gait. If Wilder continues progressing at this rate, by the time he returns to Hollywood, he'll easily pass as an experienced rider to everyone but the most well-seasoned equestrians.

Which is great. Really great. Super, duper great.

It's the returning to Hollywood part that has my stomach sinking.

Wilder's unusually quiet. I've gotten so used to him running lines or asking questions while we ride, the sudden silence stands out. I've come to like the sound of his voice, the way his words rise and fall in a gentle rhythm.

"Is everything okay?" I ask.

Wilder turns to me with a far-off look in his eyes. "Yeah. I'm just thinking."

Oof. Now I'm curious what's on his mind. If I ask, will it look like I'm prying? If I don't, will he think I don't care?

Thankfully, Wilder saves me the trouble of having to choose whether to ask. "Apparently, there's some speculation that I might not have been the best choice to play Deacon Slade."

"Oh?"

This surprises me. Even though I don't know much about Hollywood casting or which other actors were vying for the role, Wilder very much embodies the look and demeanor of a typical movie cowboy.

"One of the other actors up for the role . . . Cam Sheffield." Wilder shrugs. "Apparently, they passed on casting him because he doesn't know how to ride and Alexander told them I did."

"Oh." I sit with that a moment. "Uncle Alex must really believe in you."

Wilder gives a humorless laugh. "No kidding. But the thing is . . . lying about knowing how to ride a horse is really frowned upon in the industry. There's this Western film, *Little Big Man*, that was shot in the seventies. Have you heard of it?"

"No, but I'm sure it's one of the movies Grandpa watches on TV. He loves old Westerns."

"*Little Big Man* had a lot of famous actors in it. Dustin Hoffman. Faye Dunaway. Chief Dan George." Wilder scratches his chin. We make our way around a rocky scramble and then he continues. "Anyhow, I guess they hired, like, fifty actors who all said they could ride a horse. And when they went to film the scene, the AD—the assistant director—called out 'action' and supposedly *all* the actors fell off their horses."

"That must have been a sight."

"Probably," Wilder agrees. "When you're an extra, maybe it's not that big a deal to lie about knowing how to ride. But when you've been cast as one of the leads, and it's possible the only reason you landed the role was because your agent told them you can ride . . ." He swallows. "And you definitely can't?"

"You couldn't," I say. "Not when you first arrived. But now look at you. You're saddling horses and trail riding on the open range."

Wilder smiles, but it doesn't quite reach his eyes. "True."

I get the sense that there's more to the story. "But?"

"Cam Sheffield."

Like Wilder, Cam Sheffield's a seasoned young actor who's looking to transition from made-for-television movies to the big screen. Wilder mentioned him earlier, but I'm not sure how he fits in. "What about him? Are you worried the role will be recast?"

Wilder takes a deep breath. "Pretty much." He exhales. "I guess it's possible the studio passed on him for a different reason, but . . . lately, it seems like he's coming after the role by flexin' some new skills."

"Maybe it's less about why they *didn't* choose him and more about why they *did* choose you. Sure, Uncle Alex told the studio people you can ride, so that's a point in your favor. But I mean . . . Hollywood is known for special effects and creative filming techniques. If they really wanted Cam to play the part, they would have found a way to make it happen. Body doubles, stunt doubles—"

"Those ponies-on-a-platform that they pull around so it looks like you're on a horse," Wilder says.

"And we haven't even gotten to green screens and CGI."

Wilder smiles and my heart grows three sizes.

We amble over a steady rise and then make our way into a valley dotted with yellow wildflowers and lush green grass.

"The thing is, these past few days, Cam's been posting a ton of videos and photos of himself on horseback to his social media accounts. Hashtag born to ride. Hashtag yeehaw. Hashtag—"

"Look," I say, trying to find the right words, "it's easy to snap a quick selfie or short video on horseback, upload it, filter it, and hashtag it to perfection until the cows come home. But does this Cam guy have the skills to actually ride a horse until the cows some home?" I give a skeptical shrug. "I doubt there are very many actors who are willing to commit to this like you have."

"Maybe," Wilder mumbles.

Clearly, he's not convinced.

"Easy," I say, and Land Sailor slows. Wilder rides ahead for a moment before he gently turns Jupiter around to face me. His brow is furrowed under the shadow of his cowboy hat.

"A few days ago, you wouldn't have been able to ride Jupiter out on this trail, let alone be confident enough in the saddle to maneuver him on your own, without any instruction. And look at you now. You've come a long way in a few weeks."

Wilder chews on his bottom lip.

"Now you just have to show up to set ready to wow any doubters."

"You make it sound so easy," he says in the grumpiest tone I've ever heard from him.

"Oh, it's not going to be easy at all," I say.

Wilder's eyes flash open, and he looks surprised that the pep talk has gone from cheerleading to blunt reality.

"If you're worried about the competition and you want to ensure that the role is really and truly yours, you have to own it.

You can't just know how to ride a horse. You have to be a horseman. You can't show up as an actor portraying a cowboy. You have to be a cowboy."

Wilder gives me a solemn nod, but there's worry pooling in his dark eyes.

We can't do anything about the calendar. The hours tick by in the same way they always have, counting down to the end of Wilder's time at the ranch. But we do have control of how committed we are to turning Wilder into a true cowboy before he leaves.

After our trail ride, Wilder shows me some of the videos Cam posted. We sit on the couch in the guest cottage, hovering over Wilder's phone as he scrolls through what seems like an endless stream of selfies and reels. I do my best to focus on Cam Sheffield's dazzling blue eyes and not the fact that Wilder keeps shifting closer and closer to me.

There's a picture of Cam leaning against a picket fence with a cowboy hat tipped back on his head and a red bandana tied around his neck. *#countrylife*

Wilder's arm brushes mine, sending a burst of tingles all the way to the tips of my toes.

Then a photo of Cam on horseback with a giant red barn in the background, his short-cropped hair artfully messy. *#countryboy*

Wilder's knee presses against mine, radiating a warmth all the way to my core. I'm pretty sure my body temp just shot up a bazillion degrees.

Cam sitting on a horse with a lasso hanging from the saddle horn. *#instahorse #horsestagram*

Wilder's thigh is so close it's practically searing my skin through our jeans.

The feed switches to a video of Cam riding a horse along a dirt path.

"Well?"

I inhale sharply, and it has nothing to do with Wilder's warm breath on the nape of my neck and everything to do with the video. At least, that's what I'm telling myself.

"He's not an experienced rider," I say, jabbing my pointer finger at the phone. I'm too animated, too loud, and trying too hard to pretend that Wilder's physical proximity is not affecting me in any way.

"He's not?" he asks, glancing at me out of the corner of his eye.

"Nope." I feel the corner of my mouth turn up in a satisfied smile. "He's not using his core to stabilize himself. His toes are pointing down, not up." I pause the video. "And look, he's not even holding on to the reins. Someone off-camera is leading the horse."

Wilder turns to face me. "Are you sure?" he asks with a mixture of hope and hesitation.

"Oh, I'm sure. I've been around humans and horses my whole life."

Wilder's shoulders sag with relief. "Thank god."

"And aside from being cast in the role that Cam wants, you have something else that he doesn't."

"What?"

I reach out and give his arm a reassuring squeeze. "Me."

Wilder's warm hand covers mine and I practically melt into the couch next to him. My skin sizzles. My blood is lava. And I'm not sure I can remember how to breathe.

For a moment I let myself believe his touch is something more than just a gesture of gratitude. That I'm the leading lady in this story and he's my handsome love interest.

But this isn't a romance. It's not even a love story. It's merely a crush waiting to implode as soon as Wilder leaves.

CHAPTER 22

Wilder

"HOWDY," CASSIDY SAYS, glancing over at me. She's in the paddock with Land Sailor, who's already saddled up, and another horse I haven't seen before. "Are you ready to ride?"

"I was born ready," I reply with a grin.

We both laugh at the joke, and it feels good to have someone on my side who knows the pressure I'm under and who's willing to help. Not only that, but I also enjoy spending time with her. And, if I'm being completely honest, I'm glad that we'll be spending a whole lot more time together in our race against the clock to turn me into a legitimate cowboy.

I hoist myself up and over the split-rail fence in an easy, fluid motion that would not have been possible before I came to Silver Stallion Ranch. I haven't bulked up exactly, but my muscles are stronger and my core is solid and, after all the time I've spent in the saddle, I'm more in tune with my body.

"Is Jupiter okay?" I ask.

Cassidy nods. "He's fine. But I figured we'd give him the day off. This is Sidewinder, a quarter horse gelding."

Sidewinder is taller than Jupiter, with a dark brown mane and a chestnut coat. I reach out my hand to let him smell me.

"Sidewinder's one of the horses we use for intermediate riders. He's not quite as experienced as some of our other trail horses and he can be spirited when he wants to be. But he needs more trail experience and you need to learn how to handle different horses, so it's a win-win."

After spending a few minutes letting Sidewinder get used to me, I retrieve a saddle pad and saddle from the stable and get to work. Soon we're making our way out of the stable yard and onto the range.

The sky is blue and clear, as it's been every single day since I arrived. "Does it ever rain here?" I ask.

"Not often," Cassidy says. "But you're used to that, right?"

"Yeah. What about snow?" I ask. I try to picture the land around us covered in a blanket of crystalline, glistening white. Not the fake stuff from the Western wear photoshoot, but the real deal.

"For sure," Cassidy says. "You should see this place in the winter."

I realize that I do want to see Silver Stallion Ranch in the winter. And in the fall. And in the spring. In the short time I've been here, this place has grown on me, and part of me can't understand how Alexander ever left.

The thought of leaving reminds me that I'll be heading back to Hollywood soon. Back to my life of call sheets, wardrobe fittings, and memorizing lines. My heart squeezes in my chest when I think of the things I'll miss when I'm gone.

Birdzilla and her murder flock, who have thankfully stopped hunting me like velociraptors and now see me as the food-delivery guy.

Rambrandt and Van Goat, who always "Maa" at me and stare hungrily at my shoelaces on the rare occasion I'm wearing something other than dusty old cowboy boots.

Jupiter, the gentle and patient trail horse.

And Cassidy, most of all.

I glance over at her. At the way the soft sunlight falls on the gentle curve of her cheek. At the wisps of hair that fan out around her face. At her lips, so soft and sweet and kissable.

Leaving Cassidy. That will be the hardest thing of all. If only there wasn't so much distance between Wyoming and California.

If only there wasn't still so much distance between us right now.

I never thought a California sunset could be topped.

As a backdrop to the Ferris wheel, sunset at Santa Monica Pier has a unique blend of tourists and locals, and it's a great people-watching experience.

There's also sunset seen from the Griffith Observatory. Overlooking L.A., the view of the city and the way the light hits the Hollywood sign is incredible. Even more so during an industry event, when there are plenty of finger foods and famous people to enjoy it with.

And then there's sunset at Crystal Cove. The steep stairs that lead from the cliffs to the beach are not for the faint of heart, but the view of the sun's orange and gold rays reflecting off the ocean like it's covered in diamonds is totally worth it.

Not gonna lie, I'm surprised to find that sunset on the Wyoming range is a solid contender. Most days, we've been working so hard there hasn't been time to appreciate it. Either that, or we've been eating dinner.

Right now, the sun has only just begun to dip down in the sky, but I can already tell that today's sunset is going to be amazing.

The air is crystal clear, with the scent of sun-warmed savory sagebrush and sweet wildflowers so potent I can almost taste them. In the distance, the mountains darken from daytime gray hulking giants to the majestic purple mountains we used to sing about in elementary school. Everything around us is turning golden, almost like I'm seeing the world through an amber-tinted lens filter. But there's no filter that could make the world look and feel like it does right now.

Cassidy nudges Land Sailor into a fast trot and I encourage Sidewinder to follow along. He and I don't mesh together the same way that Jupiter and I do, but he's been very patient with me. Cassidy rides ahead toward a patch of trees, but I slow Sidewinder to a stop. I've been trying to practice starting and stopping so that it's as natural to me as riding a bike.

I take a moment to appreciate the view. This place is so picturesque, no camera could ever do it justice. But that won't stop me from wanting to reminisce over pictures when I'm back in L.A. It's hard to believe that my stay here is more than halfway through.

Last night, as I was scrolling through Instagram posts and spam emails, I realized how nice it's been to just leave my cell phone in the cabin during the day. Not having any service away from the main building has made it a lot easier to ignore the urge to check for more posts from Cam Sheffield. But one of the drawbacks of leaving my phone behind is that I have no photos of my time out here on the trail. Thankfully I grabbed it before I left this time.

Panoramic mode would be perfect for the wide valley we've ridden to, with its sloping fields dotted with yellow blossoms and the peaks in the distance. Even though I'm still not confident about executing a smooth three-sixty turn on horseback, my phone has plenty of memory. Trying for the perfect three-sixty shot will be good practice.

I hold the camera in my right hand, reins in my left, and shift my weight in the saddle just like Cassidy showed me. I gently adjust the reins and press with my thighs. Sidewinder dips his head and then pivots around. My body sways as he moves, so I'm not surprised to see the picture is more of a mess than a masterpiece. My second attempt is better but still looks like it could be a Salvador Dalí painting, with melting rocks.

By my fifth attempt, my arm is sore from holding the phone steady and Sidewinder is unimpressed by our riding in tight circles. I don't know if horses can get dizzy but I'm not sure I want to find out.

"Okay, Sidewinder," I say, giving his withers a gentle pat. "One more time around and then we can practice galloping? What d'you say?"

Sidewinder flicks his tail.

I make a split-second decision to flip the camera to video selfie mode and urge Sidewinder into another spin. As soon as we've completed the turn, I slide the phone back into my pocket and nudge Sidewinder into a walk.

I shift my weight forward and his walk becomes a slow trot. Then his trot becomes a canter. I know I promised him galloping, but I'm not ready for that yet.

Am I?

Air rushes over my face as Sidewinder picks up speed. Then we're galloping. Really galloping. My body rises and falls in the saddle as Sidewinder shoots forward, his hooves pounding over the ground beneath us.

It feels like we're flying, and in the heat of the moment, I reach up and unclip my hat so I can pull it off and twirl it over my head like I'm a rodeo cowboy. I'm a half-second away from whooping when Cassidy turns to face me.

All the breath rushes from my chest.

She's absolutely stunning with the golden sunset behind her like a giant halo. I can barely make out the lines of her face in the shadows, but a jolt rushes through me when our eyes meet. I feel like I'm racing toward my destiny. I want this moment to last forever.

That can't happen.

But a photo can.

I set my hat back on my head and slow Sidewinder into a lazy walk. I slip out my phone. After pulling up the camera app,

I snap a few shots and slide it back into my pocket. The photos are probably blurry. And if by some miracle they're not, the backlighting will probably wash everything out. But that's okay.

I might have to leave, but at least I can take the memories with me. And blurry or washed out, I'll be able to look at those pictures and remember how it felt to be galloping across the grasslands toward Cassidy, like a cowboy returning home after a long cattle drive.

Cassidy watches us approach.

"Whoa," I say, tipping my hat to her. Sidewinder prances to a halt.

"Not bad, Wilder," she says with a grin. "Not bad at all. You could stabilize yourself more with your core. And your shoulders are still a bit stiff. But seeing as how you're comfortable enough to take pictures while riding, I think you're well on your way to becoming a proper Hollywood cowboy."

"Hollywood cowboy," I say. "Not a real cowboy?" I lift an eyebrow.

"It's easy to be a cowboy for the camera," Cassidy says, looking up at me. "But being a true cowboy . . . that's a way of life."

"Well, then," I say. I slide my right foot out of the stirrup and kick my leg over. My movements are smoother and surer than they were only a few days ago. My feet hit the ground and I don't wobble.

Progress!

I take a deep breath and turn to face Cassidy.

The sky is slipping from golden to a peachy pink. Everything looks softer in this light. Cassidy's dark hair. Her smooth skin. Her parted lips.

Once again, I'm faced with a decision.

Do I say something suave like a character in a movie? That backfired last time, and I don't want to mess up again.

Do I smile and say something low risk about the weather before jumping back on my horse? It's the safest option available. I don't have to worry about losing face or bruising my feelings.

My heart races as I take a step closer to Cassidy. She doesn't back away. Her gaze darts down toward my mouth.

"No risk, no reward," I murmur, pulling off my cowboy hat.

But before I can lean in to kiss her, Cassidy sighs and draws back. She glances up at me with shimmering eyes and then she looks to the sky that now resembles a scoop of orange and pink sherbet.

"We don't have much daylight left," she says. Then, with a mischievous grin, Cassidy darts forward and pokes me. "Last one to the stables has to feed the goats in the morning."

Before I can even process what's happened, Cassidy's in the saddle and turning Land Sailor around.

"Hyah," Cassidy says.

"Oh crap." The last thing I want to do is feed Rambrandt and Van Goat. I scramble to pull myself up into the saddle. Sidewinder is already turning before I'm completely situated. Thankfully I'm balanced enough that I can slip my foot into the stirrup while he moves. "You heard her," I say, giving him a gentle nudge. "Hyah."

And then we're off.

Racing against the setting sun.

CHAPTER 23

Cassidy

"THAT DAMN TRACTOR of yours overheated again," Grandpa says, setting his glass of fresh-squeezed lavender lemonade down on the table with a bang. "I told you it wasn't worth the money you paid for it."

My father sighs. "Don't start in on this again, Dad."

Wilder shifts uncomfortably in his seat across from mine at the dinner table. We've been so busy with farm chores, trail riding, and cowboy lessons, we haven't shared many meals with my family, except on Sundays. So here we are, in our Sunday best, soaking up all the awkwardness hovering around the table.

When Wilder catches my eye, I give him an apologetic grimace. He offers me a sympathetic smile.

I wonder if his family holds on to things like ours does, or if they move past things for the sake of harmony. I can kind of understand why Grandpa's still upset with Uncle Alex. It couldn't have been easy to have his eldest son up and leave with hardly any warning after years of expecting him to take over the ranch someday. A hurt like that can fester.

But it's also ridiculous to bicker over the tractor Dad bought from the Frosts three years ago. It was one of the first things Dad did after Grandpa "retired," and I think Grandpa's still sore that Dad didn't ask him for his opinion.

Dad would have bought the tractor no matter what Grandpa said. It wouldn't have mattered if it was in perfect working condition or not. The Frosts needed the money, and everyone knows they're too proud to accept a loan. When Mrs. Frost's medical bills started piling up from her chemo treatments in Denver, Dad asked if he could buy their old tractor. I'm sure he planned to let it rust in the barn. Maybe use it for spare parts. It was at Grandpa's insistence that we even bothered to try getting it up and running.

The real problem is that Grandpa's having trouble giving up control and Dad's still trying to live up to Grandpa's expectations for Uncle Alex. So of course Dad won't admit he didn't buy the tractor because it was a good investment. And Grandpa won't just let the tractor rust in the barn.

"I would have told you it was a lemon if you'd've asked," Grandpa says.

Dad sets his fork down on his plate. He pinches the bridge of his nose and I watch as his ears darken from suntanned to fiery red.

"That thing's broke down more than it's not," Grandpa continues. "That makes it a lemon."

Mom lifts a pitcher from the center of the table and asks, "Would anyone like more lemonade?"

I see what she did there, with the whole lemons and

lemonade thing, but I don't think anyone else catches her subtle joke. Even though I'm the only person who nods, Mom tops off everyone's glasses.

Dad stares down at his half-eaten roast chicken with creamed spinach and wild rice.

Grandpa fumes over his fork and knife.

Wilder chews his food slowly and deliberately.

Sunday dinner with the Sterling family is a real fun time.

"A good tractor would be able to pull a harrow without overheating," Grandpa says, determined to poke and prod at Dad. "Those tires are worthless in mud."

At that, Dad's eyes flash to Grandpa. "What were you doing driving the tractor with a harrow attached?"

After an incident last year involving an ATV and the duck pond, Grandpa's not supposed to drive anything that's powered by fuel, not hay.

"That's beside the point," Grandpa says, waving him off.

"The hell it is," Dad says, raising his voice.

"I'll fix it," I blurt, desperate for them to stop bickering. It's bad enough Mom and I have to deal with this regularly, but Wilder's here and it's embarrassing.

Both Dad and Grandpa look at me.

"Tomorrow morning," I say. "It's probably just a gasket."

Turns out, it's not *just* a gasket.

And it's not the fuel pump.

Or the fuel line.

Or even the transmission.

What the hell did Grandpa do to this thing when he took it for a joy ride?

I'm elbow-deep in grease and grime, covered in sweat, and ready to throw in the wrench completely. Over the past few years, I've gotten pretty good at diagnosing and fixing the tractors, this one especially.

But not today.

I hold out a screwdriver and Wilder takes it from me. He sets it back into my toolbox where it belongs. "Any ideas?" he asks.

I let out a frustrated sigh. "A problem this big could mean it's the engine or the wiring. I don't have very much experience with either of those things."

"Is there a repair manual we can look through?"

"Not that I've seen." I ease myself down until I'm cross-legged on the ground beside the front tire. The ground is damp from last night's pop-up rainstorm, but at this point, I'm already such a mess, I just accept the mud. "This thing is older than my father."

Wilder's seated on an old wooden milking stool, hunched forward with his forearms resting on his knees. "Do you think we get a Wi-Fi signal here?"

"Should," I say. Mom put a signal booster in the training arena, which is right next door. He pulls out his phone and frowns down at the screen.

"Wow, that's a lot of messages," he mumbles.

"We can take a break." I could use something cold to drink.

Wilder shakes his head. "Nah. They can wait. What model and year is the tractor?"

"It's a 1952 Ferguson TO-30."

My messy bun is more mess than bun, with too many strands

187

hanging down over my face. I tug the elastic free and quickly brush it out with my fingers before pulling it back up again.

Wilder's hair, on the other hand, is perfectly coiffed. There's not a trace of dirt on his now slightly worn-in clothes. Not a streak of grease or grime on his face. Even his fingernails, which are trimmed short, are clean.

I glance down at my rough and ragged hands. At my jagged nails with their dirty nail beds. At the bloody knuckles I got trying to work one of the wrenches in between the tractor casing and a bolt.

"Okay. I found a copy of the dealer shop manual," he says, glancing up at me with a broad grin that makes my heart skip a beat. "For the new and far more powerful Ferguson thirty," he announces in his best salesman voice. "Let's see what it says."

Four hours, three wrenches, two Band-Aids, and a lunch break later, and I've just hoisted myself back up into the seat to try to start the tractor for what feels like the millionth time today.

Wilder and I share a cautiously optimistic look. He gives me a nod and I turn the key. Nothing happens for a moment and my heart starts to sink, but then the engine rumbles to life.

"Oh my god," I exclaim. "We did it!"

"We did it," Wilder shouts back.

I shift the tractor into gear. "I'm going to drive this up to the barn."

Wilder nods and gathers up my toolkit and the milking stool. We grin at each other the whole way back, me behind the wheel and him walking alongside. After I back the tractor into its spot, Wilder steps over. The rumble of the engine echoes around us until I turn the key to the off position.

I jump down from the tractor, and as I turn to offer Wilder a celebratory high five, something furry and quick races toward me. I tip back, caught by surprise by the calico blur, and ram my hip into the side of the tractor. A loud bang echoes through the barn. Trouble lets out a feral "Mrowl" at the sound and weaves between my legs like she's a downhill slalom skier.

"Trouble," I grumble as I completely lose my balance. My boot hits a bit of loose gravel and slides over it, sending me skittering, right into Wilder's open arms.

"Oof," he grunts when we collide.

The force of our impact sends us spinning around in a wide arc. Wilder's arms tighten around my waist and he twirls me like we're dancing, out of the engine-scented barn and into the fresh outdoors. His warmth seeps into me, making my insides melt like spun sugar.

Wilder stops spinning me when we reach the driveway and he gently sets me back on my feet. His hands hold my waist lightly, but my skin still sears and sizzles from his touch. When I look up at him, he's gazing back at me with those dark, sexy eyes of his, but the way he focuses on me, I feel like the only girl in the world.

"Cassidy, I need to tell you something," he says, his look going serious.

All the fizzy feelings in me seep away. Of course. I got caught up in my emotions and the excitement. What an idiot I am.

Just as I feel the heat of embarrassment rise to my cheeks, an unfamiliar dark SUV pulls into the drive. I step back as the vehicle stops before us, the windows so darkly tinted they almost match the coal-black paint. The driver steps out, adjusts his suit sleeves while giving us a nod, and then pulls open the driver side passenger door.

I catch a glimpse of long, dark hair and giant sunglasses.

"Natalie?" Wilder says.

The girl turns to us and flashes a brilliant smile. She pulls off her sunglasses to reveal glistening amber eyes framed with thick, lush lashes. She's wearing painted-on designer jeans, a crisp white V-neck shirt, and a camel-colored duster that goes all the way down to her ankles, where it brushes against her chocolate-brown suede boots.

"What are you doing here?" Wilder gives me a raised eyebrow look that lets me know he wasn't expecting her.

Still, that doesn't stop the jealousy from bubbling up inside me. Natalie Garcia, star of *The Aspen Files* franchise, looks like she just walked off a runway. And I . . .

I glance down at my clothes, covered in grease spots, impressions of tire treads, and mud.

. . . look like I *was* the runway.

"So you didn't get my messages. Or Alexander's, apparently." She takes in her surroundings with raised eyebrows. "I didn't realize how remote this place is. Do you even have reception?" She slides a phone from her pocket and takes a quick glance. "Nope. No wonder you have no idea what's going on. Well," she says with an easy laugh. "Surprise. I'm here." Without blinking her long eyelashes, she turns to me and smiles. "You must be Cassidy. Alexander told me all about you. I'm Natalie Garcia, but you can just call me Nat. I'm so happy to finally meet you."

What is even happening right now?

I glance over at Wilder, but he looks just as clueless as I feel.

"Are you also one of Uncle Alex's clients?" I ask, trying to make sense of everything. You'd think he'd have mentioned signing a star like Natalie Garcia.

"No," Natalie says.

Oh. Maybe she's Wilder's . . . girlfriend? My heart teeters on the edge.

"I only met Alexander yesterday," she continues. And then she does the most stunning thing, considering how dirty I am. And that her maybe-boyfriend just twirled me across the drive. Natalie winds her arm through mine so that we're linked at the elbow, leans over as if we're the best of friends, and says conspiratorially, "Now, where's a good place for the three of us to chat?"

"I don't understand," Wilder says, staring down at Natalie's phone. "That's not you."

"I'm well aware," she says in a dry, almost bored tone.

The three of us are seated around the breakfast table in the guest cottage. So far, I've discovered that Natalie is not Wilder's girlfriend (phew). But she is a love interest of another sort. Natalie's been cast to play one of the lead roles in *Outrider*. She and Wilder once acted together on a previous project, and it sounds like they move in similar social circles, so they aren't exactly strangers. But they haven't been in contact lately.

Until now.

"But . . ." Wilder scrunches up his forehead and leans back in his chair. "I don't get it. How did they get these pictures? And why do the tabloids think it's you?"

"We both have a similar build, I guess." Natalie studies me

like I'm a piece of abstract art, squinting and tilting her head to see if she can figure it out. "And our hair is a similar tone. See." Natalie passes me her phone.

Beneath a headline that says "*Outriders* Out Riding" is a selfie of Wilder on Sidewinder, his suave grin sparkling for the camera. Just over his shoulder is the silhouette of a figure on horseback behind him in the distance. You can't tell much from the picture. Just that the rider is probably female and the horse is gray. There's another picture beside it of . . .

"Me?" I glance up at Natalie.

Immediately I look back at the image on her phone. You can't see my face in the second photo because of the way the setting sun blurs everything, but I know for sure that this is one of the photos Wilder took on our trail ride. Sidewinder's ears and dark mane frame the bottom of the photo. Land Sailor stands in profile beside me as I face the camera head-on.

Now it's my turn to scrutinize Natalie. She and I are the same height. We do have a similar hair color, even though her hair is long and silky and mine is shorter and prone to split ends. We share height and hair color, and that's pretty much where the similarities stop. Natalie's softer and shinier, where I'm all rough edges and tarnish. It's like comparing Tiffany & Co. to Thelma's Bargain Basement.

Natalie is the epitome of a California actor, and I've never felt more like a country bumpkin. If she's anything like the rest of the girls in Wilder's life . . . Well, it's even more clear to me now that whatever is happening between us is nothing more than a summer fling to pass the time until Wilder goes home.

My brain gets it, but my heart? Not so much.

"Bottom line is that social media is going wild for these

photos. Ordinarily, everyone on our respective teams would just ignore this kind of thing," she says, directing her comments to me. "But it's building buzz. Lots of buzz. And the studio wants to capitalize on it while it can." Natalie presses her palms down on the table and smiles. "And that's exactly why we're here."

CHAPTER 24

Wilder

"**WHAT DO YOU** mean by 'we'?" I ask.

"'We' as in me and one of the studio's photographers." Natalie takes her phone back from Cassidy and runs her manicured finger along the edge of the case. "Don't worry. We're here on the down-low. The plan is to take some nicer staged photos of us riding horses, a couple of candids, that kind of thing."

"Do you think that's a good idea?" I say. "People might think you and I . . ." I wave my hand between us and then glance over at Cassidy.

She's studying her fingernails and doesn't look up.

This is such a mess. I still need to tell Cassidy how I feel. Lay it out on the table. I really like her and I don't want things to end when I leave. I'm pretty sure she feels the same way. I'd finally just convinced myself that I should get over my fear and say something. And then Natalie arrived.

". . . are a thing?" Natalie says.

Cassidy winces and sinks farther down into her chair.

"As if." Natalie says it so bluntly, I might have been offended if I wasn't knee deep in worry about how this will affect things with me and Cassidy.

Natalie and I both know that we don't actually have to be dating for it to appear that way. One photo taken out of context. A well-placed rumor. And bam. We're front page on some tabloid where it will claim we're planning an elopement in Vegas. Or something. "How's the studio going to spin this?" I ask.

Natalie looks between Cassidy and me. Her eyes are full of understanding.

"They've promised to keep us platonic. And the photos we take here will be shared as if it was a planned publicity shoot."

"And if we refuse?" I ask.

Natalie shrugs. "I'm not sure we have much of a choice. The minute you posted those photos to Instagram, it opened up a whole can of worms."

"Whoa, whoa, whoa," I say, as if I could slow this conversation to a halt like I do a horse. "I didn't post any photos to Instagram." What the hell is Natalie talking about? "I haven't done anything on social media since I got to Wyoming."

Natalie gives me a confused look. "I'm not sure what to tell you." She taps her phone a few times and then hands it over. "But you did post on Instagram. Like, yesterday."

My Instagram profile is open on the screen, and sure enough, the latest post shows pictures of me and Cassidy on our trail ride, which are now having a semi-viral moment. "I don't understand," I say, checking the time stamp. "These were posted last night."

"Yup," Natalie says. "Sometime around five-thirty or so, based on when my notifications started blowing up."

Cassidy's frown deepens, which cuts me to the core. I hate how unhappy she looks and I hate that I'm the reason. Again. She hasn't said much since Natalie arrived, so I'm surprised when she joins the conversation. "We were eating dinner at the house at that time. I don't think you had your phone with you."

It's the first time she's actually looked me in the eye since we sat down at the table. There's a smudge of grease on her cheek that I'm tempted to reach over and wipe away. Instead, I twist my fingers together until the knuckles threaten to pop.

"I didn't have my phone," I say. I know this for a fact because I left it charging in the cabin. After Mr. Sterling lectured me about phones at the dinner table my first night here, I've made it a point to not have it on me. There's enough tension in the main house at mealtime that I don't need to be adding any more.

I scroll down to read the post's accompanying text.

wildernash Paradise on earth. Sunset trail rides have me in a cowboy state of mind. #horseback #taketherins #ranching

"This doesn't sound like something I'd post at all," I say. I scroll to my previous post to compare, but once again, it's not mine. Or rather, it was posted under my account, but not by me.

This time, it's a photo I took of Rambrandt and Van Goat on my way to the chicken coop a few days ago. From a safe distance, of course, since I'm still not over the shoelace incident.

The two goats peer between the slats of the split-rail fence that separates their shed from the pasture.

wildernash Should I grow a goatee? Nah, I'm just kidding around. #GOAT #humor #jokingaround

Now, that is something I definitely would never say. And a goatee? Really?

"Who the hell is posting— Oh." I sit back and slowly set the phone on the table.

I know exactly who is posting. And why.

"This is all my fault," I say, running a hand through my hair.

"Explain," Natalie says.

"Right before I left to come here, Alexander and I talked about having my PR team run my social media accounts for me. I post semi-regularly about random stuff, but Alexander wasn't sure I'd have time for it. And there was the issue of trying to keep my stay here at the ranch on the down-low." I press my palms to the table. "We talked about announcing a social media break, but Alexander thought that might get negative attention. And not posting at all might raise concerns. If anyone from the studio noticed I'd suddenly gone quiet, they might start asking questions."

"Okay," Natalie says, nodding. "That all makes sense. But how did your PR team wind up with the photos?"

"I have the Photos app set to sync with iCloud. Before I left, I created a shared photo library to upload some selfies and other photos for the PR team to use. I must have forgotten to change the permissions." It only takes me a second to switch the settings, but the damage is already done.

So much for keeping a low profile in Wyoming.

"I'm sorry," I say. "I didn't mean for you two to get roped into this."

Natalie laughs. "Look at you, using cowboy lingo. You're really committed to the role."

"I'm serious."

Cassidy blinks as she stares down at her hands. "It's not like anyone knows it's me. And it's not like the ranch is a vacation hot spot. I doubt anyone would be able to get our location from the photos."

"And I've been meaning to get some horse time in before we start filming," Natalie says, like none of this is a big deal. "It's been ages since my last trail ride."

"We could always tell the truth. Say that it's not you in the photos," I suggest to Natalie. I'm not wild about the idea of other people covering for my mistakes.

"And then what?" Natalie tilts her head like a predatory bird to look at me. "Have the vultures out searching high and low for you and the girl in the picture?"

"No." I grimace.

"Exactly."

Natalie's back at Silver Stallion Ranch the next morning, this time with a professional photographer.

Today she's dressed in a pair of jeans and a flowery shirt with flowing sleeves. Her hair is tied in a loose braid and she has a fresh-faced makeup look. Natalie's riding boots are dark brown and slightly scuffed.

"How long have you been riding?" I ask, nodding to her boots.

"I took some lessons when I was a kid, but I haven't had much time for it lately. I borrowed these from my sister," she says.

The photographer walks over to us. "This is Nigel," Natalie says.

"Welcome to Wyoming," I say, holding out a hand. "I'm Wilder."

Nigel tucks a battery pack under his arm to free up his hand. After a quick shake, he says, "The light's good right now, so we should get started."

Nigel's got a giant camera bag slung over his left shoulder and a tripod propped on his right shoulder like a Revolutionary War soldier's rifle. His logo-free blue baseball cap is sweat stained and faded, and his slim-fitting black pants and black and white striped shirt make him look like a mime. He paces around the stable yard, looking this way and that. Probably trying to find some good backdrops.

Cassidy arrives with Jupiter and Misty Morning. Both of the horses are saddled and ready to ride.

She hasn't said much to me since Natalie showed up out of the blue yesterday, but we haven't exactly had much time to chat. As soon as Natalie left for her hotel back in Jackson Hole, it was time to feed the animals. I ate dinner alone at the cabin while Cassidy helped her mom with something over at the training arena. Then it was time to call it a night.

There's a new tension between us that wasn't there before. And not the good kind of tension, either.

The longer I let things go without saying something, the

more I think I've missed my chance. The subtle touches, the spark, the magnetic attraction are all still there. But it's like there's an invisible force field between us, making me second-guess everything.

"No, no. This won't do," Nigel mutters as he spins around in a slow circle, taking in the stable and paddock. "We need something more rustic. With more of a Western vibe. This all feels too new."

"We have an old bunkhouse that might work," Cassidy says. She glances at me, but before I can catch her eye, she turns her attention to Nigel's sandaled feet and frowns. "It's not in walking distance, though. I don't suppose you know how to ride?"

"Um, a horse?" Nigel says, giving a quick shake of his head. "No."

Cassidy looks over his assortment of gear. "Do you need all that equipment?"

"Of course," Nigel says. "I only brought the bare minimum."

I think in this day and age, a smartphone would be considered the *bare* minimum, but I'm not about to point that out.

"I'll drive you out in the ATV," Cassidy says to Nigel, then looks over at me and Natalie. "You two can follow behind on the horses."

"So?" Natalie asks, glancing at me from the corner of her eye as we follow behind the ATV at a reasonable distance. The horses don't seem agitated by the noise, but the tires are kicking up plenty of dust. I'd always assumed that the bandanas cowboys are often pictured wearing were mostly a style choice or convenient for robbing a bank or holding up a stagecoach, but now I see their true value as a makeshift dust mask.

"What do you mean?" I ask.

"Why are you hiding out in the wilds of Wyoming while your PR team covers for you on social media? There are plenty of ranches and trails in SoCal if you were looking to get in some riding. Wyoming's a long way from L.A. Wait, wait! Don't tell me." Her eyebrow arches and the corner of her mouth quirks up. "Alexander mentioned your being here is pretty hush-hush. Ooh, is it something juicy? Detox? Rehab? Plastic surgery?" She glances at me and then shakes her head. "Definitely not hair implants."

"Alexander really didn't tell you?" I say, cutting her off before she can list any more outlandish possibilities.

"No. We were too busy coordinating this spur-of-the-moment photoshoot to get into any details."

"You'll be disappointed."

"Try me."

I suppose at this point, I have to trust her. Clearly Alexander does, or he wouldn't have shared my location. "Horseback Riding 101," I say. "I'm basically here for private horse camp."

Natalie looks over at me. "Seriously?"

"Seriously. Deacon Slade knows how to ride. The studio made it very clear that whoever they cast to play him has to be able to ride, too." I shrug and nudge Jupiter to go a bit faster now that the ATV has put plenty of distance between us. "And I don't know how to ride."

"You didn't, maybe," she says, giving me an appreciative nod. "But you sure know how to ride now. How long have you been here?"

"A few weeks."

"Is that all? I never would have guessed," Natalie says. "You've picked it up fast."

"Cassidy's a great teacher," I say.

I can just make out the top of her head beneath the four-wheeler's roll cage. When I glance over at Natalie, she's staring at me in amusement.

"What?" I ask.

"Well, aren't you a smitten kitten," Natalie says with a smirk.

CHAPTER 25

Cassidy

I **HAVE TO** give Nigel credit. He's dedicated to his craft.

Maybe a little *too* dedicated.

The minute I've finished loading his gear into the ATV, he jumps into the back, positions himself sideways across the seats, and starts snapping photos of Wilder and Natalie. I'm not sure he's looked at anything besides the camera's viewfinder since we started to drive away from the stable. Also, how much memory is this guy carrying? Because all those pictures have to be eating up a ton of storage space and we're only fifteen minutes into this photo shoot.

"Those two look fantastic together," he says.

Of course they look good together. That's part of the reason they were cast as love interests for the miniseries.

I try to ignore the way my heart squeezes in response to Nigel's statement. My fingers grip the steering wheel like I'm trying to crush it to dust, and I press my foot farther down on the gas pedal as if I could just race away from the feelings that are threatening to burst out of me like an overfilled dam.

Why did I have to go and develop feelings for Wilder?

All of my self-doubt and fears come bubbling back up as we bump along the trail. How I'm not entirely sure I can trust his intentions. How we only have a few weeks left before he leaves. How there's no way I could ever hope to hold his attention the way a Hollywood starlet like Natalie could.

Dust billows up behind us. This part of the trail is worn and bumpy since it's the path we take to get out onto the open range. Soon we'll be traveling over much more rugged terrain that's more suited for four legs than four wheels. The last thing I want to do is flip the ATV, so I force myself to focus on driving.

"The dust really gives the photos some fantastic grit, you know? True grit," Nigel says in such a dry tone that I can't tell if he's attempting humor or if he's being serious. Since he's behind me and has now wedged himself against the back of the passenger seat so he can ride backward, I can't get a read on his facial cues. "Do you think you can create more dust?"

Sure, I'll get right on that.

We come to a fork in the path. The left branch is the way Wilder and I have gone for our trail rides. Today we'll take the right branch instead, to head north along the meandering and overgrown trail that will eventually lead us to the old bunkhouse. The ATV's suspension bounces and squeaks as we stutter over a particularly rough patch of dirt, and I grip the wheel tightly to keep the four-wheeler from straying off course. Clods of dirt shoot out behind the rear wheels as we slide around until we get traction. Riding in the ATV is definitely not as comfortable as sitting atop Land Sailor.

"Are you purposely driving over all the bumps?" Nigel asks with a huff. I glance back to find him pulling his camera away from his scowling face. "I'm going to get a black eye if this keeps up."

What does he expect me to do? I'm driving an ATV over what barely passes for a trail in the middle of a giant cattle pasture in Wyoming. *Of course there are bumps.* It's not like there's pavement out here.

The engine whines as we make our way up a rise, and just as we reach the top, Nigel calls out, "Stop, stop, stop," in a tone that leads me to believe something catastrophic has occurred. Maybe some of his equipment has fallen from the ATV? Or he's spotted an injured animal? Or the bumps are making him carsick?

I slam on the brakes and we jerk to a stop, a billow of dust rising up around us.

"What is it?" I ask, spinning around to face him.

"Just look," he says, pointing his camera at Wilder and Natalie and adjusting the focus.

They appear to be perfectly safe where they are in the valley beneath us. Jupiter and Misty Morning don't appear to be in any distress. I don't see anything that resembles photography equipment or hurt wildlife on the trail. Nigel hasn't puked. I must be missing something.

"What?" I ask again.

"This. This is *the* perfect shot," he says. Nigel stands so that his head rises above the ATV's roll cage, swaps out the camera lens, and then points and clicks some more.

Wilder and Natalie wend their way around a patch of scrub brush, Jupiter and Misty Morning in a relaxed walk beneath them. Wilder's cowboy hat is tipped down so that you can't see his face, but his posture in the saddle is almost perfect. There's a little too much slouch in his shoulders, but he looks like the quintessential cowboy, and since that was the goal all along, I'll allow it. To his left, Natalie sits comfortably in the saddle. Clearly this isn't her first rodeo . . . er, ride. She tilts her head toward him, a brilliant smile lighting up her face. He says something and she laughs. I can't hear it, but I watch as he joins in, and it sends a searing jolt of envy through me.

Have I ever heard Wilder laugh like that?

I'm not sure.

I don't think so.

I know *I* haven't made him laugh like that.

It's easy to picture the sound, a warm rumble that makes my blood turn to honey even if it's just in my imagination.

Natalie reaches out and playfully smacks his arm. Wilder leans in to say something. I can see why Wilder and Natalie were cast as love interests. The chemistry between them is undeniable.

"This is perfect," Nigel says, clicking away on his camera.

Yeah. Perfectly revolting.

Never in a million years would I have expected that I'd be spending July 3 at a professional photo shoot for two up-and-coming Hollywood stars at the old bunkhouse at Silver Stallion Ranch.

Yet here I am, precariously perched on a weathered split-rail fence, holding a giant silver photography umbrella and trying really hard not to be jealous of Natalie and all the attention she's getting from Wilder while a very zealous photographer does his thing.

The umbrella I'm holding is great at reflecting light, as evidenced by the soft, dreamy beams it casts on Natalie's face as she grins up at Wilder, who has this ridiculously hot, broody cowboy thing going on that really should be illegal outside of L.A.

Besides being a great reflective surface, the umbrella's also great at catching every slight breeze and gust of wind, threatening to knock me off balance. Even with my boots angled down so that my shins are pressed against the slats while I lean forward, it still takes a lot of energy to not get jolted off.

Natalie, Wilder, and the horses are in the paddock, with the rustic bunkhouse behind them. Even though it leans slightly and the roof sags, the building is sturdy. It was one of the first buildings constructed on the ranch. It doesn't get much use anymore, but it comes in handy for shelter during unexpected bad weather or when we have extra hands on a cattle drive. Before Grandma died, she used to take me up here on clear summer nights. We'd spread our sleeping bags on the dusty, old wooden bunks, using worn saddle blankets for extra padding. Then we'd spend the night stargazing or playing Uno by lantern light.

I take a deep breath and blink back tears. Sometimes missing her hits me so hard right out of the blue. If she were here, Grandma would tell me to stop being such a Sad Sally. And then she'd say, "You can't always wait for life to happen, Cass-girl. Sometimes, you have to take the reins and pick your own path."

Okay, Grandma, I think, looking up at the sky. *I'll try.*

It's interesting that my subconscious picked that quote. I wonder what path it wants me to take.

A European starling swoops down into the tall grass outside the paddock, its oil slick–colored feathers disappearing into a thick sod carpet of green and gold. The field surrounding us is mostly prairie sand reed that won't be grazed until fall, after the cattle are driven back down from the pastures farther north of us. The grass is already pretty tall here—it's been growing since May—and many of the panicles have started to flower. A rural bunkhouse surrounded by a sea of prairie grass . . . It's the perfect aesthetic for an Old West photoshoot.

"I love it," Nigel says, as if he's read my mind.

"Look over at the horses."

"Tilt your faces toward me."

All the while, Nigel's like the mole in Whac-A-Mole, dipping and bobbing around them, kneeling then popping up to catch every possible angle.

"Yes, yes. More. Gorgeous."

"The camera loves you both."

It's strange to be standing here, on the edge of the fence. On the edge of the conversation. This might be my ranch and my world, but right now, I'm the outsider. Wilder, Natalie, and Nigel have so much in common. Where they live. Where they work.

I've been relegated to the third wheel.

No, Nigel's the third wheel.

It's even worse for me. I'm the fourth wheel.

And right now, I'm invisible.

CHAPTER 26

Wilder

"OKAY, I THINK that just about does it," Nigel says, sliding the lens cover into place. He tucks the camera under his arm and pulls a small spiral-bound notebook from his back pocket. He flips it open. "Check. Check. Check, check, check," he mumbles. Then he announces, "Okay, folks. It's a wrap."

Cassidy lets out an audible sigh of relief. She closes the reflective umbrella and jumps down off the split-rail fence from where she's been the entire time.

I get her exhaustion. It feels like Natalie and I have been posing for days, even though it's only been an hour or so, at most. Now that it's nearly lunchtime, my stomach is grumbling. And with the midday sun beating down on us, I'm also mighty parched. Looks like this cowboy stuff is growing on me.

Natalie glances at her watch. "Perfect timing. We need to head out soon."

"What time's your flight?" I ask.

"A little before five," Natalie says. "If we leave now, we can grab a late lunch in Jackson Hole before we head to the airport."

We help Cassidy and Nigel load the photography equipment back into the ATV. As before, Cassidy drives ahead with him as we follow behind on horseback. The horses fall into a steady trot as if they're as eager as we are to get back.

"Cassidy seems nice," Natalie says in that polite tone someone uses when they want to pry but are pretending they don't.

I clear my throat. "She is."

Natalie waits a few beats before she just comes out with it. "Is there something going on between you two?"

"Sorta? Maybe?" I shrug. "It's really complicated."

"When isn't it?" Natalie laughs. "I'm not sure I've ever been in a relationship that hasn't had some sort of complication or another. Complications put the real in real-ationship."

"Wow, that's good," I tease. "Did you come up with that yourself?"

"I wish," Natalie says. "It was a line from this off-off-Broadway play I saw last month. But isn't it the truth?"

Honestly, I haven't been in enough actual relationships to know. I've dated and done the group hang thing, but I haven't really wanted something serious. At least, not before . . .

"Right now, my boyfriend's shooting a film in Romania of all places. He's gone until October, at least. The time zone thing is tricky, especially when we have to work around our shooting schedules. And don't get me started on cell reception. Trying to FaceTime is like an exercise in frustration if he's not in his rental apartment."

"Lack of reception, I get," I say, because it's pretty remote here, too. "This entire ranch is a dead zone unless you're near one of the main buildings and can get a stable Wi-Fi signal."

Still, it's been nice not to be tied to my phone all the time. I'd gotten into the habit of mindless scrolling while I was sitting around during shoots or scarfing down meals, but out here, there's almost zero opportunity for boredom. Lately, I've only used my phone to touch base with Mom and to keep tabs on Cam Sheffield and his low-key social media campaign to steal the role of Deacon Slade from me.

"So, tell me about *your* complicated," Natalie says.

"Now?" I reach up and adjust my cowboy hat.

"It's a long ride back and I have questions," she says.

"Okay," I say, reaching up to scratch my jaw. "I . . . I'm not great with words. At least, not the ones I have to come up with on my own. You know how you just quoted a line from that show you saw?"

"Yeah."

"Well, I'd been practicing some lines, trying to find my character while we've been out on the trail. And then I tried to tell Cassidy how I feel—in my own words—but she thought they were lines."

"Oh." Natalie gives me a sympathetic frown. "Did you use your own voice or were you channeling some movie-inspired love interest?"

"What do you think?"

She cringes.

"There have been some *moments*," I continue.

"Kissing moments?" she asks, waggling her eyebrows.

"I don't kiss and tell," I said.

211

"Knew it."

I roll my eyes. "Cassidy and I need to talk. But I've been stalling. I'm worried I'll mess up again. And then every time I work up the guts to say something, I get interrupted." I give her a pointed look. "Your timing yesterday couldn't have been better," I say with a touch of sarcasm.

"Sorry," Natalie says. And she looks like she really means it.

"I've been trying to show her that I'm serious, that I wasn't just spouting lines before. And I thought maybe yesterday she might have believed it. But then this happened and now the distance between us is greater than the Grand Canyon. And time's running out. In a few weeks, I'll be back in California, and then what? I'll be there. She'll be here. I want to try to figure it out but . . ."

"You have a few hurdles to get over, but honestly, it doesn't sound impossible to me," Natalie says as we ride into the stable yard. "You obviously like her. And I can tell she's totally into you. The distance thing is unfortunate, but yay for neighboring time zones. At least you two will only have an hour difference between you when you're back in California, and not, like, ten hours. *That's* complicated."

"True. But I still don't know what to say to her. Or how." I dismount Jupiter and wipe my sweaty brow on my shirtsleeve.

Natalie looks down at me from Misty Morning. "I think you just have to be authentic." She dismounts and comes to stand beside me. "Actions speak louder than words," she says. "The next time you work up the courage to talk to her, use this." She pokes me in the chest, hard. "Not this." Her hand flies up and she knocks my cowboy hat off my head with a giant grin.

I bend down to retrieve it and brush the dust off with my palm. "Thanks," I say, the word dripping with more sarcasm. "Good talk."

Cassidy and Nigel emerge from the shed where the ATV is stored. They're both loaded down with all of Nigel's photography gear. I rush over to grab the tripod and umbrella from Cassidy.

"Here, let me," I say, taking them from her.

My hand brushes hers and a shot of adrenaline courses through me. Our eyes meet but hers don't have the same spark they had before Natalie arrived. As if she senses what I'm thinking, Cassidy's gaze flickers to Natalie and then back to me.

Great. Now she's probably wondering if there's something secretly going on between me and Natalie. No wonder she's been aloof since Natalie arrived. Also, I'm an idiot for not noticing it sooner. Why am I so bad at this?

"Thank you so much for putting up with us," Natalie says to Cassidy.

Cassidy nods and responds but I can't make out what she says.

Natalie turns to me and winks. Thankfully, it doesn't look like Cassidy noticed, or I'd have yet one more complication to deal with.

I give Natalie a wide-eyed knock-it-off head shake.

Nigel checks his watch and says, "Our car's here."

Cassidy and Natalie walk ahead of me and Nigel as the four of us make our way to the main drive in front of the ranch house. As expected, a dark black Lincoln SUV is parked out front.

The driver helps us load everything in the trunk.

"It was an experience," Nigel says as he slides into the back-seat.

"Thanks for letting me ride Misty Morning," Natalie says to Cassidy. "She's a beautiful horse. And your ranch is wonderful. Good job with Wilder. By the time we start filming, no one will have a clue."

Natalie wraps Cassidy in a friendly hug and whispers something into her ear. Cassidy glances at me briefly and then looks away. When Natalie steps back, Cassidy's cheeks are rosy.

I can't tell if Natalie's meddling is helpful or not. I follow her around to the other side of the car and the driver pulls open the door for her.

"See you soon," I say.

Natalie gets in and settles in her seat. "I can't wait for an update. You've got this, Romeo."

I wish I had her confidence.

But just as I've been doing since I got here, I'm going to have to fake it until I make it.

The SUV's engine rumbles and Cassidy and I watch the tail-lights disappear down the drive.

As soon as Natalie and Nigel are out of sight, I turn to Cassidy and pull off my cowboy hat. My hair is plastered to my head, and I run a hand through my damp curls. Press the brim between my hands. "Can we talk?" I ask.

Gone is the suave and sure actor I was pretending to be before. Now I'm standing here as Wilder, and I hope Cassidy can see that.

She *has* to.

Cassidy looks at me with a mix of hope and apprehension. "Yes," she says cautiously.

Okay. Here we go.

I take a deep breath. "I don't . . . I just . . ." I work my jaw with frustration. Why can't I find the right words? My heart is pounding *don't mess up, don't mess up, don't mess up* and my head is completely blank.

What are words?

Cassidy's mouth turns up into a rueful smile even as the hope fades from her eyes. "It's okay. You don't have to explain."

"No, I do," I say automatically. "What I'm trying to say is that—"

CHAPTER 27

Cassidy

"CASSIDY."

Dad's booming voice makes me practically jump out of my cowboy boots. I spin around to find him striding toward us with a concerned look on his face.

"Dad?" I ask, partially to acknowledge him but also because I can tell something big's happening from the tone of his voice.

He nods at Wilder and then says, "We have a problem."

Wilder straightens up as if he thinks he might be in trouble for something. But I can tell from Dad's posture and the fact that Wilder got a nod of acknowledgment that whatever it is has nothing to do with either of us.

"The crew's been moving our herd of cattle between the grazing pastures. We brought on a few less experienced guys this season and it looks like they got a little careless with the head count. They just radioed in that at least two calves are missing. Possibly more. Ordinarily, I wouldn't worry too much, but there have been some reports of wolf pack activity just north of here."

I heave a tired-sounding sigh. "And if the wolves get to the calves before we do, they'll think they've stumbled into the Silver Stallion Buffet," I say.

Although we're some of the few ranchers who support wolf conservation efforts, we also know the danger a pack poses to our cattle. Once wolves get a taste for veal, they could keep coming back for more. Usually they cull the weaker animals from the herd, but eventually those losses add up. Plus, dining on our cattle could lead to the wolves venturing closer to the barnyard, where there's more variety: horses, goats, pigs, chickens, ducks, and barn cats.

Trouble, for sure.

Dad shoves his hands into the front pockets of his jeans. "The guys and I have a lot of ground to cover, so—"

"We can help," Wilder says, like it's the cowboy version of "Put me in, Coach." He steps forward and settles the cowboy hat on his head like he's always worn one.

I'm about to protest, but Wilder doesn't let me get a word in edgewise. "Cassidy's taken me out on a few trail rides and we've been talking about going on longer excursions lately. I think I've proven myself out there. This will be a good way to get in some real-word experience and test my skills. Plus," I say to Cassidy, "I'll be able to check some other items off the cowboy skills list."

Dad looks like he's seriously considering Wilder's offer. "We could use the extra eyes," he says, although I can tell he's not sure if it's a good idea or not.

I have my doubts.

Yes, Wilder knows how to ride now.

Yes, the additional time in the saddle would be good for him.

And yes, the experience will give him an opportunity to really immerse himself in the cowboy lifestyle.

But . . . just the two of us, alone on the trail for an uncertain amount of time, where anything could happen? Where the potential dangers are bigger than sweltering looks, kiss-swollen lips, or shattered hearts?

I can't tell if the chill that runs down my spine is from dread or anticipation.

It doesn't take much time to gather all the equipment we'll need for a day or two out on the trail. There's a ton of territory to cover and I'm not sure how long we'll be searching for the calves. Or what challenges we might face. I start making a mental list of the things we'll need.

Flashlights and batteries.

Water bottles and water-purification tablets.

First-aid kit.

Emergency two-way radios.

Swiss Army knife and axe.

Waterproof matches.

Flare gun.

Two bedrolls, plus sleeping bags.

Horse feed.

With everything heaped on the table in the tack room, it looks like we're preparing for a natural disaster.

I've already grabbed some extra clothes and toiletries from the main house. Wilder's up at the guest cottage packing what he needs. On his way back, he'll stop by the main house to pick up the food Mom's preparing for us to eat on the trail.

Staring at the heap, I think about what else we're missing.

Camping cookware.

A rope.

I debate whether we should take a tarp along, too. We might need it for shelter, but it's bulky.

Decisions, decisions.

We're in a rush and my brain is racing at a million miles an hour. I don't want to miss anything because I'm distracted. But I also can't stop wondering what Wilder was about to say before Dad interrupted him. I'm almost as anxious thinking about those possibilities as I am about what we might face out on the trail.

Maybe Wilder and I shouldn't join in on the hunt for the missing calves. Maybe we could just . . .

"Okay," Wilder says, walking into the stable with a small overnight bag Mom lent him and two bags of food she prepared. "What else do we need?"

"I'm not sure," I say, looking over the pile again.

"Wow, there's a lot of stuff we need to take," Wilder says.

"Thankfully, we can split the load between our horses." I study Wilder, looking for any sign he's not up for the search. "Are you sure about this?" I ask. "We don't have to go."

Wilder scratches his jaw. "I'm sure. If I do this, then I'll know I'm legit. I'll be able to show up on set knowing I won't disappoint Alexander. His reputation and mine will be intact." He pauses and then his eyes light up. "Plus, it sounds badass."

"It won't be easy."

"Hey, if you're scared . . . ," Wilder says. His tone is neutral so I can't tell if he's trying to bait me or give me an out.

"I'm not scared." I'm terrified.

What if we don't find the calves before the wolves do?

What if the wolves find us first?

What if Wilder is the wolf, about to rip out my poor little foolish heart?

I don't have time to dwell on it. Dad rides into the stable yard on his horse, Will Post. "I'll ride west toward the pastures there to meet up with some of the crew who are already out scouting. You two head northeast toward Hunter's Ridge. I doubt the calves made it that far, but if they have, you can flush them west."

"Yes, sir," Wilder says, dipping his cowboy hat in acknowledgment. He looks like an Old West cowboy taking commands from the local sheriff. I'm surprised he doesn't give Dad a formal salute.

Dad nods back. "Be safe out there."

"You too," I say. "Love you."

"Love you, too, Cass." Dad clicks his tongue and Will Post starts forward.

Now that I have everything laid out and divided, we can saddle our horses, load the saddlebags, and head out. Land Sailor is still fresh since he's been in his stall all day, but Jupiter's older and not used to the kind of trail riding we'll be doing. Sidewinder will be the perfect mount for Wilder, and I'm glad he has some experience handling that particular horse already.

After scarfing down a quick lunch, we head out. The midafternoon sun beats down on us as we hit the trail toward Hunter's Ridge. It smells like warm meadows and pine trees, and the songbirds chirp around us as if they're cheering us on. Big, puffy white clouds dot the sky.

"We'll take the same trail to the old ranch hand bunkhouse that we used this morning, and then continue north, northeast. The terrain starts to get hilly and becomes a rocky scramble. There's not much prairie grass in the area, so it's not likely the calves would go there. Unless they were hunted or spooked."

Wilder nods. "Besides the calves, is there anything we should keep an eye out for?"

"Cow patties and carcasses," I say. It's grim but true.

We ride in silence for a while. I keep glancing at Wilder out of the corner of my eye. The brim of my cowboy hat limits my peripheral vision, but from what I can tell, he's the picture of ease.

I, on the other hand, am not.

There's a nervous energy coiled just under the surface of my skin.

When we come to a babbling stream about an hour into our ride, we stop to let the horses get a drink. Thankfully, it doesn't get scorching hot out here in Wyoming, even in the summer. The sun can be intense, sure. But I've seen weather reports for Southern California during a summer heat wave. I have no idea how Wilder and Uncle Alex can stand living where it regularly gets into triple-digit temperatures. I think I'd melt like ice cream.

Could I trade mild summers for melting ones?

I don't know.

But then I think about how brutally cold the winters can be, with below-freezing temperatures and endless snow squalls. I don't think I'd mind being in warm and sunny Southern California then.

"You're quiet," Wilder says.

I offer a noncommittal shrug. Now that it's just the two of us, talking feels dangerous. Especially when I can't predict what Wilder might say.

"So," Wilder says.

My heart races at just that little word.

Will he confirm my worst fears: that my feelings for him are unreciprocated?

Will he admit that he cares for me, too?

I suck in a deep breath until the air burns my lungs. The anticipation's worse than whatever I fear. We might as well get it over with.

"So?" I reply, resigned to hear him out.

CHAPTER 28

Wilder

I SHOULD APOLOGIZE for being an idiot. Or ask her if she'll give me another chance. Or confess my feelings.

But I'm chickenshit.

"How long do you think we'll be out here?" I ask.

What is wrong with me?

I've auditioned in front of rooms full of casting directors. I've had lead roles in off-off-Broadway plays. I've even survived feeding Birdzilla and her ferocious flock of attack hens on the daily. But I cannot, for the life of me, get my act together and tell Cassidy that I like her.

That I want to see where this goes.

That I want to have her in my life even after I'm back in L.A.

Cassidy shifts in her saddle. "Not more than a day or two. If we can't find them by then . . ."

She doesn't finish the sentence, but I can tell what she's thinking by her tone of voice. I don't know much about calves or raising them, but I expect that there are more dangers than just wolves lurking out here on the range.

I mean, I played the Scarecrow. I know all about the predators that lurk in the murky, dark wilds. We aren't in Oz, but a Wyoming animal trio comes to mind.

Mountain lions. Bobcats. And wolves.

Oh my.

Having been a straw-stuffed man is one thing, but now I'm feeling more like the Cowardly Lion. Not only am I having trouble telling Cassidy how I feel about her, but I'm also afraid of the things that go bump in the night out here.

I clear my throat and ask, "Does this happen often? Calves going missing?"

"Sometimes," Cassidy says. "We have a large herd and a lot of wide-open space for them to roam. Every year, we record a few losses. If it wasn't for the wolf pack sightings, we'd probably still be back at the stables."

"Where's the fun in that?" I say, hoping to lighten the tension.

I miss the easy back-and-forth banter we'd settled into before everything went awry.

I miss the shared smiles. The lingering looks. The way Cassidy felt in my arms after her run-in with Trouble near the tractor.

Was that really just yesterday?

So much has happened since then.

"Have you ever been camping?" Cassidy asks.

"Does shooting a print ad for Coleman coolers count?"

Cassidy lifts a critical eyebrow. "No?"

"We shot it at a campsite. And there was a tent," I say.

"Did you sleep in it?" she asks.

"No."

Cassidy smirks. "Then you haven't been camping. Out here, we sleep under the stars."

I guess I probably should have given all this more thought before I volunteered us for the calf rescue operation. Am I prepared to spend the night outside under the open sky? It's too late to turn back now. Ready or not, night will come.

"Right. I totally knew that," I say.

Cassidy gives me the same look she always does when she knows I'm full of it. "Totally."

Our eyes meet and my chest swells when I look at her.

There it is.

There's that sparkle in her eyes.

I thought it was gone for good, but maybe not. If I can just figure out what to say to salvage this, there might be hope for us yet.

When Cassidy told me earlier that being out here was going to give me the full-fledged cowboy experience, she wasn't kidding. After hours of navigating across hills and fields, along streams and split-rail fences, we come to a random paddock in the middle of a grassy field.

"Is this Hunter's Ridge?"

"Not quite. That's still a few miles ahead on the trail. We use this place during cattle drives," she says. "This year, the fields around here are being kept fallow."

"Fallow?" I ask.

"It just means we aren't using them for grazing cattle. Letting pastures like this rest for a year or two allows for natural grass reseeding and helps the soil recover some of its nutrients."

"Oh."

"We'll camp here for the night," Cassidy says.

We ride around the fence to make sure it's intact and safe for the horses. At the gate, Cassidy hops down from Land Sailor.

My legs are stiff and wobbly from the hours we've spent in the saddle. And just like the cowboys in old spaghetti Westerns, I have a distinctive bowlegged walk when I dismount.

We pull the saddles from the horses and take their bridles off. Then we let them loose in the paddock. They happily graze on the prairie grass inside while we get to work setting up camp.

Cassidy flips open the flap on her saddlebag and pulls something out.

"Is that a hatchet?" I ask.

"Saddle axe," she says, turning it in her hand so that the blade glints in the fading sunlight.

Cassidy's a vision, standing there twirling the saddle axe like a boss cowgirl. Not gonna lie, I'm kind of in awe.

"Can you get water for the horses while I gather firewood?" she asks, pointing the axe head toward an old metal bucket hanging from a fence post. "There's a creek right over there with clean water."

I hadn't noticed it earlier, but sure enough, I can just make out the sound of running water if I listen carefully.

Cassidy double-checks that the paddock gate is latched before we head off to our respective chores. She strides toward a grove of trees while I grab the metal bucket from a rusty hook and head for the creek.

The water's crisp and a shiver races over me when it splashes my skin. I'd thought on my way over that maybe a quick dip to wash off some of the dirt would be nice, but now that I've felt how absolutely frigid the water is, I'm perfectly fine with my layer of grit and grime. I've already experienced a Wyoming swim and much prefer the warmer SoCal waters.

I rinse out the bucket, wiping the inside as clean as I can, and then fill it with water.

Thankfully I don't splash too much on my pants leg on the way back to the paddock. Cassidy's still gathering firewood. A few weeks ago, I would have stood here twiddling my thumbs, completely clueless about what to do. Or I would have just set the bucket down in the paddock and let the horses fend for themselves. But now I confidently slide the bucket handle back onto the hook so that Sidewinder and Land Sailor can easily get a drink.

It's just before sunset and the sky is a pale orange that looks so fluorescent it doesn't seem natural. A thin layer of clouds wraps around the top of the slate-gray mountains. When a commercial airliner passes over, I think about how that'll soon be me up there, heading back to California. Leaving all this behind.

Cassidy returns with an armful of dead wood and branches and drops them next to an old stone ring I hadn't noticed before. "This won't be enough for tonight," she says, brushing the back of her arm over her forehead. "But it's a start."

"I can help you gather more."

She glances at the darkening sky and nods. "It'll be easier to do while it's still light out."

We head back toward the grove, our boots trampling a path from the paddock to the trees. There's a decent-sized dead tree on the ground that looks like it was felled by beavers, if the television shows I've watched are anything to go by.

"Do you think you can drag it back?" Cassidy asks when she sees me eyeing it.

A few weeks ago, probably not. But now? "Sure."

I give it a good tug. It's more awkward than heavy, but thankfully the ground is relatively smooth and there aren't any obstacles to navigate around.

I drop the tree next to the pile of tinder and kindling Cassidy already gathered. Then I help her pick up smaller branches for the fire. My stomach grumbles by the time we've finished our fourth trip back to the fire ring. There's only a hint of pale yellow left in the sky, and it's quiet now that the songbirds have stopped their chirping for the day.

"The horses seem happy," she says after giving them a quick once-over.

"Will they be okay in there overnight?" I ask.

Cassidy nods. "They should be. It's not supposed to get too cold tonight and the fire should keep any curious predators away."

I cough. "Should?"

"Bobcats are too small to mess with horses and humans. Coyotes and mountain lions don't usually go for horses around here since there are plenty of deer, pronghorn, rabbits, and beavers to keep them well fed." Cassidy nods to the stone circle. "And, like I said, the fire should keep the bigger predators, like wolves and bears, away."

I'd thought about mountain lions, bobcats, and wolves earlier, but somehow hearing Cassidy acknowledge that they might pay us a visit sends a spike of dread through me.

"Maybe we should get more firewood?" I suggest.

Cassidy takes stock of the pile we've already gathered. "We'll be okay with what we have. Plus, I have bear spray, an airhorn, and a flare gun if we need them. I'm sure we'll be fine."

I'm glad she's sure. Me? Not so much.

Would we really be able to fend off a . . . bear? A wolf? Any giant hairy beast out for a late night snack?

I force down a swallow as my eyes scan the open fields around us for possible threats.

Cassidy reaches out and rests her hand on my forearm, giving it a gentle squeeze. My skin sizzles at her touch.

"Yes, there are predators out here. But I really, truly don't think they'll bother us tonight. There are a ton of easier dining options available to them. Plus, I haven't seen a bear around here in months."

Is *that* supposed to be reassuring?

Cassidy releases my arm and points to the saddlebags. "We came prepared. And Dad would never let us spend the night out here if he thought we'd be in any real danger."

She makes a strong point. I take a deep breath and tell myself to cowboy up. That's what I'm here for, after all.

Twilight starts to fall in earnest and, with it, the air temperature drops. I roll down my shirtsleeves and button my flannel shirt at the cuffs. Cassidy grabs a hoodie from her saddlebag and pulls it on.

"Building a campfire is on your list, right?" she asks.

"Yeah."

"Okay," she says. "Tonight's lesson: fire building."

As I clear the overgrowth from around the outside of the fire ring, Cassidy uses the axe to chop the dead tree into smaller logs, some of which she hacks into split wood pieces. As she works, she describes the different types of campfires.

Cones.

Log cabins.

Stars.

Lean-tos.

"Because we don't have an unlimited firewood supply, and we'll be using the fire for cooking and light, you should build a platform fire."

"And then we'll eat dinner?" I ask hopefully.

"Yep," Cassidy says.

I set about laying out a stack of tinder and kindling. Layer by layer, I build a wooden pyramid, starting with the largest logs on the bottom.

While I'm doing that, Cassidy pulls out supplies for dinner. She walks over and surveys the work I've done. "Looks good," she says.

She pulls a metal container from her pocket and holds it out to me. "Want to do the honors?"

The container is the same shape and size as an old film canister—the kind my grandma used to keep change in when the washers and dryers at the laundromat still took quarters. It rattles when I take it, and I unscrew the cap to find that it's full of matches.

Okay.

I've got this.

I hope.

I've never actually struck a match before. Every time I've needed to set something on fire, there's been a lighter available. It's so dark now, I can't see more than a few feet in front of my face. Some of the brightest stars in the sky have already begun to twinkle above us. Somewhere in the distance, an owl hoots. While I can still kind of see what I'm doing, I flick the match against the sandpapery side of the canister and . . .

Nothing.

Well, that's not a blow to my pride or anything.

I strike the match again, and this time it flares to life. I'm so surprised, I drop it onto the top of the woodpile and the tinder bursts into flame.

CHAPTER 29

Cassidy

THE CRACKLING FIRE flickers and flares as gray smoke wafts up to the sky.

Wilder did an excellent job of building the pyramid so that it would burn slowly and steadily. It's warm, with only a slight breeze, and tucked into our sleeping bags with our bedrolls beneath us, we should be comfortable enough out here for the night.

I've always loved camping out under the stars. Watching their distant lights twinkle in the midnight darkness. But with Wilder here, everything about tonight is new and different.

The sky feels bigger. The stars seem brighter. And my heart seems even more tender and exposed.

I don't want to wear my emotions on my sleeve. We've been out here alone all day, and the fact that Wilder hasn't taken the opportunity to say how he feels is a clear sign that my crush has gotten the better of me.

Ugh.

I promised Wilder dinner after he got the fire started, so I pull the crisp white bear-proof food bag from his saddlebag.

"I wonder what your mom packed us for dinner," he says when I ease the sack open.

At the very top is a container labeled *dinner.* Inside are a few hot dogs nestled between ice packs, two telescoping metal roasting sticks, and a few slices of white bread. I replace the lid and hand the container to Wilder. I'm about to close the bag when I notice the label on the next container: *Dessert.*

Not breakfast? Hmm.

I pull out a container stuffed with a baggie of marshmallows, two Hershey bars, and a package of graham crackers. "Go, Mom," I say.

"She hooked us up," Wilder says, licking his lips.

I glance away quickly but my insides are fluttering like I've swallowed a field full of butterflies. Being so close to Wilder is practically torture.

I want to reach out and wrap my arms around him. To feel his hands on my waist, holding me tight. The pressure of his lips. His breath on my cheek.

My heart aches with stupid, stupid yearning.

My stomach growls with hunger, saving me from completely sinking into a downward spiral of desire.

We each spear a hot dog and get to cooking them over the flames. It only takes a few minutes to get them browned, and we pull them from the roasting sticks by wrapping a piece of bread around them.

I'm pretty sure Wilder swallows his down in only two bites, and then he's getting the next hot dog prepped and ready to go.

I at least chew mine before swallowing. Still, I'm not that far behind him with getting my second one cooking. It's been a long day and our energy stores are depleted. Although this time when the hot dogs are ready to eat, we take our time.

Wilder takes a swig of water from his canteen and sighs. "I used to think the best hot dogs were the ones you get at Major League Baseball stadiums. But I dunno," he says. "These are contenders."

I wouldn't know. "I've never seen a live baseball game, let alone been to a stadium."

"That's too bad. You're missing out. I'll take you to a Dodger's game sometime," Wilder says. "You'll see."

A dizzying burst of excitement courses through my heart, but I tamp it down as quickly as it came. It's a nice thought but also a dangerous one. Because ideas like that will only compound my crush and make it worse, and I need to keep my feet firmly planted in reality. Wilder is going back to L.A., and it's not like I'll be going with him.

Still, I don't hate the idea of exploring California. What's it like to stroll along sidewalks lined with palm trees on endless sunny days? Does the sun set differently when there aren't mountains blocking the view? A part of me that I've kept buried deep wants to know.

Guilt slithers across my skin like a snake. How can I even consider leaving Wyoming when I've been dealing with the fallout of Uncle Alex's departure since birth? Grandpa's ornery enough now, even after all these years. He'd become completely impossible for my parents to live with if I left Wyoming, too.

Not to mention, who would do my chores?

Who'd fix the tractor?

Who'd take care of Land Sailor? Rambrandt? Van Goat?

Good help is hard to find, as evidenced by the fact that Wilder and I have joined in the hunt for two calves that have been missing for who knows how long before anyone noticed.

Leave Wyoming? I just couldn't do that to my family.

"Cassidy, I—" Wilder says before the crackle of the walkie-talkie cuts him off.

His shoulders sink in defeat as I pull the unit closer to hear better.

"This is Mitch Sterling to all hands. The calves have been safely located. I repeat, the calves have been located. The search has been called off."

The ranch hands all take turns calling in with confirmation that they've heard the message.

"Wilder and Cassidy copy," I say.

Dad's voice crackles through the speaker. "You two have a safe night out there and head on back to the house in the morning."

"Will do."

After a few more crackles, the walkie-talkie goes silent.

I'm relieved the calves were found safe and sound, of course. But now Wilder and I don't have a specific purpose for being out here anymore. Now it feels less like a work trip and more like a romantic getaway.

I glance up at Wilder, who stares into the fire. The planes of his face are highlighted by the glow of the flames, making him look mysterious and dangerous.

My poor heart.

Wilder brushes his palms over his thighs and turns to me. "So, now what?" he asks.

That's the million-dollar question, isn't it?

Now.

What?

"S'mores," I say. Because what better way to stall potentially awkward situations than ooey, gooey marshmallows?

Wilder wasn't kidding when he said Mom hooked us up. There has to be half a bag of the large, pillowy marshmallows in here.

"This is another first for me, you know," Wilder says.

"S'mores?"

Wilder nods. "I had a deconstructed s'more once, at this industry event. But I've never had a traditional one."

"Wait, what?" It takes a moment for me to register what he just said. "Deconstructed s'mores? Isn't that just . . . this?" I say, pointing to the ziplock baggie of marshmallows, the bars of chocolate, and the package of graham crackers.

"Pretty much," he says. "Except the marshmallows were toasted in front of us with those fancy kitchen blowtorches, the chocolate had gold flakes in it, and the graham crackers were crumbled."

"Wow," I say. "That sounds—"

"Pretentious," Wilder says.

"I was going to say fancy. But, yeah."

We both laugh a little at that. Wilder's shoulder bumps mine and I don't shift away because I'm in too deep. Tendrils of smoke curl around us like faint threads drawing us closer.

For a moment, I wonder if I should just live in the moment. To grab hold of the reins and pick my own path, potential heartache be damned.

I could stop worrying.

Stop overthinking.

Throw caution to the wind and kiss him already.

My marshmallow bursts into flames. "Oh crap," I say, pulling it back and blowing on it until all that remains is a very charred outer shell ballooned around what little sticky insides remain.

I am the marshmallow. The marshmallow is me.

Wilder glances over at my charcoaled sugar on a stick and lifts an eyebrow. "Am I doing it wrong?"

His marshmallow is a perfectly toasty brown. And his grin . . .

That smile slays me. "It's perfect," I whisper.

Wilder's eyes sparkle like the stars in the sky overhead when he says, "Now what?" again.

There is so much weight behind the question, and I get the sense that he's not talking about s'mores anymore. I glance at his lips and remember how it felt when they were pressed against mine. Who wants s'mores when I could have some more of his kisses? Sweeter than marshmallows, meltier than chocolate, and more . . . hmm, well more delicious than graham crackers.

Wilder leans closer. The fire reflects in his eyes and it doesn't matter that our days together are numbered. It doesn't matter that he's on a path toward stardom while I'm on a trail that wends its way across the range under the starry skies. The heartache will come soon enough.

But right now, it's just him and me and a night full of endless possibilities.

Our lips meet in a soft brush that has my blood turning to molten lava. Wilder tastes like dessert and fresh air. I shift closer so I can reach up and wrap my fingers through the curls at the nape of his neck. His cowboy hat goes tumbling off his head, and he pulls mine off and tosses it aside. His warm hands wrap around my cheeks as he deepens our kiss.

In this moment, here in the ink-black darkness under a ceiling of stars, I want to be with Wilder. I want to share smiles and jokes. Hold his hand and hug him close.

I want to kiss him with everything I have.

So I do.

CHAPTER 30

Wilder

WHEN WE FINALLY pull away from each other, we're breathless. My lips tingle with the memory of her mouth on mine. Firelight dances over Cassidy's face, making her glow against the dark night that surrounds us. It's so quiet, I can hear my heart pounding in my ears. Cool night air brushes over my heated skin.

We need to talk about where this is going and what happens next, but what if I tell her how I feel and she rejects me again?

I'm used to rejection. I've missed callback cuts. I've been dismissively thanked for my time. I've been passed over for roles more times than I can count. When you're an actor, it comes with the territory. But there's always been another audition, another script, another opportunity.

There will never be another Cassidy.

Or another night like this one.

This time, when I tell her how I feel, I have every intention of speaking to her as Wilder Nash. Not as an actor. Or a two-bit cowboy. Or a sweet-talking Romeo who knows just the right lines. I'm going to lay everything out there and hope that being authentic, and maybe even a bit awkward, will let Cassidy know just how serious I am about her.

Cassidy glances up at me from under her lowered eyelashes. The exhilaration of kissing her has my heart racing.

"I like you," I say, my fingers brushing lightly over the shell of her ear. "A lot."

Cassidy reaches up and takes my hand in hers. "I like you, too." Her calloused palm brushes over mine as she weaves our fingers together.

An unspoken "but" hangs in the air. I'm not about to let it hover there so it can smother us.

Us.

"I want to be an us," I blurt. There's absolutely no way anyone could accuse me of being suave right now. I'm the exact opposite of suave.

"An us?" she says.

"A couple," I clarify. "You and me. Me and you. Us."

Cassidy tips her face away and stares at the fire. I wish I could tell what she's thinking. "I . . . like the idea of an us," she says with a sad smile. "But I don't want a summer fling."

"Who said anything about a fling?"

"It's kind of implied," Cassidy says. "You're leaving soon. This"—she gestures between us—"has an expiration date."

"It doesn't have to," I say. "What if we decided to give it a shot? See where it goes?"

Cassidy's eyes sparkle with a flicker of hope. I latch on to it and use it to propel me forward.

"California's only a flight or two away. Filming *Outrider* won't last forever. I could come back when I'm on break. Or I could fly you out for a visit and—"

Cassidy presses her fingers to my mouth. "Hold your horses, cowboy," she says. "Slow your roll." She takes a deep breath and stares into my eyes like she's searching them for all the answers in the universe. "I like you, Wilder. And I'd love to try to make it work." She pinches her lips together and pulls back. "But we're from completely different worlds. Your life is filled with things like deconstructed s'mores and red carpets. And I'm just some girl from Wyoming."

"You're not *just* some girl from Wyoming," I say, giving her hand a squeeze. I tip my face down so I can look her straight in the eye. "You're Cassidy Sterling. It doesn't matter where you're from. You're the most amazing girl I've ever met. You're smart and sweet and strong. I'm serious about giving this a shot." I clear my throat. "And for the record, deconstructed s'mores are the worst."

"Totally." Cassidy bites her lower lip and sighs. "I've never been in a long-distance relationship before."

"Me neither. But that's what texting and FaceTime are for, right?"

"I just don't know, Wilder."

My breath catches in my chest.

"I want an us, too. But I don't think it's possible."

"Will you at least think about it?" I ask. Maybe she just needs a bit more time to warm up to the idea.

Cassidy nods. "Okay."

Okay is a start.

My hands find Cassidy's waist and I pull her closer. Words

have failed me but maybe my actions won't. Her lips find mine and we melt into each other.

Soon, it's almost midnight. We tuck up in our sleeping bags, our bedrolls lined up side by side between the fire and the paddock. Cassidy sighs and rests her head on my shoulder. I wrap my arm around her and hold her close. Our fingers are sticky from s'mores, our lips are swollen from kissing, and it's one of the most memorable nights of my life.

"You know how to ride and you've checked off most of the items on your list. Do you feel like a cowboy yet?" she asks in a sleepy, raspy voice.

"Starting to."

"You should," she mumbles.

I press a kiss to her temple. My heart squeezes in my chest and I close my eyes.

The birds are eager to announce that it's dawn. When I crack my eyes open, all I see are faint, wispy clouds in the pale yellow sky above me. Even though the fire is almost out, there are still a few orange embers and a thin trail of smoke rising to the sky. I'm stiff and sore from a night on the ground, but none of that matters because Cassidy is curled up by my side.

"Morning," Cassidy says, rolling onto her back to gaze up at the sky. She tilts her head toward me and smiles.

"Good morning," I say.

And it is a good morning. Not only did I survive my first overnight experience, sleeping under the stars like a cowboy, but I also managed not to mess things up with Cassidy. It doesn't matter how little sleep we got or how my muscles ache. I'm energized.

Cassidy sits up and rubs sleep from her eyes. Her hair is a bedhead mess, especially the sections that have pulled free from her ponytail. I reach out and pull a twig from her hair and toss it toward the fire.

"Thanks," she says, reaching up to try to smooth out her hair. She cringes when she feels the knots, but Cassidy's never looked better to me. Well, maybe it's a tie. She looked pretty damn hot when she was covered in grease and dirt and grinning at me after she fixed the tractor the day before yesterday.

Was it really just two days ago? So much has happened since then, it feels like forever ago. Time moves differently out here on the ranch, where schedules are dictated by daylight and hunger, not cell phone alarms and filming timetables.

"Can you build up the fire?" Cassidy asks. "I'll get the food bag."

Last night, after s'mores and some more kissing, we hung the bag in the grove of trees to prevent any bears or other animals from visiting while we were asleep.

It doesn't take long for us to get a pot of oatmeal bubbling over the fire. While Sidewinder and Land Sailor drink fresh water and munch on prairie grass, we pack up our sleeping bags and bedrolls. After we eat, Cassidy shows me how to put out the campfire and clean up the campsite so that you can hardly tell anyone's been there. We give the horses a good brush down and then saddle them up.

We don't ride as quickly as we did yesterday. Partly because we're no longer looking for missing calves and partly because we're hesitant to return to the real world. Out here, we're in our own little bubble, free of external pressures and obligations. Cassidy and I can just be. And even though I still have a few more weeks left at the ranch, I need to make the most of these quiet moments we have together because it might be a long time before I'm back here with Cassidy again.

A few weeks later, I step into the kitchen of the main house for my last Sunday dinner at Silver Stallion Ranch. My best button-down shirt has some wear around the cuffs. There's an oil stain on the knee of my worn-in jeans. And I actually think Alexander's old cowboy boots are more comfortable than my sneakers. Before I arrived, I fit in the clothes. Now the clothes fit me.

Am I a cowboy?

Maybe.

Maybe not.

But I've definitely put in the work. All I can do now is hope it pays off.

Despite the mouthwatering scent of cooked ground beef, fried bacon, and biscuits, there's a bittersweet taste in my mouth as I take my usual seat at the table between Mr. Sterling and Mitch. Julianne busies herself pouring us all a glass of sun tea. Cassidy's chair is empty. It's not like her to be late for dinner. Usually, I'm the one holding things up, much to Mr. Sterling's frustration.

A sinking feeling pulls at me. What if Cassidy's avoiding me? Have I done or said something to cause her to doubt me again?

"You're late," Mr. Sterling says, jarring me from my thoughts.

"Sorry, Grandpa," Cassidy says. She tosses a mangled work glove into the trash can. "The goats were being goats again."

We share a knowing look and my chest loosens, now that I know I'm not the reason she's late. Rambrandt and Van Goat, however, are complete menaces. I've steered clear of them since the shoe debacle, but it looks like the new ranch hand, Travis, might have learned his lesson the hard way.

"Well, food's getting cold. And cowboy casserole isn't any good when it gets lukewarm." Mr. Sterling reaches for the baking dish and gives himself a heaping serving before passing the dish over to me.

While everyone else fills their plates, Mr. Sterling leans closer and says, "You're still rough around the edges, kid." His eyes are steely. "But all the good ones are."

Was that . . . a compliment?

"Thank you?" I say.

He reaches into his shirt pocket and pulls out a piece of paper. He pinches it between his fingers and hesitates a moment before handing it to me. "It won't be the same without you around here. If the bright lights of the big town ever get to be too much for you . . ."

I unfold the paper to find his name and a phone number scrawled on it in dark blue ink.

"Well, you can call anytime," he says in a hoarse voice.

Suddenly, there's a cottony lump in my throat. "Just not during dinner," I say, remembering the cell phone incident during my first meal at this table.

Mr. Sterling bursts out laughing. "Your comedic timing has really improved," he says, as if he has a frame of reference. Which is weird, because after I embarrassed myself by laughing at his "hay is for horses" comment, I've avoided all jokes when he's around. "*Nat and Matt* was a real dud."

"You watched one of my old movies?" I ask.

He shrugs. "Wanted to see for myself if you were any good."

When he doesn't continue, I can't resist asking, "And?"

Mr. Sterling jabs his fork into the cowboy casserole. "I gave you my number, didn't I?" While the words are sharp, the smirk on his face leads me to believe he just likes giving people gruff.

Mr. Sterling is a crotchety old man, but I'm sure going to miss him. I'm going to miss them all. My eyes burn with unexpected emotion. I blink, and when I look up to meet Cassidy's gaze, she gives me a knowing nod.

As silverware scrapes against dinner plates and conversation swirls around me, I think about how, when I first arrived, I couldn't wait to get back to California.

Now I'm not ready to leave.

CHAPTER 31

Cassidy

THE REMAINDER OF Wilder's time in Wyoming was filled with stolen moments nestled between chores and cowboy lessons. We spent nearly every waking minute together trying to pack as much as possible into the time we had left. Now we're down to hours and minutes.

Wilder's jeans, which had once been pristine, are worn in, the thighs and knees faded from sweat and saddles. The rips and tears and fraying holes are from hard work. They might look like the expensive worn-in pairs of designer jeans you can buy straight off the rack, but these weren't bleached or tattered in some factory. Wilder earned his wear and tear fair and square.

Even his flannel shirt is tattered at the hem. One of the buttons at the cuff is missing. And the pocket flops down at the top where the stitching has come out. He might have looked like a Western wear catalogue model when he arrived, but with his ragged country clothes, unruly curls, and faint shadowy stubble, he now looks like a legitimate cowboy.

My heart bucks like a bronco when he looks over at me from where he stands next to Jupiter's stall and smiles. I try to memorize the curve of his lips, the way his jaw flexes, the way his eyes sparkle. It's our last morning together and I miss him already.

Am I being foolish? Should I agree to try to make a long-distance thing work? I still haven't given him an answer. I know I owe him one. I just can't seem to find it in myself to do what needs to be done. To be the cause of my own heartache.

I've always known he'd leave. That's why I tried so, so hard not to fall for him. I couldn't help myself, but now—with our relationship hanging in the balance—it feels like we're just delaying the inevitable.

As soon as he's back in California, he'll be busy with filming. School will be starting up again for me in a few weeks and I hear senior year is no joke. Pretty soon, it won't just be the distance keeping us apart. It will be everything else, too.

"Don't let worrying about future problems manifest them," Grandma always used to say.

And worrying about all the things that might go wrong is no way to start a relationship. I don't think I can get past the worrying. Heck, it seems like all I've done is worry since Wilder arrived.

If we end it now, I'll be miserable, sure. But delaying the inevitable won't make it hurt any less. I don't need to prolong the pain.

I make my way past the other stalls until I'm standing beside him. "Are you all packed?" I ask, forcing myself to keep my tone light and breezy.

"Yeah," Wilder says.

"One last ride for old time's sake?" I ask.

I realize he's only going back to California and not someplace impossibly far away like Australia or outer space. He's portraying a cowboy in a movie; he's not riding off into the sunset in the Old West. We don't have to contend with things like dysentery or high-noon shoot-outs, but the odds of seeing him again in person once he leaves aren't very good.

"I'd like that." Wilder nods. "What do you think, Jupiter?"

Jupiter's ears perk up at the sound of his name and he gives an agreeable grunt. Wilder reaches up to run his hand down the side of Jupiter's face and then scratches him under the jaw just how he likes. Jupiter closes his eyes and sighs. It hits me that I've been so self-absorbed in my feelings, I haven't even considered the effect Wilder's upcoming absence will have on the rest of the ranch.

Grandpa will be relieved Wilder's gone, because of his connection to Uncle Alex. Although, if pressed, Grandpa'd have to admit having Wilder here wasn't a disaster or a burden. I'm pretty sure Wilder's grown on him.

Dad will miss having an extra pair of hands around. He's still trying to find reliable workers to round out the crew, and even though Wilder wasn't out wrangling cattle, he was a huge help with the farm chores. Plus, I think it made Dad feel better knowing I wasn't off riding by myself.

I bet Mom's hoping Grandpa doesn't regress into his extra-curmudgeonly self once Wilder's gone and family dinners won't require his best company behavior. Which honestly isn't that much different from before, but we'll take whatever relief we can get.

As for the animals, Birdzilla and her flock will have to find someone or something else to ruffle their feathers. Trouble will miss the plate of shredded lunch meat Wilder leaves on the doormat for her after we've prepped sandwiches for our midday trail rides. And Rambrandt and Van Goat will probably miss the jump-scares they give him when they race over to the fence and "maa" every time he walks by.

Besides me, it's Jupiter who'll miss him most. Since Wilder first introduced himself, they've shared a special bond. I worry that Wilder's sudden departure might leave him depressed. I make a promise to myself to check on Jupiter whenever I miss Wilder. Maybe the two of us can help each other through when the going gets hard.

While I ready Land Sailor, Wilder saddles up Jupiter for the last time. I watch him carefully place the saddle pad and then set his saddle atop it. He might not have been born in a saddle, like Uncle Alex told the casting directors he was, but Wilder definitely knows his way around one now. I have no doubt he'll hold his own.

Thinking of him on a Hollywood set is bittersweet. After weeks of hard work and toil, he's got what it takes to portray a convincing cowboy. I can picture him riding toward the camera, a fawn-colored leather coat flapping at his waist, his Stetson pulled down just enough to shade his eyes. I'm proud of him, of course. But my heart pangs when I think about him being there and me being here. Why does Hollywood have to be one thousand and three miles away?

Tears fill my eyes and I blink them away. I don't want to spend time moping around. Not with what little of it we have left.

I hoist myself up into the saddle. Wilder rides Jupiter to the trail head and Land Sailor and I follow behind. When we hit the open range, we let the horses stretch their legs. The wind whistles past, carrying on it the smell of dry earth and warm grass. My heart pounds in time with the horses' hooves. The late July sun warms my skin.

Wilder looks over at me and grins. He lets out a whoop as we curve around a thicket of sagebrush.

"Yeehaw!" I call out in reply.

A future might not be possible with Wilder, but I can keep the memory of him tucked inside the depths of my heart. Already I can feel it cracking, shifting, making space for hurt that will sink into me once he's gone.

We rest the horses by a silvery stream that races over smooth rocks and between small boulders. Wilder sets his hands on my waist and shifts closer until the tips of our cowboy boots tap together. He peers down at me with those captivating eyes of his. I reach up and press my palm to his cheek. His lips singe the sensitive skin on my wrist when he brushes his mouth over it. So many different emotions wash over me that I feel like I might burst.

My mouth finds his and I pour everything I'm feeling into our kiss. All the giddiness and guilt, the worry and uncertainty, the joy and the pain. Wilder's arms wrap around me and he pulls me tight as if he might never let me go.

My knees go weak and I lean back, drawing in a deep, shaky breath. "Your car will be here soon."

Wilder glances at his watch and frowns. "Yeah."

I reach into my pocket and pull out the parting gift I got for Wilder. "I wanted to give you this before you go," I say. "But not in front of an audience."

Wilder's eyes meet mine and then he looks down at the small silver horseshoe in my palm. It's about the size of a quarter and has Silver Stallion Ranch stamped along the inside of the arch. "Horseshoes are supposed to bring good luck. And I wanted to wish you good luck for the film. Maybe you can keep it in your pocket or something while you're on set." I take a deep breath. "It's to remind you of all this," I say. My voice cracks and I force myself to keep it together.

The look in Wilder's eyes softens and he clasps my hand in his. The cool silver presses into my palm as his fingers squeeze around mine. His free hand reaches up and he brushes hair away from my face. "I could never forget you, Cassidy. Not you. Not this place." His eyes narrow with determination and his jaw goes tight. "I know I have to leave. But I'll be back. This isn't goodbye. And that's not a line."

But that's where he's wrong.

Wilder's words might be sincere, but he's about to become a massive Hollywood heartthrob. It doesn't take much to picture his future on the red carpet, surrounded by flashing cameras and beautiful people. Whereas, my future is here, on the green carpet, surrounded by endless chores and barnyard creatures.

It's time for me to stop fooling myself and finally accept that Wilder and I come from two very different worlds.

"I'm sorry," I say as tears threaten to break free. I spin away so he can't see how I'm wearing my stupid crushing heart on my sleeve.

"Cassidy," he says, his voice pleading. His hand settles on my arm but I refuse to turn and face him.

"It's better this way," I manage. "There's no point in letting it drag on."

The breeze swirls around us. The stream burbles. Birds chirp and chatter. It's almost like Mother Nature's decided to provide a symphonic soundtrack to the sad little scene that's unfolding.

But it's not a scene. I know, in my heart, that everything I feel for Wilder is real and true. I blink the tears from my eyes and steel myself for what has to be done. It's time to let Wilder go.

"Goodbye, Wilder," I say with a warble. I turn to face him and brush a soft kiss over his cheek, hoping that somehow he'll understand. This is me, taking the reins. Making the choice. Setting him free. "You really are a cowboy now," I whisper.

It takes all my strength to back away. To hoist myself up into the saddle. To keep the sobs at bay.

I always knew my heart would be crushed by Wilder Nash. But now it feels like my spirit is crushed as well.

CHAPTER 32

Wilder

I HAVE PLENTY of time to make a pit stop and grab a snack in the Salt Lake City airport before my connecting flight leaves for L.A., but the bag of M&M's and bottle of Coke I guzzle don't fill the hollow pit in my stomach. I'm not sure anything ever will.

I've been sucker punched.

I glance at my watch. It's almost 8:00 p.m. Cassidy is most likely done with chores for the day. She's probably watching TV or reading or ... something without me.

Sitting here wallowing in my misery won't change anything.

I pull out my phone to doom scroll, since it's basically all I'm good for right now. But my feed is filled with nothing but smiling couples and kittens. Where's the angst? The drama?

I swipe down and there's Cam freakin' Sheffield, seated on a horse, making a heart shape with his hands. *#LovingLife #Lifeisgood #LAVibes*

I toss my phone onto the seat beside me and groan.

Hashtag burn it all down.

I need a distraction or I'm going to implode.

Back in one of the acting workshops I attended, the instructor had us pick a random word from a short monologue script and think about all the possible definitions of the word. We had to select two contrasting meanings, and at the next session, we performed our pieces based on each definition. The exercise was designed to show us how interpretations can alter how we approach a scene. And how we can look for opportunities to hone our craft and stand out from the competition. Sometimes, when I'm bored or I can't get to sleep, I think of random words and all their possible definitions.

I consider this terminal bustling with people.

Terminal: A depot. A computer monitor. Fatal.

The first two definitions intersect, in this terminal filled with people bustling to and from their travels, checking their flight status on the terminals suspended above. But that last definition . . .

Yeah, I'm definitely not a ray of sunshine at the moment.

By the time I hop in the car Alexander arranged to take me home, I'm exhausted. It's weird being back in L.A., almost like I'm seeing the city for the first time. It's after 11:00 p.m., and the streets are still bustling with traffic. I glance up at the sky, but it's too bright to see the stars. After weeks immersed in the quiet sounds of nature, the cacophony of noise is jarring.

At the same time, it's good to be back in familiar territory. We drive past my favorite pizza parlor and then pull up in front of our condo. The driver helps me unload the bags. I push open the front door and am greeted by a dark apartment. Mom left a note for me on the kitchen counter.

Welcome home, Wilder.

I'm so glad you're back. Let's have breakfast after my shift? I can't wait to hear all about Wyoming!

Love you,
Mom

I'm torn between wishing she was here to greet me and being grateful that she's at her night shift at the hospital so I can have the next few hours to pull myself together. I'm really torn up over Cassidy, but I need to get my head on straight for tomorrow, or all our hard work—and all this heartache—might have been for nothing.

I was going to head straight to the studio after Mom and I finish breakfast, but I decide to walk her home first. This morning, I threw on my standard summer in L.A. outfit of a T-shirt, baggy shorts, and sneakers, but it doesn't feel quite like me anymore. I miss the soft flannel, worn-in jeans, and dusty old cowboy boots.

Even though I'm not scheduled for filming until next week, Natalie and some of the other actors have already been on set for a few days. Today I have an appointment with the wardrobe, hair, and makeup departments to finalize Deacon Slade's look. After, some of the cast, including me, will be posing for some promotional photos.

I'm just about to step out the door when my phone rings. I pull it out, hoping it's Cassidy but knowing it won't be, and see that it's Alexander.

I swallow down the disappointment and answer. "Hello."

"Wilder," Alexander says in a cautious, measured tone. I've been his client long enough now to know that this is the tone he uses when he's relaying bad news.

That I wasn't called back.

That I didn't get cast as a lead.

That the studio decided not to pick up the show after the pilot.

I inhale to stifle my nerves. "What's up?" I say.

Alexander clears his throat, which is also not a great sign. Now I'm wondering if this call is strictly professional or if he has a more personal reason for calling. Like, my getting involved with Cassidy.

"There have been some developments," he continues. Somehow, the way he says it is even more ominous than his somber tone.

My heart pounds and all I can think is that this is a worst-case scenario, career-killing situation kind of call. All the possibilities run rampant through my head.

Is he going to fire me for what happened with Cassidy?

Was the role of Deacon Slade recast?

Did the studio discover that I'm not a lifelong horseman like we'd claimed?

"You still there?" Alexander asks.

"Yeah," I say. My mouth is dry and my chest feels tight. It's a very real possibility the suspense might kill me.

"You haven't left for the studio yet, have you?"

I barely manage a "No" as my legs go out from under me. I slide down to the floor so that I'm sitting up against the wall in our front entryway. I'm not sure I can handle losing my heart and my career in the span of twenty-four hours. A beam of light from the window above the door lands on the tip of my sneakers, highlighting the mismatched shoelaces thanks to Rambrandt's—or was it Van Goat's—antics.

"Okay, good," he says. "I caught you in time. Shooting's been delayed and they've sent almost everyone home until further notice."

"Delayed?" A strange sense of relief washes over me that at least I wasn't canned, but the feeling is fleeting. "Why? And for how long?"

Depending on the reason, a delay in filming could still be bad news.

Script rewrites.

Budget issues.

Creative disagreements.

There are so many things that can deep-six a project.

"I know the why but not the how long," Alexander says. "Natalie's first day of filming was yesterday. There was some sort of accident with some rigging. It collapsed on top of her. She's gonna be okay," he says quickly. "But she won't be able to ride with a broken leg and a few cracked ribs."

I wince in sympathy, remembering how miserable I was when I broke my arm learning to skateboard when I was ten. "Damn."

Alexander grunts in agreement. "The studio's scrambling to change the shoot schedule to accommodate her absence, and

258

the writers are trying to figure out how to cut her riding scenes without having to rewrite the whole miniseries. Right now, everything's a mess over there. There's a big push for them to deliver on schedule."

"Why?" I ask. It's not unheard of for shows or movies to be delayed. Everyone just knows to expect it.

"The director's lined up for a big blockbuster right after this project's set to wrap. A bunch of A-list actors and an astronomical budget are involved, so there's not much wiggle room. Plus, a few of the other actors will have scheduling conflicts if *Outrider* filming gets pushed too far back. If the producers can't figure out a schedule that works for the studio, the director, and the leads, they may have to recast Natalie's role to keep things on track."

I take a deep breath. Poor Natalie. Based on our conversations, she was really looking forward to this project.

It's awful that she might lose her role, but my opportunity to play Deacon Slade might very well be in limbo, too. While recasting one part doesn't always mean other roles will also be reconsidered, Natalie and I have a certain chemistry. What if the casting director goes with someone else, someone I don't have that same chemistry with? I can't help but worry that Cam is still nipping at my heels and that this could be the big opportunity he's been waiting for.

Deep down, I know it's not the end of the world. Being recast would free me up for other opportunities. But I've worked so damn hard these past few weeks. Too hard to just take it sitting down.

I push up to standing, and as blood rushes to my brain, I

have a brilliant idea. "What about a stand-in?" I suggest. "Instead of having to rewrite scenes or do a massive schedule overhaul, the studio could just hire a body double."

"It won't be easy finding someone on such short notice," Alexander says. "They'd have to be an experienced rider. And they'd have to look enough like Natalie to—"

"Well," I say, cutting him off. "We both know someone who could do it. She's been mistaken for Natalie before."

There's a pause on the other end of the line. It goes on so long that I think maybe I've lost the connection. "Alexander?" I say.

"There's no doubt in my mind that Cassidy *could* do it," he says, measuring his words carefully. "But I'm not sure she *would* do it. Or that she should."

I think about my time with Cassidy. How she stepped in to save me (and my shoes) from Rembrandt and Van Goat. How she patiently showed me how to tie a quick-release knot. How she fixed the busted tractor with elbow grease and determination.

She never once backed down. She never once gave up. And I can't imagine she'd turn us down in our time of need.

As if he can hear my thoughts pinging from my phone to the cell tower to his phone, Alexander says, "It's not so simple, Wilder. For her, it's not just about showing up in L.A. to help a friend. Not with our family history." There's a familiar edge to his voice that makes him sound a lot like his father.

My stomach sinks. How selfish am I to not even consider how coming here to help me out would impact her? Figuring out logistics and school stuff would be hard enough, but making a choice like that would definitely alter the Sterling family dynamics. It was one thing for Alexander to choose to leave Wyoming on his own terms, but I care too much for Cassidy to ask the same of her.

"No," I agree, trying my best to hide the disappointment and resignation in my voice. "You're right."

"Look," Alexander says, "we'll figure something out. I have a meeting at the studio this afternoon. We should have more information then."

"Okay," I grumble.

"Chin up, kid," he says. "I'll call you later with an update."

The call ends and I stare down at the phone.

Now what?

CHAPTER 33

Cassidy

I CAN TELL from the tone of Uncle Alex's voice that something's wrong the minute I pick up the phone.

"Hi, Cassidy," he sighs. "How are things?"

"Okay," I say, fighting to keep my voice from catching. "Trouble got into it with Birdzilla again. The new farmhand forgot to latch the goat shed door again, and Rambrandt and Van Goat made a nice snack of Mom's hybrid tea rose bush this time. Oh, and the tractor's acting up again."

"Just a typical day on the ranch?"

"Pretty much," I say with a forced laugh.

"How did things go with Wilder?" he asks.

I know he's asking about riding and not romance, but it doesn't stop the tears from welling in my eyes. I sink down onto my bed and hug a pillow tight to my chest to try to keep my feelings tucked up tightly inside.

"He's a quick study. I don't think anyone will question his

ability to ride. He'll definitely make a convincing cowboy." There's a warble in my voice that I don't want to run too deep.

I take a deep breath. Exhale. Inhale again.

Gosh, I miss him.

Tears threaten to spill over and I brush them away with the back of my hand. Why is this so damn hard?

"Good, good," Uncle Alex says. But there's no relief in his words. Something's wrong.

"What's going on?" I ask.

"This stays between us. There was an accident on set," he says.

The world grinds to a halt as a spike of ice-cold fear slams into my heart.

"Did something happen to Wilder?"

"No, no. Wilder's fine," Uncle Alex assures me.

I fall back onto the bed in relief.

"Unfortunately, Natalie was injured," he says.

"Oh, wow." That's big. Even though I was jealous of her easy friendship with Wilder, she was nice. I'd for sure never want anything bad to happen to her. "I hope she's okay."

"She will be, but . . . a lot is up in the air right now."

I listen as Uncle Alex explains about the filming delays and possible recasting.

"So if Natalie's role is recast, does that mean Wilder's role might be recast, too?"

Uncle Alex sighs. "Maybe. I'm still waiting to hear back from the studio. They're currently looking into options."

"Is one of those options Cam Sheffield?" I ask, unable to hide the bitter tone in my voice.

"His name came up. But right now, they're just scrambling and spitballing."

My heart aches for Wilder and not just because I miss him. He worked so hard this summer to learn how to ride. Yeah, it started out rocky. But he showed up every day. He put in the hard work. And to think that his role as Deacon Slade might be recast because of a freak accident?

I wish there was something I could do.

Uncle Alex promises he'll keep me updated before we say our goodbyes. After we hang up, I reach out and grab a picture frame from where it lies, face down, on my nightstand. It's one of those double frames that holds two landscape photos. The top picture is me and Wilder after a trail ride. We're resting against a fence, our faces flushed from the sunshine and fresh air. His arm is wrapped around my shoulder, his cowboy hat in his hand. I'm leaning against him, my cheek pressed against the soft flannel covering his muscular shoulder. We both look at the camera with cheesy grins and squinted eyes. It feels like a lifetime ago.

Below it is a photo Wilder took of me out on the trail. I'm riding Land Sailor and my back's to the camera, my head tipped slightly to the side, so you can barely make out the profile of my face in the shadows cast by my cowgirl hat. The sun sets on the horizon, giving the picture a sepia glow that makes it seem like it could have been taken a hundred years ago instead of a few days ago.

There's bit of mystery to it, which makes it so eye-catching. It's the kind of photo that would make people wonder: Who is that girl and where is she headed?

It kind of reminds me of the photo that Wilder's PR team

accidentally shared that had everyone thinking he was out riding with Natalie.

Wait.

I grab my laptop and pull up one of the articles featuring pictures from Natalie and Wilder's photoshoot with Nigel. There's a similar picture of Natalie on horseback, facing away from the camera. Misty Morning is a different color than Land Sailor, and Natalie's hair isn't the same length or shade, but from the back, we do have a very similar posture in the saddle. So similar, that at a quick glance, I might be tempted to think it was a photo of me. And if *I* could be fooled by the photo . . .

"Please pick up. Please pick up. Please pick up," I mumble as I listen to the outgoing call ring and ring and ring. I worry that I'll be shunted to voicemail, but just as I've given up hope, Uncle Alex answers the phone.

"Cassidy. Is everything okay?" The concern in his voice is palpable.

Usually we text or email, so it's weird that I'm calling, since we literally spoke on the phone yesterday. But my plan is so bonkers, texting would take too long, and I'm not sure it would do it justice.

"I'm fine. Everything's fine here," I say. "I've been thinking." I clear my throat and forge ahead. "And I have an idea."

"I'm not going to like it, am I?" he says in a tone that's filled with suspicion.

"Meh," I say. "I think you'll come around. Mom and Dad, too. It's Grandpa I'm worried about."

"Yeesh, kid," he says. "I already want to talk you out of it."

"Could you at least wait to hear my plan first?"

"Fine," he says.

I give him a broad overview.

"Did Wilder put you up to this?" he asks after my pitch.

"No," I say. "He did not. I haven't talked with him since he left." As much as I don't want to, I know I need to tell Uncle Alex everything. The last thing I want is for this to blow up in his face because I held something back. "We didn't exactly part on the best of terms. It's possible I broke his heart? I know I broke mine."

Uncle Alex breathes deeply, the sound crackling through the phone's tinny speakers. "Clearly you still have feelings for Wilder. And don't get me wrong, I like the kid. I do. But you've only known him for a little while. Are you considering all this for the right reason?"

"For the best reason," I say.

I like Wilder. And I miss him. And there is a small part of me that would be doing this for him.

But deep down, I know why I can't get this plan out of my mind. Why it was the final thing I thought about before going to bed last night. Why it was the first thing I thought about when I woke up this morning.

"Uncle Alex, I'm doing it for me," I say. "I love Wyoming. And I can't imagine my life anywhere else. But that's just it. I can't imagine my life anywhere else because I haven't ever really *been* anywhere else. It's not that I'm unhappy here. I just get to wondering . . . could I be happy somewhere else?" Emotions well up in me until I feel like I might burst. "Will I regret this? Maybe. But will I regret not doing it?" I swallow down nerves and worry and fear of the unknown. "Yeah, I will. Because I'll never know for sure if I don't at least try."

"You sound so much like your grandma," Uncle Alex says. After a pause he says, "And I think she would have wanted an opportunity like this for you. You're absolutely sure about this?"

"Very."

★★★

"You want to do what?" Grandpa says, slamming his water glass down on the table.

"Now, hold on," Dad says, but I can't tell if he's directing his comment to Grandpa or me.

Mom gives me a sympathetic smile. "It's sweet of you to want to do this, honey," she starts, "but—"

"Just like her good for nothin' uncle," Grandpa says. "He probably put those ideas in her head."

"Don't you go accusing Alex of—" Dad says.

This is actually going better than I thought. Still, I've had enough. I'm so tired of sitting here, night after night, listening to them bicker over Uncle Alex and the ranch. And now, about me.

"Stop!"

I've never raised my voice, especially at the table, and in the stunned silence that follows, you could probably hear a soap bubble pop.

"Uncle Alex didn't put me up to it. And neither did Wilder. This was my idea. And it's my decision." I clutch my napkin in my lap with white knuckles and force myself to keep going. "I'm not planning on leaving the ranch for good," I say, looking

Grandpa in the eye. "I like it here. And I like working with the horses and fixing tractors and stuff. But do I love it?" I shrug. "I honestly can't see myself fixing tractors for the rest of my life. I can't train horses like Mom. Or run cattle drives like Dad. It's just not in me. So what does that leave for me when I take over the ranch?" I turn to face Mom and Dad. "I'm not running away from here. Or running toward there. I just want to see what else I might be able to do with my life."

"I can appreciate that," Mom says. I can tell she's trying to be supportive, even though all this is a huge surprise I've just dropped on them.

"It's a big decision," Dad adds.

"I'm not getting a tattoo. It's not like I'm taking a one-way trip to Mars," I say. "Think of it as an extended working vacation."

"There's no such thing as a working vacation," Grandpa says with a huff. He shakes his head and growls, "Leaving Wyoming just like Alex."

I heave an exasperated sigh. "Why does it have to be Wyoming or California? Why can't it be Wyoming and California?"

For the first time since Grandma's funeral, I see tears glisten in my grandfather's eyes. "I lost Alexander. I lost Betsy. I don't want to lose you, too."

"Oh, Grandpa," I say, reaching over to place my hand on top of his. "You aren't going to lose me."

CHAPTER 34

Wilder

INSTEAD OF SHOOTING on set in the studio lot, *Outrider* is being filmed on location. Unlike Silver Stallion Ranch, with its rolling fields, running streams, and groves of trees, this location is the dry, dusty hills in Santa Clarita Valley. Sagebrush and yucca are scattered around the landscape, and an occasional tumbleweed blows by.

I've just finished up in the hair and makeup trailer. It's my first day portraying Deacon Slade and I'm a bundle of fraying nerves. Instead of a nice, meaty dialogue scene or something simple, today's scenes are exclusively on horseback, and one even features me galloping across the dusty landscape on a horse. When I left Wyoming, I was feeling pretty confident about my riding abilities. But now that the pressure's on, I'm not so sure I have what it takes.

One of the assistants grabs me as I step from the trailer. "Right this way, Mr. Nash," she says.

"Call me Wilder," I say.

She nods. I practically have to jog to keep up as she guides me through the maze of crew and cast on our way to the corral. She's wearing a headset attached to a walkie-talkie and has a thick stack of paper clamped to a clipboard in her hand. I'm about to ask her for her name when she waves over a gentleman who reminds me a lot of Cassidy's dad.

"Richard, this is Wilder," the assistant says before disappearing into the crowd of people milling by the watercoolers.

Richard introduces himself as the lead horse trainer for the project. He has salt-and-pepper hair and light blue eyes, and his handshake is rough and firm.

"Nice to meet you," I say.

"Let's get you set," he says. "You'll be riding Perseus today."

Perseus is a handsome chestnut quarter horse with a blaze. He eyes me up as we walk over, and just like Cassidy showed me, I slowly lift my hand for him to smell.

Someone calls to Richard. "I'll be right back," he says.

I wave him off and keep my attention on Perseus. "It's nice to meet you," I say. "I'm going to do my best out there today," I tell him. "But I could really use your help. What do you think? Can we be partners?"

Perseus flicks his ears. I can't tell if that's a yes or a no.

Either way, we're about to find out.

Fake it till you make it.

Or in this case, act like you've been doing this forever. Like you were born in the saddle.

I square my shoulders and stride over to a now-saddled Perseus. It's almost time for the first take and my heart is pounding down with the seconds on the AD's watch. I double-check the girth to make sure the saddle is properly fastened. Then I slide my new, but beat-up-looking, costume department–issued cowboy boot into the stirrup and hoist myself into the saddle.

My heart thuds as I wait for someone to call me out for doing it wrong or being a fraud, but the only reaction I get is a nod of approval from Richard. I suck in a deep breath and force my shoulders to relax.

Unlike the horses at Silver Stallion Ranch, Perseus is trained to follow without a lead rope or reins. We make our way over to where my first scene will be shot: a short, straight, flat bit of land alongside which is a narrow track for the camera.

The director comes over. "Good to see you, Wilder."

"You too," I say.

She has a piece of paper rolled up in her hands. "Before we start filming, I'd like to see you ride the horse down to those bushes so I can get a feel for how it'll look, okay?"

I nod. "Okay."

She scrutinizes me with narrowed eyes. "You can ride, right?"

"Yes, ma'am," I say, tipping my cowboy hat. Before self-doubt can rear its ugly head, I make a clicking noise and move the reins. Perseus steps forward and I have him trot over to the bushes the director pointed out. I guide Perseus into a turn and we head back to where we started.

"Okay, then," the director says. "We've got ourselves a rider."

I let out a breath of relief. Thankfully it seems I've passed the test. Alexander's reputation is secure and I still have a job.

The director waves the paper over her head like a baton and the crew jumps to attention.

"Quiet on set," someone calls.

And then it's "Ready, set, action."

We've just finished shooting a few short riding scenes when the director calls for a fifteen-minute break. The next scene that's scheduled is the galloping-across-the-desert-toward-the-camera scene.

Perseus is a great horse and so far, we've worked well together, but we haven't had time to build up the same level of trust as I had with Jupiter and Sidewinder. I really hope that we continue to gel as the speeds increase, because the last thing I need is to be thrown from a galloping horse.

Richard comes over to take Perseus and I dismount. I give his withers a gentle rub before handing the reins over to his trainer.

"Is it okay if I give him a peppermint?" I ask.

Richard nods. "Lots of actors claim to be able to ride because of that one time at a county fair. Or because they took that horseback riding excursion on vacation in Hawaii. They think it makes them a good enough rider to play one on TV."

Oh, crap. Here it comes. I'm about to be busted by an expert. Was my posture wrong? Did I have the reins too loose or too tight? Was I supposed to ask what commands Perseus has been taught instead of just clicking my mouth to set him walking?

Richard gives my shoulder a friendly slap. "Not you, kid. Clearly you're experienced."

A sense of relief washes over me. Richard thinks I'm experienced. I'm not about to be busted. I really wish Cassidy was here so she could see all our hard work paying off in real time. My heart clenches.

Someone calls out, "Five minutes."

I grab a bottle of water from a cooler and take a quick swig. It's warm out here in the desert, and these heavy Western clothes hold the heat.

The assistant from earlier comes over. She explains how they want to film the ride, where the starting mark is, and where we'll break into a gallop. Richard brings Perseus over and adjusts the cinches to make sure the saddle is secure.

"Perseus loves to gallop, and it doesn't take a lot for him to get going. Just lean forward and give him a little squeeze and off you'll go," he says, handing over the reins.

I've slid my foot into the stirrup and am about to mount when the assistant holds up a finger in the universal sign for "Hold on a sec." She reaches up and presses a button on her headset. Nods. "Got it," she says. "I'll let him know." She turns to Richard. "The horse for Elizabeth Pike just arrived. They're bringing it over from the trailer now."

Wait, what? I thought all the riding scenes with Natalie's character, Elizabeth Pike, had been rewritten.

"Sit tight," the assistant says to me. She walks away to talk to the camera crew.

This is one of the most frustrating things about filming— the hurry-up-and-wait aspect of it all.

I hear the rumble of hooves pounding over the ground before I see the rider heading our way. A thick trail of dust kicks up behind them. The director barks, "Roll camera, roll camera, roll camera," as the nearby camera operators rush into position to capture the scene on the fly.

Someone replies, "Cameras rolling."

The wind kicks up and swirls a dust devil around the horse and rider. Sunlight causes the flecks of mica in the sand to glisten and sparkle.

A dark cowboy hat is pulled low over the rider's face. The bottom of a long brown duster flaps behind them. I blink. That rider reminds me a lot of . . .

All the air in my lungs rushes out when the rider glances up and our eyes meet. "Cassidy?"

Her dazzling smile lights up the set brighter than any key lights ever could.

"Howdy, cowboy," she says when she slows to a stop in front of me.

"What are you . . . ? How are you . . . ?" As usual, I can't find the words because real-life is off script.

Cassidy hops down from the saddle and hands the reins over to Richard.

Her hair is longer and a different shade of brown. Up close, I can just make out the wig lace around her hairline. She's wearing an Old West costume that reminds me a lot of the outfit Natalie wore in some earlier promo photos. It's different from what she usually wears, but she looks amazing.

"Surprise," she says, but there's a bit of apprehension in her eyes. Like she's not sure how I'll feel about her randomly showing up on set.

Words might be failing me at the moment, but I'm not about to let her doubt how I feel again. I step forward and wrap my hands around her face, the tips of my fingers brushing against the nape of her neck. "I've missed you," I say, then lean in for a kiss.

Our lips meet and fire courses through my veins. Her mouth is soft and sweet. Her fingers twist into my curls.

"I've missed you, too," she says before pressing her mouth to mine again.

There are a few hoots and cheers. The director calls, "Take another fifteen." But that's just background noise compared to the pounding echo of my racing heart.

Someone walks by and coughs loudly, our cue to back away and pull ourselves together. This is a film set, after all, and kissing is usually reserved for the on-camera scenes.

"What are you doing here?" I ask with a grin that's so cheesy, even Easy Mac would pass on an audition tape.

"Well," she says, "long story short: Natalie can't ride. And I can. I've been hired to be her body double slash stunt rider while she's recovering."

"That's incredible." I feel like I've been shot to the moon and I'm floating in outer space.

"Uncle Alex is letting me stay with him. He'll be my on-set chaperone. And all my school stuff is online already, because the ranch is so remote. I can do the work here just as easily as I can back home. And now you can take me to one of those ball games like you promised."

"I feel like the luckiest guy in the world," I say. My hand goes to my pocket, where I have the horseshoe charm that Cassidy gave me before I left.

The assistant catches my eye and tips her head to let me know it's time to shoot.

"They're waiting for me," I say.

Cassidy nods. She presses a kiss to my cheek and then steps back. "Go get 'em, cowboy."

I will, but there's something I need to do first. I pull off my hat, wrap my arm around her waist, and pull her in for another breathless kiss. "I've been wanting to do that for a while now," I say.

And this time, we both know I mean it.

ACKNOWLEDGMENTS

Being a published author is one heck of an adventure and a dream come true. There are so many amazing people who have helped make my second novel possible.

To my wonderful agent, Jordan Hamessley: I am so grateful for your enthusiasm and encouragement. Thank you for continuing to champion me and my writing. I'm glad to have you on this journey with me. And to the team at JABberwocky Literary Agency for welcoming me with open arms and for all the support you've offered since I came on board.

Thank you to the fantastic Wendy Loggia, who was up for going on another trail ride with me. And to my editor, Alison Romig, who has expertly taken up the reins and steered me through another manuscript. Working with you both has been an amazing experience. Your energy and excitement are contagious and very much appreciated. And to everyone at Delacorte Romance who supported this book: Thank you for making it shine!

Sarah Lawrenson is a phenomenal publicist, and I appreciate everything she's done to spread the word about my books (and her patience when I send emails filled with questions, concerns, and possibly hairbrained ideas).

Thank you to Alissandra Seelaus and Angela Carlino for

designing another adorable cover—you've captured my characters perfectly.

I am grateful to Christina Zobel for sharing her expert knowledge of horses and horsemanship and for reading an early draft and providing feedback on "horse accuracy." Any errors are my own.

To my Cold Crockpot Romance kindred spirit, Diana Gallagher. I cherish our friendship. Thank you for brainstorming plotlines with me, offering constructive criticism, and talking me off ledges when I lost my way on the trail.

I am so grateful to the community of authors I'm connected with, who offer positivity, cheering, and camaraderie, including Andrew Sass, Marty Mayberry, Brielle Porter, Erin Becker, Kristy Boyce, Dori Butler, Chiara Colombi, Becky Dean, Kristy Everington, Sabrina Fedel, Madeleine Gunhart, Tara Hannon, Catherine Hapka, A.J. Irving, Stephanie V.W. Lucianovic, Kara Newhouse, Cindy Thomas, and Taylor Tracy.

To my incredible friends and extended family who have formed an amazing cheering squad and have supported me every step of the way, including Evelyn Cadman, Andrea Champagne, Cheryl Dicks, the Dicksons, Caitlin McMonagle and Wyatt Sinclair, the McMonagles, Christi Segura, the Verocks, Aunt Carol, Aunt Ida, and Aunt Pat.

To Mom and Dad, for the experiences and adventures that helped fuel my storytelling and imagination. And for letting me "borrow" the goats. To my sister, Samantha, and brother-in-law, Austin, for brainstorming ideas, website design and redesign, and general encouragement. I'm the luckiest sister in the world. To Terry, my father-in-law, for taking on extra chores and entertaining the kids, most especially when I'm in author mode or on deadline.

To my husband, Jody, who has been by my side through thick and thin—both when the road is bumpy and narrow and seems impossible and when it's a smooth, well-marked, pleasant trail. There's no one I'd rather have by my side on this wild adventure! I love you!

Yes, I'm biased, but I still believe that I have the best kids in the universe. Brooks and Madeline, I'm so glad I'm your mom. I love you more than you can ever imagine. Thank you for helping me keep everything in perspective.

A quick shout out to Rambrandt and Van Goat, the namesakes for the goats in the book. When I was young, we lived on a small farmette in New Hampshire, and Rambrandt and Van Goat were our pet goats. My memories aren't as clear as the photographs my parents have, but I know those two were full of wily antics like the pair in the book.

And to Vienna Teng, whose music inspired the name for Cassidy's horse, Land Sailor. (Nod to the multiple unleafed authors who recommended I check out her music. Spot-on!)

To all the booksellers, librarians, and teachers who have been so welcoming and sweet: Thank you for helping to get my books into readers' hands!

And finally, to all the readers, reviewers, and recommenders who have picked up one or both of my books. I am so grateful for everyone who has reached out with kind words and shared my books with potential readers.

Thank you so much for joining Cassidy and Wilder on their starry-eyed trail ride! I wish you all clear skies and happy trails!

BOOK CREDITS

Michael Caiati—Marketing Designer

Angela Carlino—Cover Designer

Kristin Guy—Trade Marketer

Michelle Canoni—Interior Designer

CJ Han—Production Manager

Colleen Fellingham—Production Editor

Jordan Hamessley—Agent

Wendy Loggia—Publisher

Sarah Lawrenson—Publicist

Alison Romig—Editor

Tamar Schwartz—Managing Editor

Alissandra Seelaus—Cover Artist

Anything's possible under a prairie sky . . .

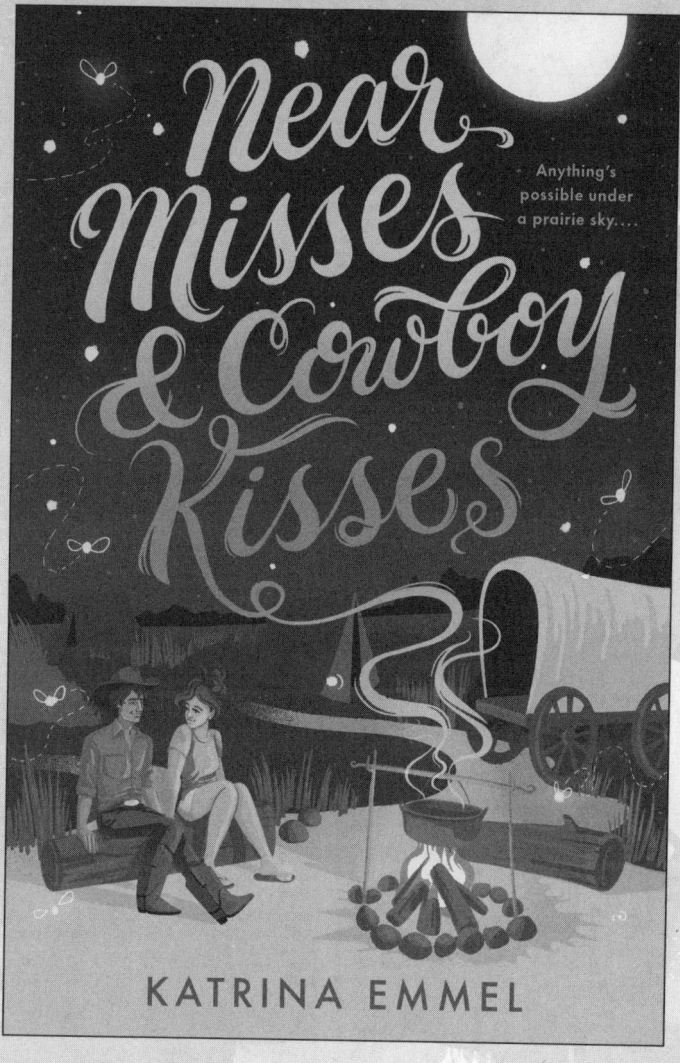

Saddle up for another romance from
Katrina Emmel!

Delacorte Romance

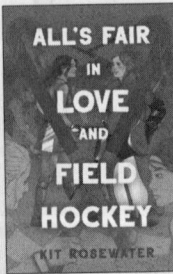

IT'S A LOVE STORY.